Centralia, W(

MW01516837

Backpack in hand, Jake rocketed forward, slamming into one of a trio of girls with such force she flew off the platform onto the tracks. His backpack dropped as he teetered on the platform edge.

"Call 911!" he shouted at the two remaining girls, both so engrossed in their phones they hadn't noticed their friend's plight.

Jake leaped onto the tracks as the train bore down, its locked wheels screeching, its horn sounding a deafening, futile blast.

The train slowed but no way it could stop in time.

It was four feet from the girl when Jake reached her. She was unconscious, her head resting on a rail already slick with her blood. He bent low, scooped her up and threw her off the tracks.

He was diving clear when the train slammed into his side. The train would have dragged him under if his feet were planted. With his body already airborne, the engine carried him forward before spitting him onto the gravel ballast on the opposite side of the tracks.

Everything seemed to move in slow motion. He lay parallel to the tracks, his face so close to the slowing train he felt the heat of the engine as the locked wheels shrieked past.

He rolled clear, tasting blood draining into his mouth from a gravel-shredded cheek. He stumbled in a daze back toward the girl.

Had he killed her? He'd knocked her onto the tracks. What the hell happened?

Praise for Ken MacQueen

"An edge of your seat thriller. MacQueen, a journalist, ratchets up the suspense and tightens the grip to the explosive end."

~ *Robert Dugoni*
New York Times Bestselling
Author of The Tracy Crosswhite series

Hero Haters

by

Ken MacQueen

Hero Haters

Cover Art by *Kim Mendoza*

The Wild Rose Press, Inc.
PO Box 708
Adams Basin, NY 14410-0708
Visit us at www.thewildrosepress.com

Publishing History
First Edition, 2022
Trade Paperback ISBN 978-1-5092-4385-3
Digital ISBN 978-1-5092-4386-0

Published in the United States of America

Dedication

To Ros, for everything.

To Patricia.
No murder on the
first page, but
hang in there.
Best wishes

Ken MacLaem

"Show me a hero and I'll write you a tragedy."
F. Scott Fitzgerald, Notebook E

Prologue

Spokane, Washington, August 2019

Local hero Anderson Wise can't remember the last time he paid for a drink at Sharkey's.

Nor can he remember an embarrassing assortment of the women who selflessly shared their affection, post-Sharkey's.

As for that last blurry night at the gin mill, he wished to hell he'd stayed home.

The bar's owner, Sharon Key, hence Sharkey's, took joy in chumming the waters on Wise's behalf for a regular catch of what she called "Hero Worshippers." She saw getting him laid as partial repayment for saving her eleven-year-old grandson Toby's life some eighteen months back.

A disaffected dad, high on crystal meth, stormed into Toby's classroom to take issue with his kid's latest report card. He showed his displeasure by shot-gunning the teacher, then reloaded and asked all A-students to identify themselves. Being A-students, they dutifully raised their hands, Toby among them.

As the high-as-a-kite shooter herded the high achievers to the front of the class, Wise, the school custodian, charged into the room armed with a multipurpose dry-chemical fire extinguisher. He blasted the shooter with a white cloud of monoammonium phosphate, to minimal effect, then slammed the gun out of his hands. It discharged into the floor sending several pellets into Wise's left foot. Thoroughly pissed, Wise ended the drama by pile-driving the extinguisher into the shooter's face.

Sharon Key, a widow in her early sixties, subsequently replaced the beer signs and dart board with blow-ups of the laudatory press Wise earned during the tragic aftermath. The front of the next day's local paper held pride of place. It carried a photo of Wise, extinguisher in hand, under the headline: *Greater Tragedy Averted as Hero Janitor Extinguishes Threat.*

The story contained a pull quote in large font which Wise came to regret: " 'It's a versatile extinguisher,' the modest 30-year-old explained, 'good for class A, B and C fires—and meth-heads'."

Said famous extinguisher now guards the top-shelf booze behind Sharkey's oak-and-brass bar.

New stories were added to Sharkey's wall five months back after Wise was awarded, with much publicity, the Sedgewick Trust Sacrifice Medallion— one of the most prestigious recognitions of heroism that American civilians can receive.

Wise's liver and a lower part of his anatomy took a renewed pounding in the weeks thereafter. So much so he declared a moratorium on visits to Sharkey's for reasons of self-preservation.

He was back in the saddle a month now, but his attendance was spotty. "This hero stuff," he confided to Key one night, while slumped in his chair. "Maybe it's too much of a good thing?"

"Ya think?" Key muttered as she took inventory of that night's limited offerings.

It wasn't just the women. Men often bought him drinks too, happy to bask in the reflected glory of a proven manly man.

Two weeks ago, some weedy academic from back east interviewed him at Sharkey's and staked him to an alcohol-fueled dinner at the city's best chop house. The brainy one expected Wise to opine on such things as "neo-Darwinian rules for altruism."

Asked him if he'd been motivated by "a kinship bond" with anyone in the room?

Er, no.

Wondered if Wise knew that a disproportionate number of risk takers are working-class males?

Nope, sorry.

And had he calculated in the moment that a heroic display of "good genes" would make him a desirable mating partner?

Cripes. Really?

"Don't know what I was thinking," Wise said, swirling a glass of something called Amarone, a wine so amazing angels must have crushed the grapes with their tiny, perfect feet. "Heard a gun blast, grabbed the fire extinguisher off the wall. Saw the dead teacher, all those kids, and a nut with a shotgun. Did what anybody would do. I spent three years in the army after high school, mostly in the motor pool. Much as I hated basic training, maybe some of it stuck. Who knows?"

The academic gave a condescending smile and called for the bill, his hypothesis apparently confirmed.

Wise fled to the restaurant toilet and took notes on the back of his pay slip. Back home, he Googled the hell out of studies on "extreme altruist stimuli," on "empirical perspectives on the duty to rescue," and after many false starts, on theories of "Byronic and Lilithian Heroes."

He kinda got the concept of "desirable mating partner", but he was pretty sure his dick didn't lead him into that classroom. Did it?

While not a reflective guy, Wise had to admit it was creepy to reap the fleshy benefits of his few seconds of glory while his dreams were haunted by visions of teacher Adah Summerhill slumped over her desk, blood pooled beneath her. So much blood. With the shooter sprawled unconscious, Wise gently lifted Adah's head. She had no pulse and her eyes, once so vibrant and expressive, were as empty as an open grave. She'd always been nice, and totally out of his league.

So, here he was, back at Sharkey's, mind made up.

Key arrived at his "courting table" and set down his Jack and ginger ale.

"Gave my notice at the school," he told her. "Getting outta here for a while. Got that Sedgewick money to spend. Someplace they don't know me. Mexico, maybe. Or Costa Rica."

Key patted his hand. "Knew this was coming, Andy. You banged every eligible female in town, pretty much. And some who shoulda been out of bounds. I'm amazed the Tourist Bureau doesn't list you as a top-ten attraction, up there with the botanical gardens."

"All I want, Shar, is to be liked for me, not for something I did because I happened to be in the wrong place at the right time. Or is that the other way 'round?"

"Hey, you're a good-looking guy. Still got that shaggy blond baseball player thing going for ya. Might've taken a run at you myself if my hips weren't shot." She patted his cheek. "Made you blush. Now don't turn into a beach bum down there. Always thought you aimed too low, mopping floors and washing windows for the school board. Time to stretch—"

She craned her neck toward the door after it opened with a bang. "My, my, here's one for the road. She was in earlier, asking after you." Key aimed a nod at the door and whispered, "Don't strain anything." And headed to the bar.

Wise looked up and…sweet Jesus.

Early twenties, he guessed. His eyes roamed from strappy sandals, up a long expanse of tanned bare legs to a glittering silver dress that started perilously high-thigh and ended well below exposed shoulders. The ripe promise of youth was on full display, like she'd dipped her bounteous curves in liquid lamé.

She drew every eye in the place as she undulated to his table. Full red lips, high cheekbones, chestnut hair piled high. Up close now, her gimlet eyes were at once innocent and knowing, like a debauched choirgirl.

"Hi, hero." Her voice was low and sultry, as he knew it would be. She remained on her feet, hands on the table, leaning low to full effect. "When you finish that drink, I *really* want to see your medal."

****

He remembered her mixing drinks back at his apartment while he retrieved his medallion from the sock drawer in his bedroom. He remembered her running a sensuous thumb over the bas-relief portrait of Philip Sedgewick as she read aloud the inscription: *"The most sublime act is to set another before you."*

That wondrous voice lingering over *"sublime act,"* like it was lifted from the *Kama Sutra*.

And like too many times, post-Sharkey's, damned if he could remember her name—that evil bitch. He awoke, bouncing in the back of a van, hands and legs cuffed to rings set in the floor. A broken-glass headache served notice of every bump in the road.

Another lost night at Sharkey's.

Wise had a dreadful feeling he'd never be back.

Chapter One

Aberdeen, Washington, July, one month earlier

Jake Ockham was one kilometer in, one kilometer to go and already in a world of pain. Lungs, legs and palms, always the damned palms, screaming *enough already*.

He'd whaled away on his Concept II rowing machine for thirty minutes, building up to this. Stripped off the sweatshirt after ten minutes, the t-shirt after twenty-five. Down now to running shoes and gym shorts, his torso gleaming with sweat despite the morning chill.

He'd rested after a thirty-minute warm-up to gulp water and to consider the need to reinforce the pilings under the creaky wooden deck before it dumped him and the ergometer into the Wishkah River below. Might leave it in the river mud if it came to that.

Full race mode now, one kilometer in, another to go. The erg's computer showed the need to pick up the pace to break the six-minute barrier, something he'd regularly shattered a decade ago during his university rowing days.

Thrust with the legs, throw back the shoulders, arms ripping back the handle. Return to the catch and repeat.

Five hundred meters to go. Eyes fixed on a duck

touching down on the river, looking anywhere but the screen.

Two hundred and fifty meters. Faster. Harder. Don't lose the technique.

Fifty meters. You can do this.

A final piston thrust of legs, shoulders, arms and...six minutes, thirteen seconds.

"Fuck!" His roar startled the duck into flight.

He slumped over the machine, gasping for air, ripping at the Velcro tabs of his gloves, throwing them on the deck in disgust. Hated those damned gloves, so essential these days.

Head bowed, he heard the cabin's door rasp open.

"Such language." Clara Nufeld, his aunt, and technically his boss as publisher of the *Grays Harbor Independent*, leaned against the doorframe.

He didn't look up. "Don't bother knocking. Make yourself at home."

"I did, and I am. Got a couple of things to show you. Right up your alley. Might be pieces for next week's issue."

She was lean and tall, in tight jeans and a faded Nirvana sweatshirt, her spiked white hair cut short. At sixty-four, she still turned heads. Jake knew her age to the day, Clara being his mother's identical twin. Connie, his late mother, fell to breast cancer at age forty-five.

So much of his mother in Clara. So much that when Jake finished high school and rode his rowing scholarship east to Pittsburgh's Carnegie Mellon University, his father, Roger Ockham, moved his accounting business to Bend, Oregon. Said it was for the golfing, but Jake suspected the sight of his late wife's twin was a constant reminder of his loss.

Connie and Clara, fresh out of university, worked for their father at the *Independent*, Clara on the advertising side, Connie as a reporter.

They took the helm of the paper after Derwin Nufeld—their dad, Jake's grandfather—collapsed and died mid-way through crafting a fiery editorial on a mule-headed decision to pull *The Catcher in the Rye* from the high school library.

After Connie's death, Clara did double duty as editor and publisher until she succeeded six months ago in luring Jake home to Washington State from Pittsburgh to take over as editor-in-chief.

This five-room stilt home, Clara's former cottage on the tidal Wishkah, was his signing bonus.

One of the dwindling numbers of real estate ads in the *Independent* would describe the cabin something like: *"A cozy oasis on the Wishkah, surrounded by nature and just minutes from the city. Fish from your deck while contemplating the possibilities for this prime riverfront property. A bit of TLC gets you a rustic getaway while you make plans for your dream home."*

After years in urban Pittsburgh, he awoke now to bird chatter and the sights and scents of the moody, muddy Wishkah—its current pulled, as he was pulled, to the infinite Pacific.

Jake gathered his shirts and gloves and cringed at a sniff-test of his underarms. "I'll keep my distance." He waved Clara inside. "What's up my alley?"

She waved two dummy pages, the ads already laid out, plenty of blank space for him and his skeleton staff to fill with stories and photos.

Jake was still adjusting to small-town journalism,

covering at least one earnest service club luncheon every week, puffy profiles of local businesses, check presentations, city council and school board meetings. And jamming in as many names as possible. He'd done some summer reporting for the weekly during his high school years, but rowing had occupied most of his time.

Clara handed off a page proof with a boxed advert already laid out. "A new doctor is taking over old Doc Wilson's practice, thank God. I swear the last medical journal that old man read was on the efficacy of leeches and bloodletting."

Jake nodded. Worth a story for sure. A few words from Wilson about passing the scalpel to a new generation, then focus on Dr. Christina Doctorow. No hardship there.

The ad for her family practice included her photo. Rather than the cliché white coat and stethoscope she wore hiking shorts and a flannel shirt with rolled sleeves, thick dark hair in a ponytail, a daypack hanging off a shoulder. A husky at her side gazed up adoringly.

Smart dog.

Jake put her at early thirties, his age more or less. He nodded approval. "Sporty. A fine addition to the Grays Harbor gene pool."

"The woman's a firecracker. Spent ten minutes haggling down the price. I finally caved. Said I'll bump this up to a half-page, but you owe me a free checkup."

"Seriously?"

"What she said, too. Also asked 'Is that ethical?' I said, 'darling, I'm in advertising. You want ethics, deal with my nephew on the editorial side.' "

Jake laughed. "Pretty good at bloodletting herself. What else you got?"

"This is so up your alley." She handed him a classified ad page-proof. "You being an expert."

Jake slumped onto a kitchen chair. "On what?"

She tapped a one-column boxed ad in the lower left. "Heroes."

"Not hardly."

He looked closer and reared back. The heading read: *"For Sale. Rare Sedgewick Sacrifice Medallion. $100 OBO."*

There was a thumbnail photo of the medal's obverse, showing the craggy face of Philip Sedgewick, a leading member of the long-dead school of industrialist robber barons. He'd amassed a fortune in textile mills, newspapers, and exploitive labor practices. Awash in cash he came to philanthropy late in life. Like others in this elite group—Carnegie, Mellon, Rockefeller, Vanderbilt, et al—their names and reputation-burnishing generosity live beyond the grave.

Sedgewick, at his wife's urging, chose to celebrate extraordinary acts of heroism. He used eight of his many millions—an enormous sum in 1901—to endow a family trust to award exceptional heroism with the Sacrifice Medallion and needs-based financial assistance. Over the past one hundred twenty years, the trust awarded some eleven thousand medallions, an inspiring legacy of courage, and yes, sacrifice.

The grainy photo in the classified ad was too small to read the inscription under Sedgewick's stern visage, but Jake knew it well. It was a quotation by the English poet William Blake: *"The most sublime act is to set another before you."*

Below the photo was a post office box address, and *"mail inquiries only."*

11

Jake shook his head. "This is nuts. The price is insanely low, insulting really. The medallions are kinda priceless."

"I wondered about that," Clara said. "The ad cost fifty dollars so not much of a profit."

"The rare few that get to auction can fetch in the thousands. We try to buy them back, prefer that to having them land up in the hands of the undeserving."

Clara cocked an eyebrow. "We?"

Jake shrugged. "I still do the occasional freelance investigations for Sedgewick. The thing is, there's never a good reason to sell these. Either the recipient is dead broke, or dead without relatives to inherit it. Or it's stolen."

"Or," Clara said, resting a hand on Jake's shoulder, "the hero feels undeserving."

He flinched. "Was there a photo of the medal's back? It'd have the recipient's name and the reason it was awarded."

"Don't even know who placed the ad. Arrived in the mail: a photo, the ad copy, and a fifty-dollar bill. No return address but the post office box."

"Pull the ad, Clara. I'll buy it and return the money. There's a story here, something's not right."

Clara toyed with her car keys. "I feel bad sometimes, guilting you back. Do you miss it, your old life back in Pittsburgh?"

His pause was barely discernable. "Great to be back in the old hometown."

"Great to earn half the salary you did in the big city? Great to prop up the family business? Great to be stuck with your old aunt?"

"Aunt doesn't cover it. I was twelve when Mom

passed. You stepped up for Dad and me."

She looked like she was about to say something, then shook her head and flashed an enigmatic smile. "A topic for another day. Gotta run."

She leaned across the table, took his hands in hers, running her thumbs lightly over his scarred palms. She raised his hands to her lips for a kiss, then turned for the door.

Chapter Two

With his letter in the mail to whoever was peddling the Sedgewick medal, Jake shut his office door and turned his attention to his forthcoming interview with Doc Doctorow.

Boom. Doc Doctorow, the headline was already written.

Next week's issue was in good shape. He had a couple of features in the can and his editorial staff of three—down from six back in the day—had plenty to keep them busy. Time enough to explore the Internet before Wednesday's interview.

Impressive. The good doctor was a much-decorated soccer striker for the University of Washington Huskies while a science major during her undergrad years.

There was even a four-minute YouTube compilation called "Tina's Greatest Hits." It includes her surgical passing to teammates, a jaw-dropping backward bicycle goal from twenty yards out, and a rocket from mid-field still at full velocity as it ripped into the net.

He replayed the video, mesmerized by her tactical smarts, her grace, power, and, it must be said, beauty. One hell of a package.

She'd transferred to the University of California at San Francisco, one of the country's top-ranked medical schools for primary care. There, she received something called the Edward Sands Memorial Fellowship for research into the "applications of gerontology in Family Medicine."

The university news release called it "*a merit-based award supporting a student with outstanding academic credentials and engaged in a promising biomedical study.*"

She could write her own ticket. Why come to this backwater?

He dug deeper, finding references to her master's thesis: "*Dead in the Water: Forensic Challenges to Identifying Victims of Aberdeen Washington's Infamous Floater Fleet.*"

What the hell?

He rose from the world's most uncomfortable chair, a wooden monstrosity in continuous use since his grandfather founded the *Independent*. He'd intended to wheel it to the dump when he took the job, but he came to see it as an incentive to get off his ass and onto the street.

He worked a kink out of his back and headed down a steep flight of steps to the dusty files of the newspaper's library. The walls were lined with cabinets holding index cards, clipping files and film negatives— a neglected resource in a digital world.

He made a note to assign a reporter to mine this trove for a regular feature. Call it *Tales from the Morgue*. Cases in point: "*Floater Fleet*" and "*Gohl, Billy,*" the two fat files he carried up to his office.

The floater fleet was an ugly remnant of Grays Harbor County's past. Aberdeen, the county's largest community, was incorporated in 1890. Sawmills, fishing, and canneries were its economic mainstays. For recreation, its transient males indulged in gambling, drinking, whoring—and homicide.

Within a decade of incorporation, Aberdeen's astronomical murder rate earned it such nicknames as *"Port of Missing Men"* and *"Hell Hole of the Pacific."* Not the sort of descriptors you'd add to the city crest.

In some cases, indigent seamen simply vanished. But scores of nameless bodies were pulled from Grays Harbor, the Wishkah and its tributaries between 1902 and 1908, many the work of a single serial killer. Estimates of the toll ran as high as two hundred men— the *"Floater Fleet,"* as locals called them.

Although the murders happened some sixty years before the *Independent* was founded, the tale was too juicy for Jake's granddad to leave buried. He'd exhume the file every decade or so when a bogus anniversary or fresh historical tidbit justified another look.

The stories inevitably focused on Billy Gohl, town bully and controversial agent for the Sailors Union, who, police claim, preyed on itinerant seamen who came to Grays Harbor looking for work on the docks and ships. He'd rob them of whatever they carried, dump their bodies, and let the Pacific hide the evidence.

The file was a treasure trove. Jake thumbed through every story the *Independent* published, every letter to the editor those generated, and even yellowed original clips of Gohl's arrest and trial. Who knows how his grandfather got his hands on those?

Great stuff: An all-caps, second-coming-sized headline from a February 1910 edition of the *Spokane Press*: *"MURDERED BY WHOLESALE. Aberdeen Police Capture Greatest Murderer Of Age."* From an April 1910 edition of the *San Francisco Call, "Sixty*

Murders Traced to Gohl. Detectives Say Aberdeen Man Littered Bay With His Victims."

The file held no stories about Dr. Doctorow's thesis. Which left the field open to Jake.

He tapped into the Theses and Dissertations section of the University of Washington website and downloaded an electronic copy of Doctorow's "*Dead in the Water*." Sometimes planting your ass in a chair pays dividends.

He read her thesis that night, sitting on his deck overlooking the Wishkah, thinking of the bodies it had flushed to sea. It was good reading in an academically windy way. He'd planned to skip the tedious notes, bibliography and reference sections at the end. But having gone that far, he bribed himself with a second beer and soldiered on.

And there it was…son of a bitch…the *raison d'etre* for her thesis.

Chapter Three

Clearfield County, Pennsylvania, June, one month earlier

"Introduce yourself once more," said the man.

"We've gone through this again and again."

"This time for the camera. I insist."

After an exasperated sigh, he said, "My name is Walter Meely. I'm forty years old and I'm the music director and choirmaster at Living Gospel Evangelical Church in Omaha."

He was in a bright white room, his arms and legs zip-tied to a heavy wooden chair. He had no idea where he was. Not Nebraska, pretty sure about that; he had hazy memories of a long van ride.

"What else, Walter?"

"How many times must I say it?"

The man in a tweed sports jacket behind the camera—a man Walter hated and feared in equal measure—shook his head in disappointment. He turned to the young man beside him, the one who'd betrayed Walter, as he grinned and jiggled a device in his hands.

"Surely you don't want my son to deploy Old Sparky again. You peed yourself the last time. Now, for your own good," the man said, oozing false concern, "what else, Walter?"

"I'm a, I'm..." Walter was crying now. "I'm gay,

dammit. That what you want me to say? Why the camera? Who's watching this?"

"Such an imprecise term, with multiple meanings. Are you *happy*, Walter?"

"No. Who's watching this?"

"An audience of the curious and concerned. They care about you, Walter. Your mother is not among them, if that's your concern. Honesty, please. Do you lay with men? I believe that's the biblical term. Are you a sodomite? A queer? A faggot?"

"Damn you." The words came out in a hoarse shout. "I'm homosexual. Does that satisfy you?"

"I'm not that way inclined. Let's continue. Are you a hero?"

"The Sedgewick people, they gave me a medal for heroism. You saw it. You have it."

"That's an answer of a sort. Describe for our audience how you won this trinket?"

This was clearly a much-told story, one he recited almost by rote. "It was late, I was driving home from choir practice. I saw an SUV overturned in the ditch. Its horn was blaring. I smelled gas and a flame was flickering at the back, small but growing."

The man waved his pipe as if to speed the tempo. "Continue."

"The vehicle was on its roof, like I said. It was crushed down and the windshield had popped out. The hood was all mangled. There was a very small opening, but I saw a man inside, kind of stunned and bloody and hanging from his seatbelt. I got him out."

"Details, Walter. Details. How did you squeeze into such a small opening? Did you injure yourself? How did you get the man out? Those sorts of things make our story come alive."

"The mangled engine hood was in the way," Walter said. "I lifted it up as best I could to make room. I cut my wrist and hand on the sharp metal, though I didn't notice at the time. I crawled in…I'm not a big man. Undid the seatbelt, and the man crashed on top of me. The fire had reached the back seat by then. I got out from under him and pulled him out behind me, I honestly don't know how."

"You are indeed small, Walter. Was it divine providence that you were on that lonely road, you, and not some hulking, beer-bellied slob?"

"The Lord works in mysterious ways. I believe that sincerely."

"You didn't come directly from choir practice?"

"No. I, ah, visited with a friend for a few hours."

"You mean you had an assignation with a choirboy, don't you?"

"Not a boy, a man. He's twenty-six. We love each other."

"Would the Lord approve, you laying with this man? Would the pastor give this unholy union his blessing?"

Defiant now, Walter thrust out his chin. " 'Judge not, lest ye be judged.' It's in the Bible."

"Haven't read it. Saw the movie. Were you afraid, Walter, crawling into that burning car?"

"I don't know. I guess I should have been, but I was just in this weird zone where the only thing that mattered was getting this poor man to safety."

"If you weren't afraid, maybe not so heroic, eh?"

Walter looked puzzled.

The man was really getting into it now, rubbing his

hands together and biting the stem of his pipe. "In that moment you were just an unfeeling bundle of reflexes and synaptic firings. Where's the bravery in that, timid little Walter Meely? What kind of hero is too afraid to tell Mummy he loves banging choirboys?"

Meely strained at his bindings. "Don't judge me," he shouted. "Why am I tied up, if you're so darn brave?"

The man smiled and nodded his head as if conceding a point. "Are you afraid now, Walter?"

"Of course. This is…sick."

"I promise you'll be unbound next time we meet. We'll have an adventure or two. A hero-quest, if you will. You, me, our little team here, and our audience worldwide. Together, we'll explore this nebulous theory of heroism. Together, we'll gain insight into a concept sadly shopworn and devalued from overuse."

He shrugged. "Or die in the attempt."

Meely, at a loss for words, bowed his head and wept.

Chapter Four

Aberdeen, Washington, July

Jake lost control of his interview with Christina Doctorow before it began.

"I'm going stir-crazy setting up my practice," she said over the phone the day before. "It's like moving into a museum."

"You don't want a story?"

"Oh, hell yeah. I'll need the publicity and I've a student debt like you wouldn't believe. But, say, you have a little recorder like reporters use?"

"Of course."

"And hiking boots?"

"Um, yeah?"

"And a couple of free hours?"

"Whatever it takes."

"Okay, ten tomorrow morning. Meet me at Dr. Wilson's antique surgery, soon to be Doctorow's Holistic Health Care. The replacement sign goes up tomorrow. You can drive us to something called the Weatherwax Marine Forest, you know it?"

"More stroll than hike, but the full coastal rainforest experience, paths through the old-growth, great birding, and wildlife from deer to occasional otter."

"Sold. Ten it is."

"You'll—"

She'd already ended the call.

****

She basked in sunshine on her office steps as Jake pulled up. She dumped a daypack in the back of his ride, then settled into the passenger's seat. He reached across the stick shift of his sporty Japanese import to shake her hand. "You picked a perfect day for this. Hi, I'm Jake."

"Hope so. I don't as a rule get in cars with strange men." She gave his hand a perfunctory shake. "Tina." She turned his palm up, running her fingers over its scars. "We'll talk about this later," she said. It was more order than request.

"Mind if I have this back? It's useful for shifting gears and such. You a palm reader?"

"No, but they do tell a tale."

Jake shoulder checked and pulled onto the street, heading west toward Ocean City and the Weatherwax trailhead. "Been reading up on you. I hardly know where to begin."

"How about after an hour into the hike." She nodded toward the backseat. "I brought my famous homemade oat bars. I assume you're bribable?"

"Not to the same extent as my aunt. Oat bars, yes. A full checkup, no."

"That's a relief, I didn't bring a rubber glove."

She flashed a smile. Arcade Fire came on the radio. She reached over and turned up the volume, closed her eyes and popped on sunglasses, bobbing her head to "Rebellion."

Jake used the opportunity to study his passenger. Thick black hair in a long ponytail hung out the back of a faded Huskies ball cap. A spray of freckles dotted across prominent cheekbones which bracketed a nose that turned up at the tip. Dark sunglasses rested above a small bump that hinted at a past break, soccer being a rough game.

He used a red light to complete his assessment. A scoop-necked sleeveless blouse revealed muscled biceps and a cascade of freckles on her upper chest. Between canvas hiking shorts and a battered pair of hiking boots was a whole lot of powerful leg. No rings on either hand.

She lowered her sunglasses. "Meet your approval?"

Apparently, her eyes weren't closed. "Purely clinical," he said. "I'm painting a word picture."

The prescribed first hour was a surprise. Rather than the torrid pace he'd expected, she'd stopped frequently along the narrow paths to study moss-draped branch and treetop, fern, fungus, and eagle. She greeted them as old friends.

They settled on a mossy patch at a secluded spot near the lake. Tina opened her pack to remove a thermos of coffee, two cups and a container of oat bars. A nearby Sitka spruce dappled the sunlight. A faint breeze carried a riot of scents: the tang of salt water, the rot of damp earth, and fusty whiffs of cabbage and mildew from a multitude of mushrooms and fungi.

Jake reached for a second oat bar. "Thought you'd bring your dog along?"

"Dog?"

"The photo with your ad has a gorgeous husky."

Her face clouded. "A bit of a fraud, that picture. I wanted to portray myself as a healthy, outdoorsy, animal-loving kind of gal." She pointed at his recorder.

"All true. But," she said, making a slashing motion across her throat, "that's not for publication. Agreed?"

"Agreed."

"The dog, Ranger, belongs to the guy I left behind. I miss him terribly."

Jake hid his disappointment. "He'll join you later?"

She laughed and shook her head. "Hell no. It's Ranger I miss. As for the guy, Ray's his name, happy to be free and clear. In our last, ah, discussion, after I discovered he was playing the field, he called me, among other things, 'assertive, controlling, and cocksure'."

"And those are bad things?"

"They speak to his insecurities and his archaic view of relationships. I mean, *cocksure*? Even his language is out of date. There were any number of reasons to dump him, but cheating, being lied to, that I won't tolerate." She looked embarrassed. "Sorry about the overshare. That damn Ray still gets me wound up." She looked at his recorder. "While that little red light is off, tell me about your love life? Only fair."

"Not how it works. I'm the interviewer, you're the interviewee."

She ran a finger across her mouth, then crossed her arms. "Waiting."

"Assertive," Jake said. "Controlling. Cocksure."

"Waiting."

He shifted his gaze to a scudding cloud and sighed. "My only major relationship in Grays Harbor was a high school sweetie named Amanda. That ended when I went to college in Pennsylvania. She's a mother now, married off and on to a sheriff in town. Trent Shane, a guy I went to school with—a bully then and remains one now. Some weeks back he warned he'd do me dental damage if I went anywhere near Amanda. Now *that's* controlling."

"And?"

"Zero interest in meddling in their toxic marriage."

"What about Judy, over in Pennsylvania?"

"Judith." Jake reared back. "How in hell? Ah, jeez, Clara's been running her mouth."

Tina flashed a canary-swallowing grin. "Can't reveal my sources, doctor-patient confidentiality. And don't avoid the question."

"We had two good years, then our paths diverged. She landed an assistant professorship at MIT—a very big deal and much deserved. Wanted me to follow her to Cambridge." He raked a hand through his hair. "The relationship was running its course. And by then, Clara was offering the editorship of the *Grays Harbor Independent*. Naturally, I couldn't resist all this power and prestige."

"Naturally."

He clicked on the recorder. "First question: Why would a woman of your accomplishments wash up in Grays Harbor?"

The smile faded. "How about we save that for another time? Let's keep it positive. It's important—personally, professionally, and financially—I make a good impression here in my adopted community. I'm sure your readers are interested in my holistic health approach—my philosophy of pushing exercise, diet and lifestyle changes ahead of pills."

Jake faked an extravagant yawn. "Oh, they'll be fascinated."

Chapter Five

Aberdeen, Washington, July

Tina Doctorow marched into Jake's back office at the *Independent* the day after publication and settled into a chair across from his desk.

He was on the phone taking notes. He looked up then returned his attention to the phone. "Thanks for this, Stanley. I'll give details of your fundraiser to Rhonda, she's our resident cat lover...No, I don't hate cats." Jake looked at Tina and rolled his eyes. "But Rhonda *really* loves them. She'll do a great job. Look, gotta run, someone just arrived with a hot news tip."

He looked at Tina, leaning forward in her chair, elbows resting on his desk. "Have a seat. Make yourself comfortable. If you're in the market for freshly spayed felines, Happy Cat Haven has a silent auction fundraiser next weekend. Great savings on kibble, litter, and two-for-one kitty cats. You heard it here first."

It was Tina's turn to roll her eyes. "About my profile," she said, hands now clasped on his desk. *'Doc Doctorow Opens Shop.'* Really?"

"Rhonda wrote the headline. I was rather busy, what with Mulvaney's Hardware burning down right before deadline. I had to cut a third of your story to slam that one in."

"You've branded me for all time as 'Doc

Doctorow.' Lacks dignity. And 'Opens Shop' is no better. Couldn't your cat-lover have written, Dr. Tina Doctorow Opens Holistic Medical Practice?"

"Bor-ing. And too long for the space. Personally, I'd have gone with Doc Doctorow Opens Up, but you weren't very forthcoming. You went on and on about exercise and nutrition and medical philosophy. It was all so…clinical."

"I *am* a doctor."

"But somewhere there's a real Tina under that medical gobbledygook. What makes you tick? What drew you to Grays Harbor? You never did say. I had to jam in a reference to your oat bars just to reveal some humanity. I've already had a reader request the recipe."

"That's not all you revealed. That photo you took of me up a ladder installing the clinic sign focused way too much on my legs and ass."

Jake grinned, guilty as charged. "It also showed the beautiful smile of a take-charge young woman, screwdriver in hand, toolbelt on waist. Hey, you chose to wear shorts."

She snorted. "I'll let you make it up to me."

"While not admitting guilt, I'll spring for dinner. Fine family dining at the Grizzly Den. They've got twenty-five different burgers on the menu and some gluten-free stuff, if you're into that."

She shook her head.

"You drive a hard bargain," he moaned. "Okay, how about Rediviva? They've a Dungeness Cappelletti to die for."

"In your dreams. For now, it's nose to the grindstone while I open shop," she said, air-quoting the last two words. "What I had in mind was a volume discount on, say, fifty copies of the *Independent*. For all the story's flaws, it's good fodder for the waiting room."

"When you put it like that, how can I refuse?" He picked up the phone. "Anna Mae, can you give Doc Doctorow a bundle of papers as she leaves, please…It's Jake, who else calls you on my office line? No, I said *give*, as in no charge."

He hung up with a sad shake of head. "Anna Mae is what you call a legacy employee. She hides her deep respect for me under a thin veneer of disdain."

Tina rose to leave. "Thanks for the papers."

"Two words, doctor," Jake said.

She stopped at his office door. "Yes?"

"Dungeness Cappelletti."

She turned and headed down the hall. Jake's gaze lingered, him wondering if she hadn't put a hint of extra swing into that very fine behind.

Chapter Six

Jake installed Erik Demidov, his best friend and former college roommate, in the river shack's guest bedroom. He'd arrived from Seattle for a weekend visit. They sipped Scotch on the deck watching the river flow and digesting Jake's five-spice duck breast, scalloped potatoes and fresh-picked green beans.

He gave Jake two-to-one odds on a five-dollar bet that an ominous cloudbank building off the Pacific coast would spare the city yet another dump of rain. Erik was back from a three-week working visit to, well, he wouldn't say. "Oh, the tale I could tell if not for my non-disclosure agreement," he said.

"You got one hell of a tan wherever it was."

"The glow of success."

While the visit was mostly recreational, Erik planned a brief meeting with Clara. He'd rebuilt the *Independent's* rudimentary website, tripling traffic and doubling revenue. "I still have a few bells and whistles to add."

Such web slinging was a favor for Jake. His real job was as a senior agent for BitBust, an international digital investigations company. If a plane mysteriously crashes, or another critic of the Russian government falls from a balcony, or suspected left-wing rioters loot a gun shop, BitBust draws on multiple video sources, satellite imagery, clandestine communications, and shoe-leather investigating to tell the real story. Maybe a shoulder-held rocket launcher brought down the plane. Maybe the critic's swan dive began with a push. Maybe the lefty anarchists were really neo-Nazis. BitBust's paying clients, at least those Erik talked about, were major news organizations, police services, besieged opposition parties of repressive regimes, and insurance companies.

Jake suspected the client list also included many clandestine three-letter national and international agencies. Some extensive BitBust investigations had to be underwritten by entities with deep pockets.

Jake knew Erik worked months and travelled widely for one such investigation before letting slip he'd delivered the goods. When he asked if the results would be made public, Erik gave a derisive snort.

His phone pinged with a text from Tina.

—*I've come up for air and worked up a heck of an appetite. Your story, for all its flaws, attracted a host of new patients. If your offer of a sumptuous dinner is still on the table, it better be, tomorrow night works for me*—

Jake did a mini fist pump and typed:

—*You betcha. Pick you up at 7:30*—

He looked to Erik, shrugged, thought what the hell and added to his text:

—*We may have a third for dinner. He's housebroken, more or less*—

Erik spent the rest of the evening prying out a scant few details about Tina.

"What was that you said about non-disclosure agreements?" Jake asked, then shrugged. "There's nothing to tell."

"Yet."

Jake went online and reluctantly booked a table for three at Rediviva. "Don't feel obligated," he'd told Erik. "You know, if you've other plans."

Erik beamed. "I wouldn't miss it for the world, I want to meet this doctor of yours."

The smile transformed to a malicious grin. "Perhaps you're disappointed? Perhaps you wish to be alone with your little kitten, your *malen'kiy kotenok*? Call her that and she'll lap milk from the palm of your hand. Such a warm language for such a cold country. But I digress."

Erik was doing his Russian shtick. He'd never been to the country, near as Jake knew, having learned the language, and his low opinion of its leadership, from his father, an embittered expat Russian Jew.

Jake threw up his hands. "Cool your jets, buddy. She's not my kitten."

"Yet. But you wish, eh? Leave it to me. I'll sip some wine, I'll break the ice, then, poof, I'll disappear."

****

Saturday evening found the three presiding over a chilled bottle of dry white and a platter of Rediviva appetizers. Tina asked how they met.

"Thrown together as roommates by the university housing authority in first year," Jake said. "Turns out we found each other's company tolerable, so we shared an apartment all four years."

"The Odd Couple," Erik said. "Different as chalk and cheese. He's Oscar."

"And he was my babe magnet," Jake said. "Women find him wildly attractive for reasons I can't fathom."

"Humm," Tina said with a dreamy smile.

"Yes," Erik said, "it is my burden."

Tina batted her eyes. "Poor you." Turning to Jake: "And lucky you."

Erik turned his full wattage on Tina, his questions extracting little beyond her carefully edited backstory. Jake could have filled in some blanks, but wisely chose not to.

Never one to let the conversation lag, Erik changed tack, recounting a BitBust case Jake hadn't heard before which involved an Internet pill mill that ground up male *pleasure pills,* packed the powder in gelatin capsules and sold them as Blue Magic, an "IQ enhancer for children ten and under."

Tina was agog. "That's appalling."

"Truly," Erik said. "They sold like wildfire, even as complaints poured in. The challenge was finding the source. The Blue Magic website was so brilliantly masked the company seemed to operate in twenty countries at once. Ultimately, we traced it to a warehouse on the outskirts of Kaunos, Lithuania. It was a mob operation, guarded like Fort Knox. Gaining access for the requisite proof was dangerous and daunting. Naturally, BitBust prevailed."

"Naturally," Jake said.

"Inevitably." Erik spread his hands, no hint of false modesty. "Our client, who shall remain nameless, was most grateful."

"Those poor children," said Tina. "What side effects they must have suffered."

Erik gave a knowing grin. "The side effects, for little boys especially, proved both a blessing and curse for the producers of Blue Magic. Parents bathing their little Johnnies and Fritzes noticed a rampant display of up-periscope from the bathwater, if you get my drift."

"Oh, dear," Tina said.

"Fathers took to sampling the product, finding Blue Magic to be effective in raising the paternal, um, IQ."

"Oh, dear," Tina said again. "I know where this is going."

Erik turned to Jake. "Your doctor friend is wise beyond her years. Yes, Tina, the complaints came from mothers. While many were initially grateful for their partners' rejuvenated affection, the sleep loss and wear-and-tear ultimately proved overwhelming."

Tina pressed a napkin to her face. "I just snorted wine out my nose," she said between fits of laughter.

Leave it to Erik to unbutton Tina's earthy side. Jake was a bit jealous as Erik proved more adept than he in the unbuttoning. It was ever thus. Tonight, his friend was as good as his word. He popped a last crab croquette into his mouth and rose to go. "I'll leave the main course to you two."

Tina looked disappointed. "Must you go?"

"I've intruded long enough on your date. I know you two have fascinating histories to share. Besides," he fanned his face with a hand, "I sense a sexual tension that's quite overwhelming."

Jake groaned in embarrassment and rested his forehead on the tabletop. "And, poof, he was gone."

"Poof? Rather crude, Jake. Just because your friend is gay…"

Jake's face reddened. "You misunderstand. It's just that he'd promised me he'd 'poof,' disappear before the entrees. And how did you know he's gay?"

"It's obvious."

"Because you're a doctor?"

"Well, he didn't hit on me. But the real tells were the sly looks between him and that waiter over there, the one with the cute butt." She rested her chin on a hand, enjoying his discomfort. "So, *is* this a date?"

"Um, ah, yeah. If you don't mind," he stammered. "If you want it to be."

"That changes everything," she said, attempting to look stern. "Economic factors are now at play. Instead of your treat, we'll split the bill. I'll not cede you home-court advantage."

The exchange seemed to clear the air. The conversation flowed as did a second bottle of wine. They grazed each other's main courses, her Dungeness Cappelletti, and his Black Pepper Beef Loin.

He walked her home, stopping outside a tired-looking six-plex, painted in what looked like navy surplus battleship gray. "Just 'til I get on my feet," she said with a head-nod behind her. "It came furnished in mid-century moldy."

"I enjoyed tonight," Jake said.

"Me, too," she said. "But let's take it slow, huh? I just got here. Is it seemly to fall for the first boy I see?"

"I have an opinion, but only you can answer that."

"Do me a favor."

"Anything."

"Don't become my patient. Wouldn't be ethical." She took his hands, running her thumbs over his scarred palms. "We haven't talked about this. And what did Erik mean we both have histories to share?"

"Plenty of time for that."

"Seriously, what could he know about me?"

Jake silently cursed Erik's tendency toward

oversharing on all things but BitBust escapades. "He stayed in my guest bedroom, which doubles as my home office. It's where I wrote the story of your office opening. He must have looked at your file. The man's an inveterate snoop."

"File?" Her voice suddenly frosty. "You keep a file on me?"

"We're a newspaper. We keep files on all prominent citizens."

"Prominent? I don't know whether to be flattered or horrified. I want to see it."

"That's highly irregular."

"It's highly essential. Erik's right, our histories are mysteries. Fair's fair, I want to know more about you. Your rowing. Your work. Those hands. Life's key moments you've artfully avoided sharing."

You're one to talk.

She stood there, resolute, chin thrust forward. "I assume you have a file, too?"

"Like I said, we're a newspaper. It's not very inspiring reading."

"Are you free Wednesday night, after the paper goes to press?"

Jake nodded, feeling trapped.

"I'll come by your office at eight, have both files ready. This won't be a date."

"More like an inquisition."

A hint of smile vanished almost as quickly as it appeared. "Goodnight," she said, turning for her door.

Chapter Seven

Erik headed home to Seattle midday Sunday, clearly disappointed at the chaste end to Jake and Tina's dinner date. "What's dinner," he asked with a sigh, "without dessert?"

"We shared a Crème Brulé."

"Have I taught you nothing?"

With Erik gone, Jake reclaimed his office. He turned to the stack of mail on his desk: two bills, three charity appeals, and a white envelope with a blurry postmark and no return address. Setting aside the bills, he ripped open the white envelope.

It contained his check torn in half, a photo and a digitally printed response to his attempt to buy the Sacrifice Medallion.

"Dear Mr. Ockham,

"Your decision not to run our advertisement puts us at a disadvantage. It leaves you as our only potential customer. As a result, we must raise the price. It is now two hundred dollars, in addition to the refund of the fifty dollars we paid for a classified advertisement you failed to publish.

"Admittedly, this is a steep price for a shiny bauble. One supposes it has some worth as a curiosity, though the currency of the term 'Hero' is overused and much debased in these slipshod times.

"Payment of two hundred and fifty dollars should

be delivered via e-transfer to the email address below. The verification code will be the word 'Sedgewick.'

"As a gesture of good faith, enclosed is a photo of the back of this medallion, containing the name of this supposed 'hero' and the purported deed that earned him this bit of bronze.

"A prompt response is expected and appreciated,

"Sincerely, Dr. B. Dawes."

Jake reread the letter, shook his head and muttered, "Pompous ass."

Words like "supposed" and "purported" never figured into his investigations. Facts are the backbone of Sedgewick's rigorous definition of heroism.

The medal criteria are simple and daunting: a civilian leaves safety and risks death in an attempt to save the life of someone they have no responsibility to help. That generally rules out family members, and soldiers and first responders unless they're off duty.

About one-in-five rescuers die in the attempt. Those investigations especially are draining, humbling, and to be honest, mystifying. Everyone's a hero in their imagination, but risking all in the split second of a crisis? Well, you just never know.

Every aspect is checked to gauge the degree of personal danger. Everything from the temperature, waves and swimming abilities for water rescues, to video evidence and interviews with participants, witnesses and first responders at the scene of a fiery vehicle crash.

And it was just such a crash that earned Walter Meely the medal now up for sale.

Jake looked at the photograph and reread the bald facts engraved on the back:

Walter J. Meely who saved Charles W. Spenser from a burning vehicle.

OMAHA, NEB.

April 9, 2016

Jake knew the story well. It was a grateful Charlie Spenser who nominated his rescuer, sending the Sedgewick Trust a photocopy of a news brief of the event. Jake handled the case from the fund's Pittsburgh offices, conducting Skype interviews with both men and the on-scene fire and ambulance crew. He also tracked down a passerby's shaky, expletive-filled phone video of the rescue.

The thing about most heroes is they're so unlike the stuff of movies and television.

He thought back to some of his cases. Why, for example, would a middle-aged black secretary at an insurance company pull her race-baiting neighbor from a burning apartment?

Why would a twenty-something high school dropout with a criminal record sacrifice his life attempting to save a six-year-old girl from a flood-swollen river? He didn't even know how to swim.

And why did Walter Meely, the organist and music director for Omaha's Living Gospel Evangelical Church, crawl into the shattered remains of an SUV to pull an unconscious Charlie Spenser from the flames?

Jake attended the medal presentation ceremony for that one, held at the Living Gospel Church, the choir stall full and the pews packed. It was Jake's first in-person meeting with Meely, all five-foot-three and one hundred thirty-eight pounds of him. It was a mystery how he even pulled Spenser, a burly warehouse forklift operator, from the wreck. For Living Gospel's pastor there was no doubt: "The guiding hands and holy power of the Lord manifested in His humble servant Walter."

The presentation was a teary affair.

Spenser practically crushed Meely in an enveloping hug. By contrast, Jake's congratulatory handshake was a model of restraint; he was aware of the wormlike scar on Meely's wrist and hand, torn open by a jagged piece of the SUV.

Later, Meely's diminutive mother, Sabina, pulled Jake aside. "Nothing like this has ever happened to Walter," she said, peering up at Jake through the thick lenses of her glasses. "To be called a hero after so many years of insults and bullying! This means the world to him. Maybe now he'll meet a nice girl," she said, giving Jake's arm a squeeze, "move out and get a place of his own."

Jake had taken an instant liking to the guy.

He flipped the photo back on his desk. He couldn't see Meely selling or surrendering his medal. Not willingly.

"Supposed hero?"

Fuck you, Dr. Dawes.

Jake would buy the medallion, if only to get it out of those cynical hands—then he'd find out what happened to Walter Meely.

Chapter Eight

Clearfield County, Pennsylvania, July

Professor Dawes, as he demanded to be known, peered through the eye-slots of the locked doors of his two guests. "Up and at 'em. I've arranged a playdate this morning."

He elicited a low moan from Meely's cell and a spirited "Fuck you" from the new guy.

It was a week since Meely's arrival and four days since his video debrief. The online audience grew impatient. It took longer than expected to round up a second contestant, who was installed just three days ago with the usual bitching and moaning.

The original thought was to grab a girl, add some sexual tension to the mix. Meely's predilections rendered that moot. So, in a bit of a rush job, they nabbed a kid named Reggie Obergon. Well, a kid of fifteen when he snagged a Sedgewick medal eleven years ago for diving off the side of a disused Michigan quarry to rescue a ten-year-old boy who'd tumbled into the icy water.

The hated Jake Ockham hadn't investigated this case, but Obergon would do.

The kid and his mom were picnicking on the reclaimed hillside when he strayed too close to the quarry's edge and slipped in. All the mother could do was scream, which got the attention of Obergon who was at the unofficial swimming hole with a couple of buddies.

It was spring break. While the ice was off the water, the boys had yet to screw up the courage for the season's first ball-sucking plunge from their usual ledge. Until Mommy screamed.

Reggie reacted instantly, taking a running leap from the lip of the quarry, a twenty-five-foot drop to the water. He reached the hypothermic boy just as he slipped below the surface. With his own strength sapped by the cold, it was all he could do to get them to a low gravel beach, where he put his Boy Scout CPR to good use.

As always, the Sedgewick description was a bloodless recitation of facts. It was the online news accounts that captured the professor's interest. Reggie was an unremarkable working-class kid. He told reporters, *"I just jumped, didn't think. Lucky I didn't know how cold the water was."*

One of his friends, basking in the reflected glory, said *"When it comes to not thinking, Reggie is an expert."*

The Sedgewick citation made much of the quarry's three-hundred-foot depth, as if you couldn't drown as easily in ten feet of water. And since the kids were eventually going to dive in, Dawes reasoned, where's the heroism in that?

The rescue was in a hard-luck township in southeast Michigan, which would have spared him from the professor's attention. But bad luck for Obergon, his layoff from a Detroit auto plant inspired him to take his welding papers to Pittsburgh, the Steel City. He would still have escaped notice if a Detroit newspaper hadn't done a ten-year retrospective on the rescue. Turns out the kid Obergon fished out became a Rhodes Scholar. The Pittsburgh papers ran an *AP* version of their adopted local hero.

Pittsburgh was just two hours by van from the professor's home. Obergon's fate was sealed. Walter Meely had yet to take the measure of his fellow prisoner. Reggie Obergon was not the trusting sort. "How do I know you're not a fuckin' plant?" was his response to Meely's tentative greeting as the new guy pounded the walls, turned the air blue.

The rage in Obergon's voice smothered a whole mess of fear, Meely surmised. He could relate.

It was the second day before Obergon shared his name. He'd returned from his own video interview, which did nothing to improve his mood. "They tell me you got one of those hero medals too," he called through the cell door.

After Meely explained he'd crawled into a burning SUV to rescue an accident victim, Obergon said, "Least you were warm. I froze my nuts off pulling a kid out of a quarry."

After a pause, Walter asked, "What do you think they've got against heroes?"

They tossed around theories but got nowhere.

Obergon said, "There's three of them, by my count. Two guys and that piece of ass who picked me up in a bar. Called herself Blaze."

He mimicked a female voice, " 'Oooh, show me your medal. I want all the details.' I took her to my place, gave her a look-see. I says, 'So, what are you gonna show me?' She says, 'Anything your heart desires but let's have a drink first.' About the last thing I remember 'til I woke up in this shit hole. That the same deal with you?"

Meely hesitated. "More or less."

Chapter Nine

Aberdeen, Washington, July

Jake clicked "send" at 6:30 p.m. Wednesday, electronically shipping the final four pages of that week's edition to a regional printer fifty miles east in Olympia. It had been decades since economics dictated the *Independent* mothball its own small Goss press.

The headline on this week's line story read "*Fam-Values Group Demands Right to Vet Library's Young Adult Collection.*"

Jake's photo showed a dozen pinch-faced protestors marching outside the library and carrying placards that said, "*YA Books Create Young Atheists*" and "*It's Public —Not PUBIC—Library*"

Jake stirred the pot with a raging editorial, asking if they'd *"excise the naughty bits in the Good Book while you're at it?"* He sat as he wrote in the very chair where his grandfather died while defending the right of J.D. Salinger to "corrupt" an earlier generation of adolescents.

It was the perfect seat for writing such editorials, so damned uncomfortable it instantly put him in an aggressive frame of mind. Beneath his editorial he reprinted an excerpt of his grandfather's half-finished diatribe, under the headline "*Stupid Idea Then, Stupid Idea Now.*"

With the paper put to bed, he headed to a diner around the corner for a take-out burger and fries. He ate at his desk, careful not to spill mustard on two files with the power to kill or cure his ailing love life. He was sorely tempted to excise offending parts of both Ockham, Jake, W. and Doctorow, Christina, S. but having just written a thundering defense of freedom of expression that would be the height of hypocrisy. Also, dishonesty is no way to start a relationship, if that's what this became.

At close to eight he put on a pot of coffee and girded his neglected loins for battle.

At one minute after eight there was a knock on the *Independent's* front door.

He let her in with a bow.

She handed him a plastic container. "Spelt brownies," she said.

"Humm?"

"An ancient grain, packed with protein, you being a red meat guy."

"Yum. Come on back, coffee's on."

The files, and a thermal carafe of coffee and fixings were arranged on a scarred low table overlooking the building's side driveway. He wheeled his late grandpa's desk chair to the table. "Use this," he said. "It's my favorite."

With preliminaries out of the way, he waved to the files. "Choose your poison, me or thee?"

"Me first," she said. "Shouldn't take long."

She picked it up, looking surprised at its heft. Jake had arranged her personal details chronologically. The first sheet she pulled out was a printout of her birth announcement, retrieved from *newspapers.com*.

"Really?"

"Trust, then verify. You seemed too good to be true. Had to make sure you weren't an angel fallen to earth."

"Jesus."

There were a couple of items from the *Tacoma News Tribune* of her high school sporting exploits on the soccer pitch and volleyball court, also plucked from *newspapers.com*.

The next four pages stapled together caused a visceral reaction as Jake knew they would. There was a slight tremor as she flipped quickly through the pages. She turned them over and set them to the side. They were stories from the Tacoma and Seattle papers dated Dec. 18, 2006, and others in the following days.

The headlines were variations on a theme of "Prominent couple" or "Tacoma lawyer and beloved base doctor" killed in late-night rollover on state route 151. The stories said the couple—Tacoma criminal lawyer Andrew Doctorow and his wife, Sandy Doctorow, a popular civilian doctor at the Madigan Army Medical Center—were killed while returning from a Christmas party at Joint Base Lewis-McChord.

Subsequent stories said what was initially thought to be a single-vehicle crash was now a hit-and-run investigation. Paint scrapes on the driver's side suggested they may have been sideswiped by a passing vehicle on the divided highway. *"The couple leaves behind two children, Curtis Doctorow, 21, and Christina Doctorow, 19, both university students."*

Tina looked to Jake, eyes hard, mouth pursed. "They never found the other driver. Thank you for not printing that."

"Not relevant."

She looked wounded.

"Not relevant to my news story. Very relevant to your life. I, ah, lost my mom to cancer when I was twelve."

She nodded then locked eyes with him, her gaze softer, reappraising. "Twelve. So young. Blows a hole in your life, doesn't it? I'd thought myself an adult until then, away from home, living in residence. Are you too old at nineteen to consider yourself an orphan? I threw myself into sports. Sweat therapy, I guess."

"I had my dad, and Clara. And rowing helped a lot, one form of pain crowding out the other."

Tina sped through more pages, her university years, plenty of sports triumphs and academic awards, pausing briefly at a printout with a reference to her undergrad thesis, *"Dead in the Water: Forensic Challenges and Limitations to Identifying Victims of Aberdeen, Washington's Infamous Floater Fleet."*

Hard to miss, Jake had circled it in ink, adding a question mark.

She turned over the page without comment and added more on top, as if to prove it was of no consequence. Transcripts of their hike/interview, and a clip of the resulting story were next in the folder. The last item was a fat manila envelope.

Jake braced for the worst.

She opened it, skimmed the top pages then threw them down on the table. They were lurid historical pieces on the infamous life of Aberdeen serial killer Billy Gohl. Her face reddened, her eyes blazed. "What's this got to do with anything?"

"I tend to over-research."

She turned over the yellowed, century-old news clips of Gohl's trial and arrest. Next, she picked up a fat photocopied excerpt from a local history book, *On the Harbor: From Black Friday to Nirvana*. The extract was a meticulously researched historical essay, *The Ghoul of Grays Harbor*. It was the single best piece on Billy Gohl Jake had seen.

He'd used yellow highlighter on part of the opening paragraphs: *"police were eventually able to link Gohl to nearly forty murders, though many historians believe the number could be as high as 200."*

She flipped through the pages, lingering on Jake's scribbled annotations and highlighted sections, looking for something she obviously didn't find. She shifted uncomfortably in the chair, though not uncomfortably enough to stop reading. "What has any of this trash to do with me?"

"There's one last item in the file."

It was a copy of Tina's undergrad thesis on the Floater Fleet. She immediately turned to the bibliography and references. She focused on two circled citations in particular: *"Doctorow Family Bible"* and *"Doctorows: A Private Family History."*

Affixed to the thesis was Jake's crudely drawn family tree and a bullet-point history, both dating from 1900. It was the year Gohl, a German-born career criminal already suspected of murder, arrived in San Francisco after leaving a trail of wreckage from Australia to Alaska and the Yukon Territory.

In San Francisco, he met and impregnated a dancehall girl named Annie. She refused his demands for an abortion and gave birth to a son, Billy Jr., in late 1900, putting Gohl's name on the birth certificate. Gohl denied paternity, gave her fifty dollars and threatened to "teach Billy Jr. to swim if you come begging for more."

By 1902, he'd moved up the coast to Grays Harbor, eventually marrying Bessie Hager, another dancehall girl. He used his position as a union official to rob and kill itinerant seafarers.

In San Francisco, Annie was transformed by motherhood. She took a clerking job, meeting and marrying a local bookkeeper and church deacon named George Doctorow. George adopted Billy Gohl Jr, who became William Doctorow after a formal name change. The couple had three other children. William was nine when his birthfather was arrested. He didn't learn of his parentage until Annie confessed in a letter on her deathbed in 1919, after contracting Spanish Flu.

"I have that letter," Tina said, her voice tight and cold. "I suppose that will be 'relevant' when you destroy my reputation."

"I'm not terribly adept at tracing family trees," Jake said, his voice hard. "But by my count you are Gohl's great-great-granddaughter. I did think it relevant at the time. You'll recall I asked you why, with your credentials, you'd come to a backwater like Grays Harbor."

"And you'll recall, I didn't answer. So, Mr. Ace Reporter, you've opened a grave for my reputation. What's your next story? 'Doc Doctorow, Part 2, Serial Killer's Bastard Kin?' That should get you out of this backwater and onto a big-time newspaper."

"Ace reporters often ask questions when they already know the answers. The responses, or non-response in your case, are revealing."

"I'm sure you can read all kinds of pop-psyche

bullshit into my motivations. Maybe I'm a 'Fallen Angel,' " she snapped, throwing up her hands in finger-quotes. "Damaged goods, here to atone for Great-great-granddad's sins."

"An ace reporter would do that," Jake said, his voice quiet. "What I am now is a small-town editor who happens to love this community, and who appreciates our need for quality doctors. Look at the retrieval date on the printout of your thesis."

She stood, arched her back, then reached for the thesis. The date was on the university library's fronting page. "Yeah, so?"

"So, I knew all this before our interview. What I read into your obfuscation was that you're eager to fit in here. And that you have personal and financial reasons not to carry that family burden into a new town and a fledgling practice."

He shrugged. "Being a hick reporter, I left it out."

She stood, holding her thesis, twisting her back and shoulders. She seemed momentarily at a loss for words, then said, "Your favorite chair is a piece of shit."

Jake gave a tentative smile, unsure if the storm had passed or this was a brief respite in the eye of Hurricane Tina. "Take the thesis and family history home with you," he said. "Shred it for all I care."

"I know you reporters love your files. Be a shame to waste all that paper. I was proud of that thesis. It was an excuse to process an ugly bit of family history. That's all it is: ancient history."

Jake nodded, not believing it.

She scooped up his file. "This, I'm borrowing. I don't get you, Jake Ockham."

"Just a simple guy. Simplicity is pretty much a

family doctrine."

"Why don't I believe that? Maybe there are clues here to what bubbles underneath."

Jake walked her to the front and locked the door behind her.

"When you find out," he said, munching a brownie, "let me know."

Chapter Ten

Aberdeen, Washington, July

After days of ominous silence Tina phoned Jake at the office. "The fallen angel has a file to return."

He angled for dinner, but reluctantly accepted trekking up the Aberdeen hillside for afternoon coffee at Grays Harbor Community Hospital, of all places.

She held down a corner table in the hospital coffee shop, looking very medical in blue scrubs. It stirred unsettling memories of a mother ravaged by cancer. And years later, of excruciating weeks in a burn unit. Dreams die in hospitals.

She looked up with a smile. "An Americano, please. Black."

He nodded, took her order to the counter and brought back a latte for himself. *She did smile. Can't be that bad.* He noticed his file on the table. *Well, maybe.*

He stirred in a packet of white death, groping for something to say. "As hospital coffee shops go…"

"Yeah, pretty good coffee." She swept both hands down her front. "Like my ensemble?"

Still at a loss, he said: "Hospitals scare me."

"Debt scares me. As I did a combined residency in family and emergency medicine, I got myself a one-shift-a-week gig in the ER to help with the outrageous costs associated with the opening of my practice. Once a week will keep my skills sharp."

She patted the buff folder. "Lots of raw data here. I doubt the *Independent* has many files with a ten-year spreadsheet of rowing machine scores. Far more impressive, by the way, than your college GPA."

He shrugged. "One plays to one's strengths. Ergometers never lie and those rowing machine scores helped get me the scholarship. That got me into the rowing program. And the rowing program trumped my tepid interest in an airy-fairy English program. Would have preferred a pure journalism department to dissecting the works of Faulkner, Steinbeck and Fitzgerald, if Carnegie Mellon had one. There's something obscene about poking at the innards of a perfect novel like *The Great Gatsby*. Takes the wonder out of it."

"It's rare to hear 'pure' and 'journalism' in a sentence, but I take your meaning. It would be like looking for God during an autopsy, lots of amazing plumbing but where's the magic once Elvis leaves the building?"

"At the Heartbreak Hotel, one assumes."

She tilted her head and gave a quizzical smile. "Where your Olympic dreams also reside?"

Jake cringed. "Ouch. Those were pretty farfetched. Probably wouldn't have happened even without the injury. I thought it was the end of the world at the time. You can look at it clinically and think it's selfish, obsessive, narcissistic even, to spend years of your life chasing a stupid piece of metal on a ribbon. But damn, I wanted it bad."

She swiped at a coffee ring on the table. "Do you feel differently now?"

"Yes and no. With rowing behind me, I had time for family and friends, for life and for journalism. I discovered I was actually pretty good at it. Journalism, I mean. But hey, in 2008, the year I was to try out for the national team, the Canadian men's eight won gold in Beijing. For the rest of their lives, they'll know that in that place, at that time, they were the best in the world. *The best*. No one can take that away."

"Like the fire did," she said, reaching for his hands, unclasping them and turning them scars up. "Do they still hurt?"

"They're sensitive. Before the burns, I had calluses so thick I trimmed them with razor blades. I tried a comeback after the injury, even swallowed my pride and wore gloves in training, very uncool. I couldn't row past the pain." Her hands were wonderfully warm. "My coach said it was more mental than physical. Maybe he's right."

"You call it 'the injury.' You have every right to say 'the rescue.' "

"Yeah, well…I dragged an unconscious kid named Brad out of that house. Which is how I got burned. He wasn't breathing. I knew his mother was in an upper room, but the stairs were blocked and on fire. It was suicide to try to reach her. I played it safe, thinking I'd try to bring the kid back with CPR."

"A good call."

He shook his head. "Brad's eleven-year-old sister, Kristy, didn't see it that way. She came on scene as I was thumping on her brother. Their mother—Shannon was her name—was trapped upstairs. We watched her die. Little Kristy was screaming like a banshee, calling me a coward for not saving her mother. I can't disagree.

Ever see a woman die?"

She tilted her head, incredulous.

"Sorry, doctor, stupid question."

"I was a resident, green as grass, when they wheeled a young girl named Ebony into the ER. She'd bailed off her skateboard, but regained consciousness in the ambulance. She aced all the cognitive tests. I diagnosed a mild concussion and the supervising doctor agreed."

She reached for her coffee. A slight tremor showed as she set down the cup. "I arrived next shift to learn she was comatose in the ICU from an undiagnosed brain bleed. Seventeen, and she wasn't coming back. My supervisor insisted I accompany him to give the shell-shocked parents *The Talk*. The one about all the lives that could be saved with Ebony's organs. I hated my supervisor for that. I hated medicine. I hated my failure."

It was Jake's turn to squeeze her hands.

"My supervisor said, 'You'll never forget your first death. All you can do is learn from it and from other mistakes we all inevitably make. Weigh this against the lives saved if you *don't* run from your profession.' "

"And here you are," Jake said with a smile, "pulling a shift in the ER, facing who knows what fresh hell tonight. As for me, what have I learned? How would I react in another life-or-death situation?" He shook his head. "Don't know. Don't want to find out."

"See," Tina said, "this conversation would have ruined a good dinner. I—" She frowned and reached for a pager clipped to her waist. "Seems my fresh hell is a multi-vehicle crash. Ambulances are six minutes out."

She handed over his file. "Let's put the past behind

us and take a look—a slow look, please—at what might be ahead."

She was almost out the door when she turned and called out, "Almost forgot. I had lunch with Clara yesterday."

"Huh? Why?"

"Like you said, 'Trust, then verify.' She's heading out of town. Wants a chat with you when she returns."

"She's already left me a turnover note."

"Not business. I think it's personal."

And she was gone.

Chapter Eleven

Clearfield County, Pennsylvania, June

The professor and the young guy herded Meely and Obergon into a windowless van. A small aluminum boat was trailered behind. They were gagged and cuffed, jammed beside an anvil, a spool of wire and a roll of plastic snow fencing.

Eventually, they stopped at a farmhouse that had seen better days. The young guy hammered on the unlocked door and did a quick walk-though. "No one home."

"As promised," the professor said.

During an earlier meeting, the professor gave the owner one-thousand cash for rental of an arena tucked deep in the trees. And for the use of Gus and Stud, for what the professor called a private show.

"Gus is what we call your bait dog. Helluva fighter in his day but not long for this world," the owner said during the negotiations. "Still, cost ya five hundred if he goes down."

The guy—improbably named Scooter—was a lean, mean five-foot-eight, transplanted Alabama cracker who'd moved operations north when things got hot in his home state. His face was leathered from sun and cigarettes. Could be fifty, could be seventy.

The professor found him on the Dark Web, source

of all good things.

"Now Stud, a purebred pit that boy," Scooter said, "past his prime but hellfire-mean. Got another season in him, with luck. A two-grand penalty if he dies, though I doubt Gus can do him much damage. Just in case, I'll take an extra thousand death insurance deposit. Refundable, of course."

"Of course."

"Sure you don't want me to dog wrangle?"

"Best for both of us if you stay clear," the professor said.

"A word of warning, friend," Scooter said, driving his hands in the front pockets of grubby jeans. "Narc us to the cops or the fuckin' SPCA and you're dog food."

"Nothing to fear from us," said the professor, creeped out by this runty psycho. "Just leave 'em chained and watered inside the arena. All we need are four clear hours and total privacy."

This morning, Scooter and his rusting stake truck were nowhere in sight the professor noted as he and Brad drove down a rutted lane walled by trees, pulling up beside a pickup parked by a weathered barn.

Blaze was sunning on the pickup's hood, looking fine in denim cut-offs and a tight white t-shirt. Nothing but soft skin under either article of clothing, in the professor's considered opinion.

"Hi, boys," she said, working on a Hazzard County drawl. "Got the lights, cameras, and generator ready to go but there's no way I'll get near those fuckin' dogs."

The prisoners were unshackled and led outside, each with a cuff dangling from one wrist. "There's a gun on you," the young guy told them. "Don't do anything stupid."

Blaze said, "Smile, boys."

After the two dangling cuffs were locked together, the blindfolds were removed. The sunlight blasted Meely's retinas. When his eyes adjusted, he saw the young woman filming from her cell phone.

"I unite you in holy matrimony," she said, giggling. "You may kiss the...hero."

"You may kiss my ass," Obergon said.

Both male captors pulled blue hoods over their heads with wide slits for eyes and mouths. Embroidered patches with HH logos were sewn on the masks at their foreheads. The captives had similar HH patches on their blue sweats.

Blaze aimed her phone at the young guy. He fished a coin from his pocket and turned to Obergon. "Heads or tails?"

"Why?"

The young guy sucker-punched him in the gut. He gasped and folded, dragging the cuffed Meely with him.

"Wrong answer. Your turn, Wally."

"Tails, I guess," he said.

"Figured you'd go for tail."

He flipped the coin, opening his palm for the camera. "And Wally wins."

The professor waved his pistol. "Inside, gents. *Hero Hatr,* canine edition, begins."

****

Meely was first assaulted by the smell of rot and dog shit. Then came the noises, a deep barking that built to a full-throated rage, and the *thwang* of heavy bodies slamming into chain-link. The dogs weren't visible, but the sounds stopped the prisoners cold.

It evoked memories of a dog attack when Meely

was six years old. He still carried the scars on his leg inflicted by their neighbor's psycho German shepherd. The memory of it haunted his nightmares for years. But he was no longer a scared little boy. Some people—his mother, his friends—saw him as a hero. He didn't define himself that way, but in these past few months, and especially these past days, he'd shed the paralyzing fear that had constrained his life and his choices.

He'd seen his captors' faces. He was a dead man—if not today then soon. He'd prayed on this and made his peace. The raging barks and growls stirred memories of a favorite Bible story. He looked to the sky as a gun in his back prodded them forward.

They were led into a barn-like arena. In its center, three-foot-high wooden walls enclosed a packed earth floor. Bright lights cast stains on walls and floor in stark relief. Crude tiers of wooden benches lined three sides of the box. Bolts of sound-deadening insulation were jammed between the studs of the barn walls. Red lights glowed on two cameras set high on tripods.

The men were pulled to a six-foot length of chain attached to an iron pipe set in concrete. A second cuff was snapped on Obergon's right wrist. The cuff's free end was locked to the last link of the chain.

Meely was still cuffed to Obergon's left wrist. It reminded him of an old movie on late-night television about two escaped convicts, one black, one white, chained at the wrist and chased by dogs. He couldn't remember the title, but it didn't end well.

The hooded professor stood in the center of the arena, mimicking the stentorian voice of a ring announcer. "Allow me to introduce the contestants. Cuffed to the chain is Reggie Obergon, twenty-six and one hundred eighty pounds in my estimation. To his left: Walter Meely, forty. Maybe one hundred forty pounds soaking wet. Wally won the toss. He's our designated hero, rewarded with the wider range of motion."

He turned to Obergon: "Reggie is the designated victim."

"Victim?" Obergon yanked at the chain, almost pulling Meely off his feet. "What the fuck?"

"Relax, Reggie," the ringmaster said. "Surely you realize luck is all that separates hero from victim. You're free, both of you, to forge your destinies. Indeed, we've placed an anvil to your left for that very purpose. To your right are chisel and mallet— potential tools of salvation."

He stepped out of the box. "Your lives, gentlemen, depend on courage and cooperation."

Looking to one of the cameras, he spread his arms in an expansive gesture. "That and avoiding Gus and Stud."

"Fuck me," groaned Obergon.

With that, gates opened at opposite ends and two dogs, acting on training and instinct, charged into the ring, slamming into each other in a collision of muscle and bone. They snarled and bit and then backed off, unaccustomed to humans in their battlefield.

Obergon sobbed and thrashed in terror, their shared handcuff ripping into Meely's wrist. Meely thought of his mother's long-ago gift of a children's Bible story book. Inside was a painting of the Old Testament prophet Daniel, punished for his uncompromising faith by being thrown into a den of lions.

The caption under the painting went something

like, "And Daniel emerged unscathed, saying: 'My God hath sent His angel, and hath shut the lions' mouths, that they have not hurt me.' "

Expecting no such miracle, Meely prayed, *If it is to be today, O Lord, may the end come quickly.*

Chapter Twelve

After his coffee date with Tina, Jake stopped at the newspaper to drop off his file. He set it on his desk, hesitated, then eased open its cover. Having lived in Pennsylvania most of his adult life, he'd never looked at what the *Independent* staff deemed worth saving. The contents unsettled him, like someone defining you by reading your diary. Tina must have felt the same way.

He sped past his early history. He sighed and pulled out a wad of news clips from the events at a hard luck farm in Washington County, outside tiny Gambles, Pennsylvania.

Eleven years ago. When everything changed.

The first story was the front page of Pittsburgh's largest newspaper. *"Burns kill Olympic Dreams As Carnegie-Mellon Rower Rescues Washington County Teen From Tragic Fire."* He went as far as the byline: *"By Travis Barnes, Special to the Post-Gazette,"* before flipping it over. "Asshole."

He'd relive the past on his terms, not those of Travis Fucking Barnes.

It was a Sunday afternoon, March 2008, his weekly chance to get off the Allegheny River and break out of Pittsburgh for a solo dry-land run. That week's choice, by random, was the rural countryside, twenty-five miles southwest of his campus apartment. He'd parked his cranky econobox in the empty lot of a Presbyterian church on Linden Road. The service over, the congregants had presumably moved on to worldly pursuits.

He locked his wallet and phone in the trunk and jammed the keys in a pocket of his Spandex running shorts. He strapped on a camel-pack of electrolyte water and stuffed a handful of protein bars in its side pocket—fuel for his six-thousand-calorie daily diet— then jogged right onto Linden Road. He wondered still about the randomness of fate. *What if I'd turned left?*

He had three more Sunday runs planned before putting his newly minted English degree on hold to head to New Jersey for national team trials at U.S. Rowing's Princeton Training Center. The Beijing Olympics, just months away, were out of the question. He was six-feet-two-inches and two hundred pounds, small by Olympic standards for the eight-boat, but he'd work his ass off for a shot on the U.S. team bound for London in 2012.

He got the tryout invitation on the strength of his sub-six-minute ergometer scores over a simulated two-thousand-meter course. Numbers don't lie, they were world-class for his age, an unfailing measure of power, endurance and pain tolerance. That damn machine went nowhere, but in his mind, he'd rowed the equivalent of the Atlantic and back again.

Linden Road was empty that late afternoon. He thundered into the turn to Ross Road, gravel crunching underfoot. The chirp of the season's first robins and the *conk-a-ree* of red-winged black birds. Glancing up, the sky flickered and glowed above the trees, faint at first, then joined by plumes of black smoke. Maybe someone burning brush? Maybe not.

He found another gear, lungs screaming as he rounded a corner and saw, at the end of a long, winding lane, a tired two-story wood-frame house engulfed in flames. His phone back in the car, no other houses in sight. He bent over on the weedy front lawn, hands on knees, catching a few ragged breaths. He looked up, horrified to see a woman in a closed window on the second floor. She gesticulated wildly, the window obviously stuck, shouting words he couldn't hear over the roar of flames and the crackle of tinder-dry wood.

He searched the lot for a ladder, saw nothing but a battered wheelbarrow and an axe leaning against a stack of firewood. He pointed to the barn set some forty yards back and mimicked climbing a ladder. She shook her head a frantic no, pointing down to the first floor.

Smoke curled from cracks around the heavy wooden front door. Jake pulled off his camel pack and his t-shirt, drenching it in the last of his water. He tried the door. Locked. He sprinted for the axe, slamming it against the lockset until the door yielded. He wrapped the wet shirt around his face, and bending low, ran into a wall of smoke.

Incongruous amidst the maelstrom, a sports channel on a big-screen TV in the empty living room previewed that evening's Flyers game. The kitchen was fully engaged, the wall behind the stove a sheet of flame, backlighting a lone pot on a back burner. A support beam crashed between the hallway and the upper staircase, setting off a swarm of sparks. It landed on an inert body slumped at the foot of the stairs. The beam, now aflame, pinned the legs of what appeared to be a young male. Impossible to be sure, Jake's eyes streaming from the smoke.

He peeled the shirt off his face, slamming it into the beam, knocking back the flames near the body's legs. He found a broom and tried prying up the beam. The wooden handle snapped. He slid the broken handle under the smoldering beam, grabbed either side to lift it off the upper leg. The heat so unbearable he couldn't clear the body's left foot before he had to let go.

He was dizzy from the smoke and coughing violently. There was nothing else he could do but wrap his charred shirt around his hands and lift away the beam, the wood glowing red and sparking. The fire's roar was momentarily blotted out by a bellowing scream. His own.

He lifted the body in a fireman's carry and ran out the door. He collapsed on the grass a safe distance from the flames, gasping for fresh air, lawn spinning, lungs aching. It was twenty long seconds before he was able to roll over and inspect the still body of a teenage boy. There were no apparent burns on his face and upper body. No signs of life.

The ground floor and front porch were now fully ablaze. He was torn. It was suicide to attempt to reach the woman…but the anguish and terror on her face…

As for the boy, perhaps there was hope. Cardiopulmonary resuscitation, CPR training, was an essential part of rowing first-aid. He tilted up the boy's head, pushed down on the forehead to clear the airway, and blew two deep breaths into his gaping mouth. He linked both hands on the boy's chest, locked elbows and pushed hard, hoping he didn't break any ribs.

He bit down on a cry as pain surged, scraps of his

polyester running shirt melted to his ravaged hands. Stuffed the agony in the vault where hurt goes a thousand meters into an all-out race.

He pumped thirty times. Not expecting a miracle and not getting one.

He continued the machine-like cycle: two breaths, thirty pumps. Repeat. Getting nothing in return but guilt and pain.

The woman was no longer at the window.

Dammit, kid, breathe. Betting the farm on you.

He heard the crash of glass. A porcelain toilet tank top smashed through the upper window and landed on the porch roof. At the same time a car roared up the drive and skidded to a stop.

Thank Christ.

He kept pumping, looking up as the woman pulled down flaming curtains.

A girl ran from the car, pointing to the window, screaming, "Save my Ma!"

Two breaths, more pumps. Jake shouted, "Anyone know CPR?"

"No idea," said the driver of the car, a pot-bellied man in his fifties with a cell phone clutched in his hand. "Called 911. Was drivin' Kristy home, my daughter's friend, and we come up on this. God what a mess."

"Find a ladder," Jake shouted, still bent over the boy. The girl's cries turned to a frenzy of rage. "Save my ma, you coward!" She kicked and pummeled his back with growing ferocity.

"Ain't no ladder," shouted the driver, running from the barn. "Fire department's on its way."

Jake pumped on, for all the good it was doing.

There was more breaking glass and an unearthly

scream. The woman got halfway out the window before collapsing onto the glass shards trapped in its frame. She groaned, shuddered, her blood cascaded down the outside wall until she went still.

Jake stopped long enough to turn the girl from the hellish vision. She was a scrawny little thing, but she fought him like a wildcat, clawing, punching, and spitting out a string of obscenities.

Finally, sirens sounded in the distance. Nothing for it but to keep going. Two breaths, thirty chest pumps. Repeat. Don't think. Don't stop. Don't feel. It seemed an eternity before a firefighter carrying an oxygen bottle and facemask pulled him off and took over.

A fire captain guided a ladder truck closer to the house. "Anyone else inside?"

"Dunno," Jake rasped. He turned to the girl, who avoided his gaze. "Kristy, anyone else?"

She shook her head, eyes flashing fury. "Just my Ma and Brad."

The ladder extended to the gory scene at the upper window. Two ambulances and a Sheriff's Department cruiser tore into the yard, their revolving lightbars casting the scene in eerie reds and blues. The fire captain rushed to the deputy. Jake, disheveled and shirtless, joined them.

"Gonna need the coroner," the captain said in a low voice.

The deputy, a slim woman, late twenties, gave a grim nod. "On it."

He nodded toward the girl, watching expressionless as firefighters attempted to reach the woman impaled on the glass. "Have paramedics check the girl," he told the deputy. "Then get her down the road a piece, she doesn't need to see this."

Men on the lawn showered two firefighters on the ladder struggling to carry down the body. The captain shook his head. "My guys have risked enough, gonna let it burn."

Jake and the deputy walked to the huddled girl. "Her name's Kristy," Jake said, his voice a ragged croak. "She's in a bad way." He turned toward the house. "That's her mother."

"I know, we've had past dealings," the deputy said. "I'm so sorry, Kristy. Come with me."

The girl turned a hostile gaze to Jake. "Get me away from this fucking coward."

The deputy gave him a lingering look, taking in his soot-streaked face and bare chest, his blistered, bloody hands and forearms. He shivered from cold and shock. "We need to know how you fit into this. But," she said, pointing to one of the ambulances, "right now you need medical attention."

Minutes later, as a paramedic tended to Jake's burns, a blanket now hanging off his back and shoulders, the deputy turned at her cruiser and called out, "You got a name?"

He pulled off an oxygen mask. "Jake...Jake Ockham."

She eased Kristy into the front passenger seat. "Talk soon."

Kristy locked eyes through the cruiser's side window. Even now, eleven years later, he remembered how her look of naked contempt left him wounded and shameful.

Chapter Thirteen

Aberdeen, Washington, July

Jake left the file on his desk and carried his memories home. He poured a Scotch and took glass and bottle onto the deck. Tonight's belated dinner was strictly single malt. The night was cool and threatened rain. He wrapped a blanket around himself and slumped into a chair, feet on the railing as the insect choir and gurgle of river swept him along.

And so we beat on, boats against the current, borne back ceaselessly into the past. Jake raised his glass. "Thank you, Scotty Fitzgerald," he whispered, "you beautiful, gifted fuck-up."

He picked at scabbed memories of that fire and its aftermath. Brad, fate unknown, was loaded into the first ambulance to leave—lights and siren, tires churning grass and gravel as it fishtailed onto the lane. Jake was loaded into a second ambulance headed for nearby Monongahela Valley Hospital. He prevailed on the two paramedics to stop at the church parking lot to retrieve his phone, wallet, and street clothes from his car.

"Oh, yeah," the guy riding in the back with Jake had said. "Gonna need that wallet."

He'd stared at his hands. They'd been cooled and cleaned with sterile water and covered with enough bandaging to wrap King Tut.

"Hate to break it to you," the paramedic said, rooting in Jake's shorts pocket for his car keys, "won't be driving anytime soon."

"Least of my worries."

The paramedic waved the recovered keys. "Since we're now on intimate terms, you can call me Hank. Guy at the wheel is Frank."

"Really?" Jake threw him a skeptical look.

Hank was bald as an egg, a brown egg. His shoulders and arms spoke of hours in the weight room. Frank was easily as tall as Jake, about fifty pounds lighter, pale as a cadaver with an unruly shock of blond hair. Both appeared in their mid-forties and looked like mismatched salt-and-pepper shakers.

"I shit you not," Hank said. "Hank 'n' Frank, we're semi-famous in the Monongahela Valley. I'm gonna park your fine, ah, vintage auto-mo-bile behind the church. Be safe there."

As Hank moved the car, Jake sucked oxygen in the ambulance. His hands throbbed; his head and lungs ached. In the span of an hour, he'd witnessed a woman die horribly, he'd failed her son, been pummeled and bitten by her hate-filled daughter, and—let's be honest—saw his Olympic hopes crash and burn.

Hank returned and had a quiet conversation with Frank, punctuated with a low whistle. He opened the back door and dropped Jake's gym bag on the floor. "Frank got some news on the radio," he said, his face cracked in a toothy grin. "The kid came alive in the back of the wagon part way to Pittsburgh. Ain't a lick of doubt he'd be ART if you hadn't pounded the bejesus outta him."

Hank hollered to the front of the van. "Hey, Frank,

we're haulin' a he-ro!"

Frank chirped the siren. "Yup. Now let's get him to the damn hospital."

Jake had taken a moment to collect his thoughts, brushing off his oxygen mask to dab tears coursing down his cheeks. His voice croaked as he asked, "What's ART?"

"My bad. Not a term for the general public," said Hank. "It means Assuming Room Temperature. Not a good thing."

****

Jake was assigned to a private room at the hospital, "on account," the duty nurse said, "of you smelling like a forest fire." He'd spent the night adrift in a fog of painkillers.

"Expect you'll be here another night," she said next afternoon, "then the doc wants you up in Pittsburgh at UPMC Mercy. Got a world-class burn center there. They'll see about those hands."

She redressed his wounds, clucking in disapproval. "Bad enough you burned them, second- and third-degree, but you made a right mess of them afterwards."

Jake glanced briefly at his ravaged palms, then turned away as she bandaged them.

Afterwards, she'd rested a hand on his shoulder. "Hank 'n' Frank spread the word. That was a righteous thing you did."

She was a heavy-set Hispanic woman with gray hair and gentle eyes. Jake looked at her nameplate. "Thank you for your care, Valentina."

She turned at the door. "Like it or not, you'll carry this with you the rest of your life. Look at those hands with pride, hear? There's a lady sheriff waiting to see you. Okay with that?"

Jake nodded.

The sheriff's name was Julia Evans. She listened attentively as Jake recounted the events of the past evening, tactfully lowering her head to take notes those times he broke down.

"Her name was Shannon Nichol, a single mom," Evans said after a moment's silence. "Nothing you could have done, Mr. Ockham. I was there, remember?"

"Kristy doesn't see it that way."

"She had to dump her grief somewhere. Lost her mom, the house is a pile of smoldering rubble. Doubt they'll ever find the cause of the fire."

"What will happen to the kids?"

"Right now, Kristy is with Victim Services. She's eleven. And—" Evans checked her notes "—Brad is thirteen. Expect they'll go into Family Services and foster care, God help 'em. But maybe there's hope of a fresh start."

Evans was silent for a long beat. There was something left unsaid. He asked, "You'd said you knew the family?"

She sighed. "Not in a good way. A parade of domestic calls back when their old man was alive. And worse. We suspect he had a, ah, history with his daughter. He was nailed with child porn on a phone he'd forgotten at a bar. That was enough—finally—for Shannon to seek a restraining order."

"You said he's dead?"

"Guess it's public knowledge in these parts. Some of it." She shrugged. "Suicide, so the story goes. Was out on bail last year on the porn charges and violated his restraining order by returning to the house.

Apparently topped himself in their barn. Shannon said little Kristy found the body and carried the pistol to her. Investigators found her prints all over the gun. I was called in to interview them. Their suicide story held. With the forensics so muddied, no way to prove otherwise."

"Jesus, she would have been ten years old."

"Yeah. As far as the Sheriff's Department was concerned, if suicide was how it went down, he did the world a favor."

Jake left the "if" of that sentence unexplored.

Evans closed her notebook. "Brad's up at the Mercy in Pittsburgh for at least another week, then back and forth for months as an outpatient. Some nasty leg burns."

Jake flinched.

She rose to leave. "Keep what I said about the family to yourself, huh? Told you more than I should."

He nodded. "They've suffered enough."

"Anything I can do for you?"

He'd waved bandaged hands. "Can you make a call, please? I need a couple of friends to pick up my car and drive me to Pittsburgh tomorrow. I'm headed for that burn center, too. Rather not shell out for an ambulance."

His roommate Erik was away on a work term. Evans reached a guy from his English lit class who was eager to help.

Big mistake, Jake realized later. He'd trusted the wrong guy.

****

Jake refilled his glass, not for the first time. A chill wet fog off the Wishkah hinted at a looming downpour.

He was grateful for his blanket and his glass of anti-freeze. The wrong guy he'd phoned eleven years back was Travis Barnes. He caught a ride to the hospital with another university buddy and insisted on driving Jake and his car back to Pittsburgh, claiming, "Hey, what are pals for?"

He'd machine-gunned questions all the way to the burn unit. Jake, stoned on painkillers, shared the sad, gory details. Barnes neglected to mention he was packing a concealed recorder and was milking Jake for a story.

Like Jake, he was an aspiring reporter. "A couple of years of newspapering to build street-cred," he'd confided in first year. "Then network TV, baby, where the big bucks are."

After a fitful first night at UPMC Mercy's burn unit, Jake found Barnes at the foot of his bed. "How ya doing, bud?" he'd asked with a grin. "Expect you'll get the royal treatment; I told them all about your heroics."

Jake cringed.

Barnes leaned in as though sharing a confidence. "I hear that kid Brad wants to see you."

Jake had wanted to offer Brad condolences and to erase any notion that his mother died so he could live. He couldn't imagine the kid carrying that burden.

Brad had looked up with a start when Jake entered the room. He'd no idea who he was until Barnes introduced him. Barnes had lied, Jake realized too late.

"Don't remember a thing," the kid said, offering a weak wave of one hand. "My sister promised to fill me in when I'm stronger."

"I'm sorry for your loss," Jake said.

Brad turned away, the answer his lame comment

deserved. Barnes filled the void with leading questions and aimless chatter. He cajoled the two into a quick "personal" photo, to remember the "awesome bond" they shared.

Kristy walked into the room, saw Jake and made to leave.

"Hey," Barnes said. "Don't you want to thank the guy who saved your brother's life?"

"Oh, yeah," she said, glaring at Jake. "He's my hero."

She stormed out.

Next morning, a burn unit nurse set that day's *Post-Gazette* on Jake's bed as if bestowing a great gift.

He was front and center. That headline about burns killing his Olympic dreams ran below the awkward photo Barnes had snapped in Brad's hospital room. A pull-quote from Kristy, totally out of context, read, *"He's My Hero."*

Both byline and photo credit read *"Travis Barnes, Special to the Post-Gazette."*

Jake scanned the story with mounting fury. Not only had Barnes betrayed him, but his story focused on Jake's so-called *"heroic sacrifice."* As though the loss of the children's mother was secondary to *"the death of Ockham's hard-fought Olympic dreams."* As though watching a woman burn alive was heroic.

Barnes further torqued the piece with English major bullshit about Jake's *"Sophie's Choice conundrum, seconds to decide who lives, who dies."*

Pretentious asshole.

He swept away the paper and rushed to Brad's room to apologize. He was sleeping. Kristy sat in a visitor's chair; the front page of the paper crumpled on the floor. Her lips curled. "You disgust me. This story is bullshit."

"I agree," Jake said. "I had nothing to do with the article, Kristy. I—"

She reached for the call buzzer. "Get out before I call security."

"Okay. Okay. You've every right to be upset. Tell Brad I'm sorry."

Jake stumbled into the hall, swiping at his tears.

Barnes had phoned that night. "Talk about a win-win, buddy. That weeper made you famous and got me a summer internship at the *Post-Gazette*. Seriously, how much did you love it? Some surprise, huh?"

"What I think, Trav, is when my hands are up to it, I'm going to punch out your fuckin' lights."

Those were the last words he spoke to Barnes, who wisely steered clear of Jake in the final weeks before graduation.

****

The mist turned to full-on rain. Jake shed the sodden blanket and carried the decimated bottle inside. He tried to work out a dull ache between his shoulder blades. An ache that came from cold and tension, and Travis Fucking Barnes.

Chapter Fourteen

Pittsburgh, Pennsylvania, July

It was Friday and Lyla Watkins left the school where she taught remedial mathematics to a slumped and somnolent group of summer school kids, her briefcase stuffed with assignments.

Her idealism as a new grad of the Master of Education program was taking a beating, as the world-weary principal had warned her. "A few of these kids are flat-out dim, most are just bone lazy. Do what you can to get them passing grades. If they walk out of here with a diploma, there's still hope for them."

She was sure her energy, enthusiasm, and recently acquired pedagogy was lifting a few out of their summer torpor, those who could tell their numerators from denominators. Plan was, get some teaching experience under her belt and apply for the doctoral program. Aim high, make a difference.

A young man fell in step with her as she headed for a nearby bus stop. "Miss Watkins?"

She gave a quick assessment as any sensible young woman would. He was tall and good-looking in a rangy, country boy way. He seemed shy, almost embarrassed and apologetic at approaching her. Threat level: low. "Yes?"

"Hi, I'm Phil," he stammered. "Paul's big brother.

Paul in your class?"

She was still getting the names sorted, this being her third week. Paul, in the back row by the windows, quiet and unremarkable. Not disruptive, she would give him that. She stopped and nodded. "Paul seems a nice young man."

Phil gave a vigorous shake of his head, his grin revealing a crooked incisor. Never had braces, obviously. When you grow up poor you notice such things. "That's a relief, you saying that," he said. "Our family life is kinda…complicated."

"How so?" She noticed her bus speed past the stop. Damn, the next one was thirty minutes away.

"Ah, jeez. That your bus?"

She shrugged.

"Say, maybe I could tell you over a quick coffee, there's a shop just down the street, I'm parked out front. Paul lost his way after Mom died. Seems you're the first teacher to make a connection with him in a long while."

"Glad to hear that," she said, though in truth Paul seemed as consistently lethargic as ever.

"Coffee? Please?" He looked at her heavy briefcase. "I can even give you a lift home?"

"A quick one," she said. "Just so I'm back for the next bus. I'll pass on the ride, thanks, I've got errands to run." She figured the threat level was low, but why take a chance?

They walked down the street and took a table on the street-side patio. "What do you want?" he asked. "My treat?"

"Just dark roast, please, cream and half a sugar." She watched as he fixed the coffees at the condiment table inside, his back to the window.

He returned juggling two cups and a cheese scone. "Thought we could share," he said.

"About Paul?"

Phil launched into a sad tale of family dysfunction as they sipped their drinks.

"What a brave little guy," Watkins said. "I don't see any evidence of that in his demeanor."

Little guy?

"Adopted. Paul is adopted. Say, you're looking real tired."

"Need to…go."

She fumbled for her briefcase and tried to rise.

He took it from her hands. "I got this," he said. He linked arms with her and guided her spaghetti legs to his van.

****

She awoke with a five-alarm headache. Must be the mattress, which was moving. What kind of mattress moves?

Not a mattress, just a blanket. She reached for her aching head, but her arms were stretched unmoving above her head. Heard the rattle of metal on metal, like she was handcuffed. Legs, too.

Handcuffs, what the hell? Her stomach rebelled and she vomited. Felt the warmth of her bile as it soaked her blouse, the stench disgusting her. Lucky she wasn't gagged, or she'd have aspirated.

No, not lucky. What's the word?

Unlucky.

And feeling stupid for getting herself in this mess.

Also pissed off and terrified.

This time, the threat level was off the charts.

Chapter Fifteen

Clearfield County, Pennsylvania

"What-cha thinkin', Daddy?"

She settled on the arm of his wing chair and kissed the top of his head. His thick hair, the grey now dominating the black, was infused with his pipe tobacco scents of vanilla and cherry.

"What am I thinking, aside from your need to enunciate? How lucky I am to have you in my life. And pondering next steps in our journey."

"And where shall those steps lead us, Daddy dearest?" she said in an affected upper-class English accent.

"To Washington State." He smiled and reached for an envelope on his side table. "This arrived today. He's taken the bait. I've come to think his unexpected move to the West Coast is more blessing than inconvenience. The delays allow us time to refine the experiments, while delivering a broader geographic sample."

A pout clouded her features.

"We've taken our time reeling him in. Revenge, as they say, is a dish best served—"

"Revenge," she interrupted, "is a dish best smashed over his head, and force-fed down his fucking throat."

He smiled at her wordplay. "I know you're impatient, but the moment is nigh." He tapped the ash from his pipe, then set about refilling it. "I'm sure you'll agree our trial runs were invaluable, even if the last one went off script."

"Feeling better, Daddy?"

"I hope I proved last night I've returned to form."

She smiled and bobbed her head. "And then some. But, man, what those dogs did was some scary shit. Gotta say our last guests totally paid their way. By the time I finished the edits, it made for awesome video."

" 'Oscar-worthy', one of our clients wrote in the comments section. I gave our subscribers a sneak peek at our latest research assistant this morning. She's a fine-looking specimen. And I've shown them a news clip of her potential roommate, a real media darling."

He fanned the file folder, as if to quell a hot flash. "Their chemistry could be combustible. So much so, our regulars offered up eight new potential subscribers for me to vet."

"Care-ful," she said, drawing out the word.

"Always." He gave her leg a lingering squeeze, then handed over a file. "Here are Mr. Wise's particulars. Your job is to pick him up. With your brother's help for the heavy lifting."

She flipped through the clips. "Spokane? Really? He *is* kinda hot. I'll give him that."

"You have all the attributes for the job." He shot her a knowing grin. "I'd recommend wearing my recent purchase. It leaves me weak in the knees, I can only imagine what it'll do for a young buck half my age."

"Age is just a number, Daddy." She gave his shoulder a squeeze and kissed his neck. "Leave it to me, it'll be like shooting fish—"

"In a lamé dress. But that's Part Two of what

promises to be a busy week for you and your brother. Part One is a delicate operation."

He handed over the envelope. "Your, ah, friend wrote us a personal check. We won't cash it, of course, too risky. I'll demand an e-transfer in my next correspondence, made out to my alternate identity."

She studied the check. "It lists his home address. Convenient."

"Indeed," he said. "I've Google mapped the address. It's a nice piece of riverfront. Quite isolated. It may suit our needs, but I prefer to draw him here."

"When?"

"Patience, dear. If Part One goes as planned, and I admit that's not a certainty, his reputation will be in ruins long before the denouement. Meantime," he picked up a box from the floor by his chair, "Please become proficient with this."

She looked at the box. "A point-and-shoot camera?"

"Small and discreet, with a thirty-times optical zoom and high-definition video. His downfall rests, literally, in your deft hands. If you and your brother succeed—and I admit there's a host of imponderables to overcome—he'll wish he were dead, long before we grant that wish."

She looked puzzled as she unboxed the camera.

"I'll explain once your brother gets dear Lyla fed and watered. Meantime, pack a week's worth of clothes. You two leave at dawn tomorrow." He blew her a kiss as she rose to leave. "Don't forget that dress."

They gathered in the library that evening for what the professor called "a final post-mortem of our last quest."

He handed them brandies in crystal snifters and waved them to wingback chairs arranged in front of an unlit stone fireplace. "The Sedgewick Trust website is a glorious legacy," he told his adoptees, speaking in what the brother called "his lecture hall voice." "A digital catalogue of more than a century of death and disaster.

"Did you know the first award went to an eleven-year-old newsboy from Sedgewick's *Daily Pennsylvanian*? He broke into the locked basement of a burning textile mill and rescued eight girls—child laborers—before succumbing to smoke inhalation. The *Pennsylvanian* glossed over the inconvenient fact that Sedgewick also owned the mill."

If he noticed the 'we've-heard-this-before' look that flashed between brother and sister, he chose to ignore it.

"Think of it, thousands of medallions awarded, the details recorded on the website. It's our menu of mayhem: fires, car crashes, murders, drownings, and—yes—animal attacks." He shifted uncomfortably. "So many ways to put our guests to the test—to sift a few, rare authentic heroes from the one-day wonders. Reggie Obergon being a prime example of the latter. His was not a noble death."

The brother blew out a breath as if broaching a sensitive subject. "You've got to admit Wally was the real deal."

The professor reddened. "I would have preferred he make the point in less dramatic fashion, but, yes, his was a heroic death. While our sample size is minimal, it appears sexual orientation is not a determinant."

His smile tightened. "That he died off camera was tragic. That he died prematurely was disappointing. I would have loved other chances to test his mettle."

The daughter abruptly set down her snifter, sloshing brandy onto the side table. "I had to shoot him, for chrissake, he was about to take another stab at you. As for my camera work, did you really want video all over the Dark Web of a chisel jammed up your ass?"

The professor pushed both palms downward in a placating motion. "I'm not being critical. As a social scientist, it's essential to evaluate past experiments to tweak those going forward. The fault, if there was one, rests with my experimental design. As dramatic as the dog attack was, events were not entirely in our control."

"The audience loved it," the daughter said.

"That they did. The real hitch was the challenge of disposal. Even in a state this large, there are limited places to discard problems with discretion and permanence."

"Reggie gave us the solution," the daughter said.

"True, dumping them in a deep lake, wrapped with an anvil inside snow fencing, did the trick. A fitting *homage* to Reggie's water rescue, though such subtlety would have gone over his head." He snorted. "Literally, come to think of it." He swirled his snifter. "While you two are on your road trip I'll mind the farm and devise new quests, both cinematic and scientific. Ideally, they'll also obviate the need for disposal."

He turned to his laptop. "With Mr. Sedgewick's assistance, naturally. His trust's website is the ultimate resource: eleven thousand ways to die."

Chapter Sixteen

Aberdeen, Washington, July

A busy week passed since his coffee date with Tina. The car crash that abruptly pulled her away proved nasty enough to warrant an inside news brief in the next issue. No one died—fortunate for them—and for Jake, who hated writing such stories.

He hadn't had a chance to speak with Clara. She was in Bend, Oregon, one of her regular visits to Jake's father, Roger, who handled the newspaper's accounts. No doubt she packed her clubs, Roger a master at writing off green fees as business expenses.

He phoned Sabina Meely, Walter's mother, who was frantic with worry. "He didn't come home from choir practice. It's been a month, and not a word. I'm shattered," she said between sobs. "Walter would never hurt me like this."

She'd phoned the police, of course. "They didn't find him, but they discovered he was gay. Imagine! After that, they stopped looking, as if that explained everything. Maybe he ran away with a lover. Or worse, that his secret life was unbearable. Happens all the time, they said."

She broke down again. Jake held back news that someone was selling his medal.

"I know my son." She choked out a bitter laugh.

"Not everything, obviously. But he would not…would not…end things. If only he'd told me, I'd have understood."

"He's a good man, Sabina. I'm looking for answers, too. Please keep in touch."

Jake next opened an email from Jonathon Foley, the investigations manager at Sedgewick Trust. He'd already emailed him scanned copies of the ad, the medal photo and the insulting letter from Dawes.

After rowing blew up for Jake, he'd taken a reporting job at the *Pittsburgh Post-Gazette*.

Four years in, he wrote a profile of Lyla Watkins, a renowned high school point guard bound for Portland State University. That is, until she came upon a Vietnam vet whose wheelchair fell onto the tracks of Pittsburgh's commuter T-line. She dragged him clear, but the lead car sideswiped her, shattering her left shoulder. Bye-bye hoops scholarship.

Jake could relate. He wrote the hell out of her story. It drew the interest of the Sedgewick Trust organization which, after its own investigation, awarded Watkins a Sacrifice Medallion. Sedgewick had a practice, dating back to the founder's era, of using former reporters to vet the circumstances of potential medalists.

He himself had been nominated for a Sacrifice Medallion after Brad's rescue. He'd refused to be considered, telling the Sedgewick investigator, "I left his mother to die."

Years later, as Foley recruited him, he'd said: "You'll come to the Trust with a unique perspective. You'd be a medalist if you'd tried to rescue her. You'd also be dead."

"There's that," he said and took the job.

Jake opened this morning's email from Foley. *"This is creepy. Not impressed with the Omaha cops' initial investigation. I'm prodding them to do better. The Sedgewick name still carries weight, even in Nebraska. Glad you're on the case too. You're a digger, that's why we hired you. It certainly wasn't your looks. Keep in touch."*

Jake worked through the rest of his inbox, discarding junk, forwarding relevant news releases to his staff. Nothing from Tina. But—oh, joy— there was a juicy anonymous tip. Jake, aware of the good doctor's wish to take things slow, saw the leak as a chance to entice her into a Sunday road trip.

The email offered Jake exclusive details of a pending plan by Amtrak and the federal government to add passenger rail service to Aberdeen from the mainline at Centralia, some fifty-five miles inland near the I-5 corridor.

"A formal announcement comes in two weeks, but I have the final drafts of the funding agreement and press release. I've a running dispute with the daily rag in Aberdeen, so I'm willing to leak these documents exclusively to you this Sunday.

"The following conditions apply:

"You identify me only as a senior Amtrak employee.

"You don't contact Amtrak in advance of Sunday.

"You're on the platform of the Centralia station at 3:59 when the Amtrak Cascades pulls in. I'll disembark, blend into the crowd and discreetly hand off the package. Have an open backpack, and don't attempt to speak with me. I'll reboard immediately.

"Stand close to the platform edge near the train engine, but with people in front of you to hide my hand-off. I have your photo from the Independent website so don't send a surrogate.

"If you accept these conditions, send an empty email to this private address with "Yes" in the subject line."

Which Jake did immediately, though it all seemed rather cloak and dagger. For that matter, extending passenger rail to Aberdeen seemed farfetched, despite years of lobbying by Grays Harbor Chamber of Commerce types. Apart from beating the competition to a major news story, Centralia, an hour and a bit inland by car, was one of his favorite small cities. He knew from their one and only dinner Tina was desperate to add some retro charm and personality to her utilitarian apartment.

"Centralia is stuffed with outlet malls, and people come from across the state to its antique and collectables stores," Jake told her over the phone.

"I'm in," she said.

"The Antique Mall alone has fifty dealers and there's a pile more—"

"Hey," she interrupted with a laugh. "You had me at antiques. I'll pass on the outlet malls."

"Fair warning," Jake said. "I have to be at the train station there at four o'clock to pick up a package. Shouldn't take a minute. That gives us time to shop and have lunch. And the old train station is a beaut, on the National Register of Historic Places, it's—"

"Shaddap already. You've closed the deal, and I've got a waiting room full of patients. Pick me up at, say, nine o'clock Sunday. That work for you?"

"Perfect."

It was perfect.

A perfectly agreeable companion, offset by perfect weather. A perfectly exhausting shopping experience ending with a perfect Mexican lunch at La Tarasca. Then on to the station, where the *Amtrak Cascades*, its warning bells chiming, was slowing to a stop.

Jake left Tina on a bench with her purchases and wove through the crowd at the tracks.

He stood behind three schoolgirls who crowded the yellow-lined lip of the platform, texting furiously on their phones. He wanted to tell them to wait farther back from the tracks but didn't want to sound like an old scold.

He towered above them. No risk his mysterious confidential source would miss him.

It was just after four p.m., as the train pulled in, when things went perfectly to hell.

Chapter Seventeen

Centralia, Washington.

Jake, backpack in hand, rocketed forward, slamming into one of the trio of girls with such force she flew off the platform onto the tracks. The backpack dropped as he teetered on the platform edge.

"Call 911," he shouted at the two remaining girls, both so engrossed in their phones they hadn't noticed their friend's plight.

Jake leaped onto the tracks as the train bore down, its locked wheels screeching, its horn sounding a deafening, futile blast. The train slowed but no way it could stop in time.

It was four feet from the girl when Jake reached her. She was unconscious, her head resting on a rail already slick with her blood. He bent low, scooped her up and threw her off the tracks.

He was diving clear when the train slammed into his side. The train would have dragged him under if his feet were planted. With his body already airborne, the engine carried him several feet before spitting him onto the gravel ballast on the opposite side of the tracks.

Everything seemed to move in slow motion. He lay parallel to the tracks, his face so close to the slowing train he felt the heat of the engine and brakes as the locked wheels shrieked past.

He rolled clear, tasting blood draining into his mouth from a gravel-shredded cheek. He stumbled in a daze back toward the girl. Had he killed her? He'd knocked her onto the tracks. What the hell happened?

She was pale and still as death, but blood still coursed from her head wound. Had to mean she was alive, right? He took an inadequate wad of tissues from his pocket and pressed it to her wound. People rushed forward now from across the tracks. "Don't move her. Don't move her," he shouted. "She needs a doctor."

He pulled out his phone. The screen was cracked but it was operational. He pushed redial on his most recent call. "Tina, come around the train, there's a girl hurt bad...Yeah, I'm fine. She's unconscious. A head wound. Don't know what else. Hurry. Please."

****

Things were already out of control in the time it took for Jake to be patched up and checked over at Providence Centralia Hospital. Tina had tended to the girl until the ambulance crews arrived, then helped load her onto a backboard. She'd talked herself into the five-minute ride in Jake's ambulance.

She stayed with him while a young resident doctor cleaned gravel and grit out of the cuts on his cheek and disinfected and stitched deeper gashes on his face and battered side. His left arm, rib cage, and left thigh were developing what promised to be spectacular bruises. No broken bones.

The doctor gave Jake a sample bottle of pain killers and a prescription for more. "You're going to be stiff and sore as hell by morning," he said, pausing at the door of the small treatment room. "But, man, you were hit by a train. Do you know how lucky you are?"

"Yeah, lucky me. Thanks, doc."

Tina leaned in, inspected the dressing, turned his face to the uninjured side, and gave his cheek a gentle peck.

"Lucky me," he said, quieter this time.

There was a knock on the door and a smiling nurse popped her head in. "How's our hero doing?" She turned to Tina and handed off two shopping bags. "You'll want these. Someone at the station saw that you'd left them on the bench and drove them over. Sweet, huh?"

"Sweet," Tina said. "I'd forgotten all about them."

"Another reason why Centralia is one of my favorite places," Jake said.

The nurse beamed. "I feel blessed to live here. And I've just met its newest hero."

Jake looked puzzled.

"You on the Twitter?" she asked.

He nodded.

"Punch in hashtag #CentraliaTrainRescue." She turned for the door. "I'll leave you be."

Tina worked her phone, then tilted the phone so they could watch the replay together. A brief shaky video all of five seconds long was all over social media. It showed a blur as the camera swung from a black smudge on a blue sky to Jake leaping onto the tracks, lifting the girl to safety and being hit by the rolling train. Screams and sobs were heard over the blast of the train's air horn.

The Twitter feed evolved at warp speed.

The girl on the tracks was identified in posts by her friends as twelve-year-old Summer Zhang. One of her friends was looking away from the tracks, videoing a soaring eagle. Summer's yelp of fear caused her to swing back, the camera phone capturing the rescue almost by accident.

Now #WhoisMysteryHero was trending.

Jake groaned and handed the phone back. "This is why I hate social media. This is a fucking lie."

"But you rescued the girl? Incredibly courageous by the way."

"It doesn't show that I knocked her on the tracks."

Tina reacted as if from an electrical jolt.

"Someone slammed into my back, full force. Out of the blue. No warning. I'm a big guy, not easy to knock me off my feet, but it was one hell of a push."

"Like, on purpose?"

"It had to be deliberate. I don't know who, don't know why. I do know I'm no hero. I put that girl on the tracks."

She rested a hand lightly on his shoulder but said nothing.

"Do me a favor," he said. "Pull some strings, please. See how she's doing."

Tina returned with bad news. Summer remained unconscious and in guarded condition. "Her vitals are strong, no spinal injuries, thank God but she's obviously concussed. It's too early to assess how traumatic the brain injury is."

By this time however, Jake's battered phone was going nuts. Twitterverse had somehow outed MysteryHero as @IndyEdJake, editor of the *Grays Harbor Independent*. Thereafter, new hashtags were added: #ClarkKent, #FasterThanASpeedingBullet and #MorePowerfulThanALocomotive.

Email and phone messages piled up from every

media outlet in Centralia and Grays Harbor County, as well as the *Seattle Times*, the *Associated Press*, and Clara.

He ignored all but Clara. He texted her, squinting at the cracked screen.

—Home soon. Not a word of this on our website. NOT A WORD. It's going to get ugly—

And it did.

Chapter Eighteen

Before heading home, Jake stopped off at Centralia's red brick police station to file a report, determined to head off trouble at the pass. On what had been a quiet Sunday, it was clear the front desk cop wasn't plucked from the A-team. Officer Preston, according to his nameplate, was beefy and balding. Jake's claim that he was pushed toward the tracks added an unwelcome complication to an accident that had already rat-fucked his afternoon.

"Saw the video, it's all over the place," Preston said. "You lookin' for a commendation, or what?"

"Looking for whoever pushed me."

"Look, no idea at this point how the kid ended up on the tracks. My guys are still interviewing witnesses at the train station, and waiting at the hospital, hoping the girl wakes up."

He took a rudimentary statement, a painfully slow process as his sausage fingers hunted and pecked the keys. It took an act of will for Jake—his cheek on fire and his left side aching and stiffening—not to snatch the keyboard and write the statement himself.

"Our suits will be in touch when the reports are in, and we get some clarity on this mess. 'Preciate you coming in," Preston said with little conviction. "Saves us hunting you down."

Tina drove them back. "In all the excitement you

never got your news tip."

"Yeah, wondering about that." Squinting, he checked his email, no further messages from his mysterious source.

After a debate over logistics, Tina stopped in front of her apartment. "Are you sure you can drive from here? I could taxi back from your place. Or," she said after a pause, "you can stay here. I'll give you my bed."

Jake bit down on a temptation to say he'd take a rain check. "I had a lovely day, until the *Amtrak Cascades* arrived. Sorry things went south."

"Don't be," she said, helping him out of the passenger's seat. "As second dates go, it was, um, unique. And instructive."

Jake looked puzzled.

"Shopping and lunch were fun, in a superficial way. But actions speak louder than anything in your file. I saw a different side of the self-contained Jake Ockham."

"That would be my left side. Very colorful," Jake said, stifling a groan as he settled behind the wheel. "As for self-contained, Dr. Doctorow, I say, Pot. Kettle. Black."

She gave what Jake interpreted as a you-got-me kind of shrug. She stood by his car door holding her shopping bags.

"Look," he said through his open window. "I know how this will play out. If I were you, I'd pretend not to know me for a while."

She leaned in the window. "Naw, that's a dumb idea." She kissed him lightly on his bandaged cheek.

****

Jake awoke the next morning, his fears realized.

The technicolor mess that was the left side of his body was the least of his concerns. Groaning in pain, he leaned over to grab his home-delivered copies of the Aberdeen daily and the *Seattle Times*.

What hurt more were the front-page headlines.

The local paper announced, *"Aberdeen Man Risks Life, Pulls 12-year-old From Path of Train. Modest Hero Avoids Spotlight."*

The *Times* offered, *"Mystery Hero In Centralia Rail Rescue Identified as Aberdeen Journalist."*

Both stories were thin on detail, Jake having ignored all interview requests.

He powered up his laptop to access the *Independent's* website, knowing he'd be pissed off. It carried a file photo of Jake over an AP version of the story with an added qualifier: *"Ockham, 33, was recovering from his injuries Sunday night and was unavailable for comment."*

He'd gotten into it last night over the phone with Clara, who was still in Bend. He'd wanted no mention in print or online. She'd demanded a story. "Look, we're a newspaper, and you're news."

"It's gonna blow up in our faces, sure as shit."

"Maybe so. But we have a pact with our readers. Remember when your grandfather got nicked for a DUI back in the day? He took the heat, put the story on front, *and* wrote an editorial apologizing to readers."

He knew she was right.

"Like I need your permission? I am the publisher, for now at least."

"You're not getting a quote from me, that's for damn sure. We both know the real reason you're running the story."

"And that is?"

"An excuse to post that shitty little video clip."

"It's driving eyeballs to the *Independent*, no shame in that. Only thing better than a click-generating viral video," she said with no hint of apology, "is *our* click-generating viral video."

Jake's dad, always a man of few words, got on the line. "I'm proud of you, Jake. Jumping in front of that train was brave. And terrifying. And kind of stupid."

"Thanks, Dad. You're right on two of those three. But take my advice and don't go bragging yet. There's more to this than meets the eye."

They said their good-byes with Jake still pissed at Clara.

On Monday morning, he phoned Anna Mae at the office, brushing off her congratulations and her bitching about an ever-growing stack of phone messages. "Chuck them in the recycle bin. I'm working from home today. And don't, under any circumstances, forward calls here."

By ten a.m., several visitors had hammered at his door. He didn't respond. He unplugged his landline, shut off his cell, and ignored the emails bombarding his laptop. There was no response from his Amtrak "source."

Why the silence? He plugged in his landline long enough to phone Amtrak's media relations offices in Oakland, California, which handled queries for the U.S. West. He reached an Estelle Brown and asked if there were plans to extend passenger rail to Grays Harbor County.

"Where's that?"

"Aberdeen, Washington State."

"Uh-huh?"

"About an hour west of Centralia."

"Ah, now you're talking. So, this isn't a story about a girl on the tracks there Sunday? Had plenty of inquiries about that."

"Ah, no."

"Was traumatic for our engineer, I'll tell you. Anyway, where'd you hear we're pushing out passenger service all the way to this Grays Harbor?"

"A rumor I picked up."

"Seems unlikely in this climate of retrenchment, but don't quote me on that. I'll look into it. Give me your contact info. Could take a few days—this is head office stuff with a side order of federal government relations."

"I understand. Much appreciated."

"Word of advice," she said, "this sounds shaky. I wouldn't put anything in print 'til you hear from me. It'd cause us both a world of trouble."

"Wouldn't dream of it," he said and repeated his contact information.

"Ockham? Ockham? Hey, are you the guy who—"

"Bye, Ms. Brown, thanks for your time."

He hung up, certain the rumor was a dry hole. So, why lure him to Centralia? He unplugged the phone and turned to two other nagging issues: the inevitable wait for the other shoe to drop, and Clara's cryptic comment: "I am the publisher, *for now at least.*"

As for the other shoe, it dropped at four that afternoon in the form of heavy boots on the front porch and a thunderous pounding on the door. Through the peephole Jake saw the leering face of Aberdeen Deputy Sheriff Trent Shane.

He unlatched the door and invited him in, gesturing wordlessly with one arm. Shane brushed past, eyes sweeping the kitchen. A hand rested on his holstered sidearm, as if Jake might ambush him with his carving knives.

He'd not been entirely honest with Tina when he'd told her about his high school sweetheart Amanda Shane, *née* Langello. True, they'd split up when he left for university, but there had been a brief, very brief, reprise when Jake returned to take the editor's job. In their dating days, she'd radiated the same sizzle as actress Marisa Tomei. They even shared an uncanny resemblance, the same lithe figure and expressive Italian features.

He remembered snuggling up to young Amanda in the Langello's rec room to watch a video of *My Cousin Vinny*. Jake roaring with laughter as Amanda did a fine imitation of Tomei's star-turn as mechanic-turned-expert-witness Mona Lisa Vito.

They'd gone for a drive later that night in his father's borrowed Buick, parking at a favorite rural lane. "Ms. Vito," Jake had said with a meaningful glance at the backseat, "you're supposed to be some kind of expert in automobiles, is that correct?"

"Get me outta this dress," she'd said in Vito's nasal Brooklyn accent, "you'll find out soon enough."

That was then.

Within weeks of Jake's return, he was alone having a pre-dinner drink at Billy's Bar & Grill when Amanda bumped into him, accidently on purpose, she'd admitted later that night.

"Buy a girl a glass of wine?"

She still looked good...if a little weary. He rose

and invited her to share his booth. The wine turned into a seafood platter, and a night in her bed.

"Trent and me, we're not together anymore," she'd said. "He has Sam tonight, for a change. Sam's four, the best thing that's ever happened to me." She'd looked at Jake. "One of the best."

Jake knew it was a mistake, even as he parked in front of her modest two-story clapboard house. The vibrant light he remembered had leaked out of her. The girl, once determined to move to New York City, now rarely left Grays Harbor County. "Even Seattle freaks me out."

A photo of Sam rested on the fireplace mantle beside one of Shane in his sheriff's uniform. Jake wondered how "not together" they really were. Still, they'd made love, two lonely people stirring embers of the past.

"It's not there between us anymore is it," she'd said later, staring at her ceiling.

His head slumped to the pillow. "No, it isn't. I'm sorry."

She shrugged. "Just wanted to see. Can you stay the night, please?"

Jake came down next morning to find a smashed driver's side window and a citation for parking too close to a non-existent fire hydrant. Courtesy of Trent Shane, no doubt.

Now, Shane tromped uninvited through Jake's house, opening both bedroom doors and the bathroom, clearly unimpressed with its rustic charm. "Got orders to haul you to Centralia," he said finally, by way of greeting. "Cops wanna question you about shoving that girl on the tracks. Hope you've got a good lawyer.

Could be attempted murder. Could be worse, if the kid don't wake up."

He walked Jake to his idling cruiser, the light bar flashing unnecessarily. "In the back," he said with a sneer. "Won't cuff you, on account of us being old pals." He looked at Jake in the rear-view mirror. "Hero to zero in twenty-four hours. Gotta be some kind of record."

The rest of the trip was made in silence.

Chapter Nineteen

Spokane, Washington, August

"I thought Ockham was gonna die," Kristy said. "That woulda ruined the plan."

"Hey," Brad said, "I shoved him just hard enough. Who knew the crazy fuck would jump on the tracks?"

"I want his death slow—and ugly."

"Well, it woulda been ugly."

Brother and sister sat side-by-side in their shared Spokane motel room, watching a laptop replay of Jake and Summer Zhang's swan dive onto the tracks. Brad hit replay. "Our clients would've loved a quick death, they jones over all kinds of twisted shit. You seen the *TrainGore* channel? Jesus, bodies looking like they dropped from a high rise, or been torn apart by wild animals. That slow-mo vid of a head rolling into a ditch? Guy died so quick, didn't have time to wipe the surprise off his face. Gotta wonder, was the head still alive as it rolled down the tracks? The brain sayin', 'I am so fucked.' "

"You're sick."

"I learned from the best, didn't I? You got raves for your closeup of the dog ripping up poor ole Reggie. A few more like that and *Hero Hatr* will become our ticket to the big time."

"Wonder how Daddy plans to finish off Ockham?"

she asked. "We're taking a lot of chances with this road trip. Shoulda pounced before he moved west."

"You love suspense. Like how you divided the train station video, stopping just as the train hit him, everyone wondering is he dead or what? Very Hitchcock. Then running around the train to film him crawling to that kid. Posting that a day later drove our viewers crazy."

"Our viewers don't need to drive," she said with a grin. "They already live in Crazytown." Kristy opened a thumb-drive on the laptop. "And now to Mr. Wise, the pussy hound."

Heads bent close, they poured over a dozen news clips and TV interviews their father had downloaded. They skipped over the prof's scholarly monograph drawn from his dinner interview with Wise—his analysis debunking his and other heroic acts. Heard it all before.

Some evenings, he'd read aloud his old scholarly papers from his time as a social science lecturer at Elmdale Christian Women's College in New Bethlehem, Pennsylvania. It usually inspired Brad to drain his drink and head for bed. For obvious reasons, the latest monograph he posted on the Dark Web didn't carry his real name.

The monograph's title *"Anderson K. Wise, Reaping the Rewards of a Rash Act: Blue-collar Heroics as 21st Century Aphrodisiac."* The work was credited to "Dr. B. Dawes".

Brad shook his head. "Such bullshit. What does that even mean?"

"A bunch of ten-dollar words to describe a pussy hound."

She scrolled down the laptop screen. "Your job tonight is to scope out this Sharkey's place, see if Wise is there. If he is, watch, but don't approach. If not, ask when he usually shows up. Discreetly. Daddy met him weeks ago on his scouting trip to Washington State. He really wants this dude. And with Meely gone, we're down a body, so don't draw attention."

"That's your department. What's your bait?"

"I'll show you, Daddy bought it for me."

She sashayed to her bed, shedding her sundress. Nothing underneath but a hint of a g-string. She pulled a glittery item out of her suitcase and wriggled into the dress, cupping her breasts to adjust the cleavage.

She spun around, wiggled her behind. "Zip me up."

She twirled a couple of times to display the goods then looked her brother up and down. "Was gonna ask what you think," she said with a smirk, "but it's pretty obvious."

He colored. "I know what you and Dad get up to."

"He got us outta that shithole foster home, didn't he? Anyway, it's not like we're related. He likes 'em young, so why not share the goodies?"

"I went through his desk once," Brad said. "Liking them young caused that college of his to demand early retirement—when he was, like, forty-five."

"He told me he was happy to go. They didn't appreciate his field of study, especially in a state where the Sedgewick name is splashed all over everything. It's not as if he needed to work. Got pots of money and that big old mansion when his mom kicked off."

She plunked herself beside him on his bed and turned her back to him. "Help me out of this, will ya?"

Chapter Twenty

Centralia, Washington, August

It was clear on arrival at police headquarters that Jake was knee-deep in dung. The first clue was the smirk-fest when Shane handed Jake off to a Centralia detective named Harry Brewster.

He was in pressed khakis, desert boots and wore a shoulder holster over a button-down shirt. He was about Shane's age, mid-thirties, and judging from the fist-bump greeting and a couple of inside jokes, they were asshole buddies from way back.

Brewster glared at Jake and led them to a bare-bones interview room. "The kid's awake—and talkin'. Now it's your turn."

Jake had prepared for this eventuality. The *Independent's* lawyer, while adept at business and libel law, had placed a Centralia criminal lawyer on call.

"Name's Sue Price, she's got twenty years' experience busting balls," the attorney told him. "Brace yourself, clients call her Sue Pricey. Doesn't come cheap. Cops and prosecutors call her names that'd make a Hells Angel blush—goes claws-in to any and all tussles."

Jake phoned her from home earlier to fill her in on his vague understanding of events at the train station.

Brewster leaned across the table. "This is just a

chat, understand. We're still at the evidentiary phase and that little gal just woke up. You're not under arrest, so no need to Mirandize you. Yet. Have to say, though, it looks bad, best to get your side of the story on the record."

He turned to Shane, like an idea just came to him. "Hey, Trent, what say you sit in on our chat? Be nice for Mr. Ockham to have a hometown boy at his side."

Shane grinned. "Glad to, detective. Can be a comfort to have a friend in the room."

"That's kind of you, Deputy Sheriff Shane," Jake said. "Since you guys are being so swell, I'll make a call, loop another friend into the conversation." He stood, trying to hide a jolt of pain. "Be right back."

If the twenty-minute delay perturbed Brewster and Shane, it paled in comparison to their reaction when Sue Price steamed into the room. She was what Clara would call a big-boned woman, though she carried the weight with style.

"Fuck me," Brewster muttered under his breath.

She was early fifties, Jake estimated. Flawless skin under light makeup, short black hair highlighted with copper. She wore a flattering bespoke business suit, walked like a panther on improbably high heels, and flashed a nut-sized diamond ring that probably bankrupted her last client.

"Hey, Jake," she said like they were old pals, though they'd never met in person. "Leave the talking to me, that's what you're paying for."

She turned to Brewster and wrinkled her nose at Shane. "Okay, boys, what you got?"

Brewster ran through the allegation that Jake had pushed Summer Zhang onto the tracks. "From what I hear," he said, looking at Shane, "Mr. Ockham has a hero complex, so we contend he created this crisis to enhance his reputation."

Price gave a derisive snort. "Enhance? My client was hit by a train. If anyone was *enhanced*, it was Summer Zhang. Saving her life damn near killed him."

"I kinda doubt Summer or her folks see it that way," Brewster said. "We're coordinating with her and her parents to draft a sworn statement. She's still heavily medicated, so the DA doesn't want that to happen until at least tomorrow."

"Most certainly," Price said. "We don't want drugs impairing her recollection. Naturally, we'll want a copy of her statement."

Brewster waved a hand as if shooing a fly. "In due course. And we, naturally, expect Mr. Ockham to come clean. Happy to take his statement right now."

"In due course, detective." She gave Jake the high sign. "We'll take our leave. I assume you'll be transporting my client home?"

Shane spoke for the first time. "Not possible, Detective Brewster and I have further business to conduct."

It was Jake's turn to smirk. "As I recall, Detective Brewster proposed that he and Deputy Shane make plans tonight for, how did he phrase it? 'A pussy patrol.' "

Shane colored. Brewster glowered. Price rose to leave. "I'm sure the womenfolk of Centralia are breathless in anticipation. Let's go, Jake."

Outside, she offered Jake a ride home. "Not sure that cheap shot helped your cause, delightful as it was."

"Whatever. Thanks for your help. If it's all right

with you, I'll phone Quality Taxi. I'm pretty sure their meter-rate is lower than yours."

"Smart boy." She turned serious. "We have to get on top of this. I'll need a deposition from you, the whole nine yards. When and how I use it is still to be decided."

"Can I do that in Aberdeen, use the paper's lawyer or a notary?"

"Bad idea. We'll do it at my office. Aberdeen is small-town. Odds are, whatever you said would be gossip gruel within the week."

Turned out Price underestimated the rumor mill. Just two days after visiting the cop shop, Jake was front-page news again.

Chapter Twenty-One

Clearfield County, Pennsylvania, August

Lyla Watkins couldn't make out the words, but there were two male voices, one angry and agitated. She rolled off her camp cot and pressed an ear to her thick wooden door.

Male one said, "What the hell do you want, you sick fuck?"

Male two responded, "You want food, asshole, lose the attitude."

She heard a door close, a bolt slam home, and the creak of footsteps on stairs. Two thunderous kicks bracketed a creative string of oaths. Then the familiar *twang* of springs as a heavy body settled on the sort of shitty cot that also accessorized her wooden prison.

She'd been locked here at least a week. She was already losing track. Today's arrival was the first break in a routine marked by three dubious meals a day and a daily emptying of the malodorous honey bucket tucked in a corner of her eight-by-eight cell.

On the first day the meals were delivered by either a woman or the guy who'd snatched her. They'd first look through an eye-level door slot and order her face-down on the cot. Then, for about a week, an aloof older man acted as warden. Twice, he'd snapped a handcuff on her left wrist and led her naked to a bathroom and shower combo in the corner of what was obviously the deep cellar of an old house.

It was creepy, his eyes roaming her body. He snapped the other end of the cuffs through the link of a chain attached to an eye bolt inset into the concrete wall. She had enough play in the chain to use the toilet and, sweet luxury, for a tepid shower. Her vomit-stained clothes were exchanged for a set of blue sweats. Both top and pants carried a large HH, in gold embroidery.

Lyla had asked her young jailer: "What's HH?"

"Find out soon enough," she said. "Gonna make you famous again."

Again?

She shivered, not just from fear. The cellar was extraordinarily deep, dug perhaps as a shelter from hurricanes and tornadoes. A chill permeated its bones. Another cell similar to hers, empty until today, also backed onto a dank concrete wall. The other three walls and lowered ceilings were made of heavy plywood braced at floor and ceiling. She'd thrown herself at her cell's door and walls and got nothing but sore shoulders.

"Scream all you want," the woman said the first night. "No one will hear."

Each cell had a continuously burning lightbulb inset in the ceiling. To get a decent sleep, she stood on her cot and gave it a half-turn. She heard the scrape of footsteps as the new arrival explored his cell. There were more thunderous crashes as he tested its limits. He sounded big. Maybe they could find a way to ovcrpower their captors.

"Hi," she said in a tentative voice. "My name is

Lyla. Lyla Watkins."

There was a long pause, then, "Who are you?"

"I'm locked up too," she said, "more than a week now."

"What the fuck is going on?"

"Wish I knew. Did they drug you, too?"

"Yeah. I'm sick as a dog from whatever shit she slipped me. Got the world's worst hangover. Where are we? What's your name again?"

"Lyla. Don't know for sure but I think we're still in Pennsylvania someplace."

"Still? Jesus, I'm from Spokane. Means they bounced me across the whole damn country."

"What's your name."

"Ah, yeah. Name's Anderson Wise. Andy to my friends. Gotta sleep off this headache, then we have to figure things out."

"Sure. Hey, they give you fresh clothes?"

"Yeah, some sweats."

"Me too. With lettering?"

"Um, yeah. Got big HHs on them."

"Same as mine. Like we're on a team or something."

"Not a team I want to join. Hoping I wake up and this is just a bad dream."

"Oh, it's real. And scary as hell."

Chapter Twenty-Two

Clearfield County, Pennsylvania, August

Anderson Wise was hauled at gunpoint from his cell. The vixen from Sharkey's, whose name he still couldn't remember—if he ever knew it—held the weapon. Two men, one older, one younger, spun him around, cuffed his arms behind his back and guided him up the stairs and into a windowless room. It was stark white and brilliantly lit. They uncuffed him only to zip-tie him to a stout wooden chair. Didn't say a word before leaving him with a headful of bleak thoughts.

He faced a professional-looking camera on a tripod. Three chairs were arranged beside the camera but out of the shot. He had no idea if it was running. Just in case, he mouthed "fuck you" while glaring at the lens, wiggling his middle fingers as best he could. He'd vacillated between fear and anger these past days. Mostly fear, his kidnappers making no attempt to hide their faces.

He and Lyla discussed this at length, in voices just loud enough to reach each other's cells. He'd never actually seen her, but he liked her frankness and poise.

Anderson said, "They're going to kill us, aren't they?"

Lyla responded, "They're going to try."

"Why?" he asked.

"Why *us* you mean?" she returned.

They groped for commonalities. Common enemies.

She was a teacher from Pittsburgh. He was a school janitor from Spokane, almost two thousand miles away. They agreed they were pretty lame targets if their captors were waging war against the education system.

Anderson asked, "Are you rich?"

She said, "Not even close."

Anderson said, "Me neither, so it's not for ransom. What else?"

Lyla said, "Um, I'm black. Could it be a race thing?"

Anderson said, "I'm white, but—"

Lyla said, "Let me guess, some of your best friends are black."

Anderson laughed. "Well, half my rec baseball team is, and we're pretty tight." After a long pause he said, "My favorite teacher at my school is—was—black. She's dead."

Lyla said, "Sorry."

"Me, too. Wish I'd…Ah, never mind."

Lyla said, "Keep thinking, Andy. We'll figure it out. Don't hold back. It's like we're locked in plywood confessionals, and I'm not even Catholic."

He said, "Me neither, so we have that in common."

"That narrows the field," she said. "There couldn't be more than, what, two hundred fifty million non-Catholics in America?"

He said, "They're going to kill us, aren't they?"

"They're going to try."

****

Anderson figured it was an hour before the three

filed back. They carried water bottles, setting one on a side table beyond Anderson's reach.

"Thanks for nothing," he told the older man, recognition dawning now that he had a clearer view.

The woman turned on the camera, and the three took their seats.

"No Amarone this time," the older man said.

"You pretended to be a professor," Anderson said. "Asked a bunch of stupid questions."

"I *am* an academic. My questions weren't stupid. It's your vapid answers that reveal a sad lack of self-awareness—not atypical among your kind."

"My kind?"

He turned to the two others seated to his left and right. "Shall we begin?"

They hammered him with questions for hours. Often the other two repeated the same question, as if expecting a different answer, as if searching for lies or inconsistencies. They asked about his level of schooling, his relationship with his deceased parents, his sexual orientation.

"I concur. Definitely hetero," the woman said, gazing at Anderson with a sick smile. "I remember the bulge in your jeans, right before you passed out."

They asked about his "post-rescue experience." What was the public response? Did he relive the experience in dreams or nightmares? Did the "heroic status" enhance his desirability as a potential mate? They hammered away at that last query, demanding to know the number of sexual partners he'd had before and after the "experience."

He refused to give a tally, until the younger man blasted him with a taser. When he recovered, he offered an estimate that probably underreported the total.

The young guy gave a low whistle. "Fuck me. That's a heap of poontang for a few seconds work swinging a fire extinguisher. You shoulda got on your knees and thanked that shooter."

Even Anderson was quietly embarrassed, having not kept a running score. It made him think of his friend Sharon, the owner of Sharkey's. What did she get him into?

Finally, questions turned to the awful events in the classroom. What were you thinking? Were you motivated by thoughts of glory or fears of inadequacy? Did you have the hots for that dead teacher? Had you fucked her? Why didn't you save her? What took you so long?

As he'd told the professor over dinner the first time they'd met, he wasn't thinking much of anything. He just acted. The inquisitors weren't satisfied. They dragged him again over the same ground. The questions stirred a vague memory he'd tried to bury. He'd seen the shooter enter the school. He was at the end of a long hall, silhouetted by sunlight blasting through the door behind him. He carried something at his side.

Maybe an umbrella? Or maybe he just hoped it was an umbrella?

Something raised his hackles enough to paw his pockets for his phone, remembering he'd left it in the furnace room. He walked toward the man, who'd ducked into the first classroom on the right. Adah Summerhill's class. He was almost there when he'd heard the shotgun blast. That's when he'd grabbed the extinguisher and pulled a fire alarm. What if he'd run down the hall? Could he have saved Adah? Was he too self-conscious, afraid of overreacting and looking stupid? Was he just afraid?

Anderson was now a blubbering mess—hating his weakness, and the obvious joy his tears gave the interrogators. The woman turned off the camera, but only after he'd composed himself.

"Thank you for your time, Mr. Wise," the professor said, as if this was a job interview.

They cut the zip ties, lifted him to his feet and cuffed his hands. He fell back in the chair, his legs too weak to support him. The woman got on her knees and massaged his legs. Her hands strayed to his crotch, getting nothing for her efforts. "Pity."

They walked him with difficulty down the stairs and into his cell. They undid the cuffs and steered him to his cot. He fell back on the mattress. The tears returned. Lyla must have heard his cries but said nothing.

He finally broke the silence. "Weird question. Have you ever done anything...heroic?"

There was a long pause before she answered. "Some people think so."

"I've found our missing link."

Chapter Twenty-Three

Centralia, Washington, August

Jake fidgeted in Sue Price's book-lined conference room. It was four days since the train-station incident. He'd finished his deposition, which was video-taped, voice-recorded and transcribed by a nimble-fingered secretary using a courtroom steno machine. Seated shoulder to shoulder, he and Price discussed next steps at one end of a teak conference table large enough to land a Cessna.

Two copies of Summer Zhang's sworn statement sat in front of them along with porcelain mugs of coffee bearing the Price & Co. logo rendered in gold-leaf, and a plate of oatmeal-chocolate cookies. Price, dressed in another smashing business suit, was not calorie averse.

"The good news is," she said, "she can't ID who pushed her. She—"

A harassed-looking associate knocked and entered. Late twenties, white shirt, sleeves rolled to the elbows, silk tie ratcheted tight around his neck, he signaled toward the door. "Can I have a private moment?"

She frowned. "I've made it clear Mr. Ockham has my full attention until eleven a.m."

He blushed. "It's about Mr. Ockham's, um, situation."

"Then out with it, Gregory. Sit. Have a cookie.

And loosen that tie; your head's about to explode."

He fumbled with tie and collar. "Thank you, um, no. I'm gluten-free."

"Tragic. You do realize I'm charging Mr. Ockham by the quarter hour?"

"Sorry." He ran a hand through thinning brown hair and nodded to her closed laptop. "A new video from the train platform has surfaced. The *Aberdeen Daily News* called for comment, and now we're inundated with calls from other media outlets. And that Detective Brewster is demanding a meeting."

"You've not responded, I trust."

"Certainly not. But it's not good. Not good at all."

Price hammered a password into her laptop and pushed the machine over to Gregory. After a few quick keystrokes, a video opened on the screen.

It showed Jake moving behind the three girls at the platform's edge. He stared down the tracks, looking preoccupied as he slipped off a backpack, moved it in front and opened the zipper. Random crowd noises were soon drowned out by the dinging bells and rumbling diesels of the approaching train.

Without warning Jake's head snapped back as he slammed into Summer, knocking her in front of the approaching train. The tight focus on Jake offered no view of anyone behind. The video swung to follow her trajectory, mouth open in shock, flailing arms unable to stop her head slamming onto the rail. It captured Jake's jump as the thunderous base of a horn and the shriek of locked wheels replaced the cheery bells of the arriving train.

The video blinked off after he disappeared behind the train. It picked up from a different perspective.

Now, Jake was across the tracks, bent over the unconscious child. As a crowd formed, he seemed to wave them away.

The Twitter version, already going viral, carried the hashtags of #JakeTheSnake, #FakeJake and ending with #BoycottGHIndependent.

Jake buried his face in his hands. "I'm so screwed."

They replayed it a dozen times, freezing the picture at key moments. It raised more questions than answers. They huddled over Price's laptop and hammered out a brief statement. Price instructed Gregory to distribute it far and wide.

"Jake Ockham is grateful that Ms. Zhang is recovering from the horrific accident at Centralia Station. He wishes her well and requests the Zhang family's privacy be respected during this traumatic time. He issued the following statement:

"I'm sure the Zhang family has as many questions as I have about the devastating incident. Two widely circulated videos show portions of the accident. Both are deeply disturbing but neither show the whole truth. I was intentionally pushed from behind by an unknown assailant, and to my deep regret I was unable to stop colliding with Ms. Zhang. I welcome the investigation by the Centralia Police Department and am confident it will support my version of events. I urge anyone at the station that afternoon to contact police with witness statements, photographs or video that may aid the investigation. I will have no further comment as police conduct their enquiries."

Jake looked to his lawyer. "What now?"

She shook her head. "I won't sugar-coat this. Barring a miracle, I expect you'll be arrested in the next few days. It's my hope, though, this appeal for witnesses turns up exculpatory evidence. At the least, it should stir up enough chaff to delay a decision to lay charges."

He slumped. "I'll need time to make arrangements at the paper. I've already told the publisher, that's my Aunt Clara, I have to step down as editor until this is resolved. She agrees. Luckily, she'd already hired a recent layoff from the *Seattle Post-Intelligencer*. She was going to edit our online edition, but she'll step in as acting editor. I meet her tomorrow."

"Get to know her quick; the wolves are at the door," Price said. "I know you're nervous but you're losing the plot here. Your only priority is keeping your ass out of jail. With your permission, I'll give Detective Brewster your statement in hopes of forestalling the inevitable."

"Please do. It might buy me a few days to do my own digging."

"I'm not so sure that's wise," she cautioned. "Brewster will see it as stepping on his investigation."

"With luck, he'll never know. I've no faith in the guy. He was fitting me for an orange jumpsuit even before this latest video."

Price checked the time and handed him the last cookie. "On the house."

Chapter Twenty-Four

Back home, Jake sped through the messages on his home and office lines. He killed all media inquiries without listening to the fawning entreaties. He pounded the "press seven to delete" button with such regularity he almost killed a message from Estelle Brown, the Amtrak spokeswoman.

"Hi, Mr. Ockham. First off, please accept my belated congratulations, I hadn't realized during our earlier conversation I was speaking with a hero."

Jake cringed. Obviously, the message was left before shit met fan.

She continued. "Down to business. I'm told there are no plans to extend passenger service to your city, not now or in the foreseeable future. If you need a quote, use this: 'Unfortunately, there is no conceivable scenario where an extension of passenger rail service to Grays Harbor County is financially feasible. Amtrak remains committed to its current bus link from Centralia to Aberdeen. Satisfaction surveys show it has strong support from our passengers.' End quote. It seems like your source had a bad case of wishful thinking, Mr. Ockham. Grateful you didn't run with a bad rumor. Bye."

Jake saved the message. Inevitably, Brewster will ask why he was at the station, if not to push sweet little Summer Zhang in front of a train. This voicemail and the archived emails from his alleged source should make the case *someone* wanted him at the station.

He'd been set up, but why?

It was one of many questions to chew over with Erik Demidov, whose analytical mind and mad skills in the cyber world were coupled with a ruthless streak. How that coexisted with his unyielding loyalty and bubbling sense of fun was among life's mysteries. Erik's success as a founding partner in BitBust stemmed in part from an ability to put himself in the mindset of the most venal, corrupt and amoral sociopaths imaginable.

"You'd make a great master criminal," Jake once told him.

Erik had clapped hand to heart, pretending to be hurt. "Never, *dorogoi moy*…But my clients?" He gave a waddaya-gonna-do kind of shrug.

Erik, to Jake's relief, left a message asking if it was all right if he arrived tonight.

Jake returned the call. They'd already been in touch. Jake initially called to vent, but Erik insisted on being more than a sympathetic ear. Now he was in full investigative mode. "Two people almost died, my friend. This stinks like a Russian outhouse. I'm finishing a case report this afternoon. I'll be at your place by seven, in time for dinner. We've got digging to do. And I must discuss my website tweaks with Ramona Williams, your new online editor."

Jake was stunned. "That her name? How do you even know about her?"

"Clara called a week back, asking me to check her out. She's a righteous hire, Jake. My contacts tell me her layoff at the *P-I* had little to do with finances and much to do with her jealous and insecure supervisor. Surprised you're out of the loop."

"One of many recent surprises, your apparent expertise in Russian outhouses least among them. Ms. Williams, by the way, will be acting editor. I'm stepping down until I'm cleared. *If* I'm cleared."

"Good. Getting you out of this steaming pile of *gavno* is a full-time job. I'm bringing steaks and two bottles of a California red so divine you'll kiss the ground in gratitude. It's from a case gifted by a grateful client for services rendered. We'll leave it at that. All I ask is a decent bottle of vodka in your freezer. "

"You've got it."

Jake cleared his phone messages. Their content had turned on a dime from laudatory to vitriolic. No surprise. History is rife with heroes toppled by feet of clay. It's why he'd known his fall from grace was inevitable. It's why he'd loved his job researching accidental heroes for the Sedgewick Trust. There was no agenda to their deeds, just the purity of reflex, action, and result.

It's why he still took occasional freelance assignments from Sedgewick, vetting potential West Coast medalists. Many didn't make the cut. Those who did left him humbled and inspired.

Clara arrived at his home in mid-afternoon in a whirlwind of sympathy, angst, and rage, her hugs squeezing him like a human stress ball.

"Easy, dear," Jake said, hiking his t-shirt to display bandages and a body bruise in transition to vomitus shades of greenish yellows and browns.

She burst into tears. "I'm so sorry."

"Aww, jeez, Clara, it didn't hurt that much."

She pulled a tissue from her purse and dabbed her eyes. "I'm so sorry about everything. Sorry you jumped in front of that train. I can't unsee those goddam videos, they're everywhere. The comments section of our website is appalling; I'm surprised you haven't pulled it down."

"I haven't looked," he admitted. "It's a devil's playground of spineless trolls and anonymous cowards. All heat, no light. Let them vent. I'll leave it to Ms. Williams, our new acting editor, to deal with. I hope you were going to inform me of her hire before I found her sitting at my desk?"

"I'm sorry, Jake. Things got crazy for you, and I wanted to grab Ramona before someone else snapped her up. She's brilliant. You'll love her." She did her patented eye-brow arch. "You didn't return my calls from Bend."

"Childish, I admit. But you ignored my warning that running the train video would blow up in our faces."

"I made the right call, and you know it. Besides, it was nothing compared to what the *Daily News* just puked online." She fumbled with her phone and thrust the screen in Jake's face. *"Independent Editor Stonewalling Investigation Into Allegation He Pushed Teen Onto Tracks."*

The story, quoting "a source close to the investigation," captured Jake's testy exchange during Brewer's attempted interrogation. It claimed, "Sources say an arrest is imminent, a remarkable downfall for *Independent* editor Jake Ockham, just days after his own newspaper trumpeted his alleged heroics."

It noted, *"Ockham refused repeated interview*

requests from this newspaper." It did grudgingly add the statement he and Sue Price drafted and promised more details in the next day's print edition. Naturally, the story carried a link to the latest "damning video, obtained by the *Aberdeen Daily News*."

"Yeah," Jake said. "Obtained by the *News*, and every other paper, website, TV and radio station in Washington State."

Jake handed Clara two items from his cluttered desk. "Here's a statement I've drafted announcing my decision to step down until this issue is resolved. It is temporary, right?"

Clara took the paper and left his question unanswered. "Thanks, I'll box this on front and announce Ramona William's hire as acting editor."

He handed her the card Trent Shane tossed on his kitchen table the day he hauled Jake to Centralia. "He'll deny it, but Shane is the 'source close to the investigation,' should Ramona want to match the story. I recuse myself from any and all comment."

With muted enthusiasm, he invited Clara to tonight's dinner with Erik.

She sighed. "No can do, many fires to put out. We're hemorrhaging advertisers like you wouldn't believe."

She gave Jake a hug. Gentle this time. "Cheer up, honey. We'll get through this. Your dad arrives tomorrow night, in case you didn't know. He's worried sick."

"Of course, I didn't know. Why would he inform his only son of his arrival?"

"Don't pout. He'll stay with me. We'll catch up over a nice dinner at my place." She sailed out the door, leaving yet more unanswered questions in her wake.

Feeling a need to punish himself, he changed into workout clothes, donned gloves and hauled his erg machine onto the deck.

Thirty minutes later, his left side was in agony. If his scarred hands were on fire, his bruised side was in too much pain to notice. He sat on the machine, watching the Wishkah flow, calming his breathing, slowing his heart rate, letting the pain subside. Two ducks banked in the wind and skidded to a landing, riding the current downriver as they bobbed for food. High above, an eagle rode the thermals, broad wings barely moving as if contemplating dinner options, meat or fish?

Acting on instinct, a fat rabbit on the far bank dove into the rushes, taking itself off the menu. Seafood it is, reminding Jake to pull scallops out of the freezer. Pan-seared on a bed of oven-crisped pancetta and crushed peas, they'd go great with Erik's steaks.

Couldn't imagine life without the Pacific and these rivers that fed it. Couldn't imagine life in prison. He sat some more, lost in thought, as the Wishkah flowed on.

Chapter Twenty-Five

Erik arrived at seven and set his bounty on the kitchen counter. He'd texted two hours previous, saying there'd be a third for dinner.

He opened both wine bottles to breathe. "You really do need a decanter; your student days are long past."

"I had one, you broke it."

"Oops." He shrugged. "Months ago. Buy another for heaven's sake."

Erik unwrapped brown butcher's paper to reveal three fat, beautifully marbled rib eye steaks. "Dry aged forty days—the sweet spot in my humble opinion." Next came three plump cobs of corn. "Passed a farm stand on the way here. I was powerless to resist. Hope you don't mind."

"Tis the season. Leave on the husks, I'll chuck them on the barbecue with the steaks," Jake said. "What I mind is the lack of consultation about including a mystery guest. We've much to discuss."

With no hint of apology, the former roommate said, "The guest arrives at eight. Dinner around eight-thirtyish? Okay?"

Jake nodded. "Time enough to walk a couple of dirty martinis to the deck and do some scheming. I see this as a three-olive situation." They pulled chairs away from the outdoor table and sat side-by-side facing the river, feet propped on the deck railing. "Your thoughts on the new video?" Erik asked.

"Aside from its general unhelpfulness and curiously wide distribution? The video is totally focused on me, like the shooter knew what was going to happen. I'm working on the assumption that whoever lured me to the station is also connected with the video shoot."

"Agreed."

"It's clear, the way my head snaps back, that I was violently propelled forward. Notice how anyone behind me, the pusher specifically, is not visible. A neat set up and a nice frame job."

"Also true. If I had to guess, it was an attempt to paint you as a cold-blooded killer. You may have ruined their intent by risking life and limb to save the girl. No one could have predicted you'd jump in front of a train."

"Me included." Jake plucked an olive from his swizzle stick. "Heartless villain or fallen hero, they win either way."

"I'm assuming, as you obviously are, that you're the target and not little Miss Zhang."

Jake nodded. Second olive down, drink level perilously low.

"Just to be sure," Erik said, "I dug into the background of the Zhang family. The parents are second-generation Americans living the dream. Dad's an engineer, mom's a pharmacist. Three kids, house paid for, not so much as a parking ticket between the lot of them."

"Which brings us to the big question," Jake said. "Why?"

"Why you, specifically? Or why are we holding empty glasses?" Erik retorted.

Jake waved in the general direction of the kitchen. "Fill your boots. Don't want my taste buds numbed by another martini. Be a waste of the wine you brought."

"Good point. A couple of beers, then?"

"Have a growler of Belgian ale, lowish alcohol. Great for deck-sipping. Mugs are in the freezer."

Drinks recharged, they returned to the big question. "Who have you pissed off lately?" Erik asked.

"Personally, no one recently. Well, Trent Shane, the sheriff. He's hated me since high school. I used to date the gal who's now his wife. Sort of."

"Sort of dated her? Or his sort of wife?"

"The latter. Not a happy union."

"Ah, have you been in contact since? Any, um, dating I should know about?"

Jake avoided the question. "Doubtful a high school romance is at the root of this."

"Okay." Erik looked skeptical. "How about controversial stories?"

"There's a family values coalition most unhappy with an editorial I wrote, but I don't see a bunch of book-burning blue-rinsers conspiring to kill me. That said, there is a side project I've been looking into, not sure it's even a story. Just kind of—"

There was a knock on the door. Jake looked at his watch. "Our mystery guest?"

Erik smiled, his turn to wave in the general direction of the kitchen. "One way to find out."

Jake opened the kitchen door to find Tina Doctorow, looking amazing in a flowered sundress, strappy sandals, a floppy-brimmed hat, and sunglasses.

"Hi, Jake," she said, looking uncharacteristically shy. She waved to an idling taxi. The driver saluted and backed out of the gravel drive. "You look surprised," she said. "Weren't you expecting me? Erik said—"

"What I am is thrilled, Tina. Welcome to my humble abode."

She had a white sweater draped over one arm and held a hemp bag, which she handed to Jake. "A bottle of wine in there, the same white we had at dinner, I hope that's okay. It should still be cold. And a dessert."

"Spelt brownies?"

"No," she punched him playfully in the arm. "A pecan pie, from Mom's old recipe book. I'm not much of a baker."

He pulled the pie out of the bag and set it on the counter. "A thing of beauty," he said, eager to make up for the stunned look he'd greeted her with. "I'll save the wine for the appetizer course." He tucked it in the fridge. "We're having drinks on the deck, what can I get you?"

She scrunched up her shoulders. "Do you have the makings of a gin and tonic?"

"Absolutely."

She looked around the kitchen as he made the drink. "This is amazing, especially for a guy," she said, running her gaze along the row of chef-quality pans hanging over a kitchen island, and taking in an Italian espresso machine, a high-end food processor and a knife block.

"So sexist. When I rowed, I burned through a minimum six thousand calories a day. Eating was such a necessary evil, I wished there was a trapdoor into my stomach to save time and all that chewing. When I quit rowing, or rowing quit me, I fell in love with eating again. Quality, rather than quantity."

She cast an appraising look at his physique. "You could bounce a quarter off that stomach. Obviously, you've dialed back the calories."

He gazed fondly at the pecan pie.

He handed her the G & T and pulled the remains of the Belgian growler out of the fridge. "I'll give you the two-minute tour then we'll join Erik outside."

It didn't take long. The kitchen opened into a living room. Off it were two bedrooms and a bath. She touched his arm as they turned for the deck. "I hope it's all right, me being here? Erik said you wanted me to come, but you looked kind of shocked."

"Erik would only say we're having a mystery guest. I assumed it was his latest boyfriend. Seeing you at the door was the best thing that's happened to me all week long."

She smiled and seemed to relax. "After the week you've had, that ranks me above a police interrogation, a false accusation of attempted murder, and a public shaming. I suppose I'm flattered."

"I'll have to work on my compliments. Your radiant beauty leaves me tongue-tied."

"Better," she said as Erik rose to meet them.

They gathered around the glass-topped table—Erik looking pleased with himself, Tina taking in the river view. "This is so perfect," she said, turning to Jake. "Your place, this view. I can almost feel my blood pressure lowering."

"It calms me," he said. "Until I contemplate the fine line between rustic charm and decrepitude. I'm amassing a frightening number of handyman tools.

Anyway, time to get the appetizer started. Erik, how do you want the steaks seasoned?"

"Leave it to me."

It was a perfect night for outdoor dining. Tina volunteered to set the table, which left just enough time for Jake to confront Erik. "Would it have killed you to tell me Tina was coming?"

"And ruin the surprise?"

"Don't get me wrong, I'm thrilled. God, she looks wonderful."

"Jake, Jake, Jake, I was shocked she asked directions to your place. This can only mean you haven't bedded her yet. Disappointing."

"We've only just met."

"Get on it, boy. Even in this one-horse town you won't be the only guy eager to tap this natural resource."

"Thanks for the advice, Dad. And so elegantly phrased."

The pan-seared scallops were washed down with Tina's white to great acclaim. As Erik cleared the plates, Jake placed the corn on the pre-heated barbecue, letting the cobs steam as the husks charred. Then the steaks, medium rare for Tina and Jake, blood rare for Erik, accompanied by a salad of local tomatoes, red onion and cucumber.

The setting sun painted the horizon. Tina captured the vivid cloud-streaked oranges and yellows on her cell camera before firing off a couple of shots of her dinner companions. "A night to remember."

"No fair," Jake said, "you caught me with steak in my mouth."

"A refreshing change from your foot," said Erik.

Jake turned to Tina. "Help me with dessert?"

She warmed the pie in the oven while Jake fired up the espresso machine. "Thank you for coming," he said. "You made my night."

"Two handsome men, how could I refuse?"

"Please don't take this wrong," Jake said, cringing at his awkwardness. "I want more of these nights. Many more. I think you're wonderful."

Her smile faded. "There's a *but* coming."

"I'm toxic, and it's only going to get worse until I'm cleared. If I'm cleared. Hell, my lawyer thinks I'm going to be arrested."

"Still waiting for that but."

"You're building a medical practice, the last thing you need is to be tied to the local pariah. I know it's presumptuous, we're not even a couple, but I think you should keep your distance." He shook his head, kicking himself for risking a relationship he desperately wanted to flower. "Um, just for the time being."

"Is that what you really want?" Her voice so soft it was almost lost in the steam and gurgle of the coffee machine.

"Absolutely not. But maybe what you need."

She raised one of his hands to her lips for a kiss as delicate as a butterfly's wings. "I'm a big girl. I'll decide what I need. We're already taking it slow. Maybe too slow, but I'm enjoying peeling back your layers without emotions getting tangled in the sheets. Um, maybe I'm being presumptuous."

"Egyptian cotton, with a thread-count off the charts. Ready and waiting for…whenever."

They carried coffees and desserts outside, where Erik basked in the flickering glow of two hurricane lanterns. He polished off his pie, declined his share of the last of the wine and, with a sly smile, announced he was turning in after a long day.

Jake and Tina put up a token protest, which was duly ignored. Had he turned back, he would have seen they were holding hands.

Chapter Twenty-Six

Clearfield County, Pennsylvania, August

Anderson Wise woke to a ferocious pounding on his door followed by a similar assault on Lyla's cell.

"Time for some fresh air." It was the young guy. He unlocked their doors, a pistol in hand. The girl was beside him, carrying handcuffs.

"Arms in front out the door and no funny business," he said. The woman snapped cuffs on them and they were led up the stairs.

It was Wise's first look at Lyla. She smiled and nodded, all that needed saying already shared in their plywood confessionals. She was tall, maybe five-nine, and leaner no doubt than she had once been. An elastic band pulled thick black hair tight to her scalp, a tail of wild curls cascading behind. He locked on Lyla's fierce, intelligent gaze. He hoped she read in him a determination not to fail her.

The older man waited in the kitchen. "We're going for a drive," he said with an expansive smile. It was one a.m. on the kitchen clock.

"You two look sleepy," he said in an attempt at sympathy. He handed each a small thermos. "Made you coffee."

They loaded into two vehicles. The professor drove a British SUV. Anderson was in the back, along with the young guy still holding the gun. Lyla was led to the shotgun seat of a smoke-belching Detroit relic of the '80s, overdue for the wreckers. The woman buckled her in then poured her a cup of coffee, like she actually gave a shit.

She got behind the wheel and both vehicles headed down a narrow road past field and forest.

The professor powered down the windows, opening the vehicle to the night sounds of rural Pennsylvania; choirs of cicadas, crickets, and katydids sounded above the hum of tires. Fireflies blazed in the darkness, as fleeting as a camera's flash.

Anderson sipped coffee and tried to let the night chorus calm him. He couldn't overcome the dread this false freedom carried. What is the life expectancy of a firefly? Weeks? Months? Better odds than his, for sure.

An hour later, they rattled down a lane at the side of an unharvested corn field. They stopped at a wire fence, extinguishing their lights. Anderson saw Lyla was asleep, her face resting against the old car's side window. He was a nervous wreck and she nodded off. Amazing.

The three captors exited the vehicles, the woman fussing over Lyla before taking what looked like a camera bag from the back seat. The three pulled on ski masks. Lyla slumbered on.

The professor, holding the gun now, ordered Anderson out of the car. The young guy pulled bolt cutters from the SUV and cut a section of fencing, the wires twanging like broken guitar strings. He got behind the wheel of the K-car, Lyla still inside, drove through the gap in the fence and humped out of sight over a hillock. Tires clattered on gravel, then brake lights flared and went dark. A car door shut and he returned, leaned on a fencepost and checked his watch. No sign of Lyla.

The professor said, "The app says five minutes."

The woman clipped a small black box to the chest pocket of Anderson's jacket, adding strips of duct tape to the clip to reinforce its hold.

"This stays on, or you die," the professor said.

Anderson looked down, recognizing a newer, smaller version of his own sport video camera. The low rumble of heavy diesels joined the night sounds.

The girl pointed a video camera at Anderson and the professor spoke. "The sound you hear is an approaching train. Unfortunately for Lyla, her car is stuck on the tracks. You, Mr. Wise, have a choice. You can return to my vehicle and sip your coffee. No harm will come to you, I've even placed fresh pastries there for your enjoyment."

He unlocked Anderson's cuffs and glanced at his watch. "Or you can make a probably futile attempt to extract Lyla from the path of a southbound Canadian Pacific train hauling softwood lumber and running hot. She'll be comin' round the bend when she comes," he said in a sing-song voice. "In two minutes."

Anderson wheeled and sprinted for the fence opening. It was too dark to see the young guy stick out a leg, launching him into the air. His hands broke the fall, coarse gravel shredding his palms. He scrambled to his feet and sprinted to the car. The sweep of the locomotive's headlamps illuminated a distant row of trees as it rounded the curve.

The car doors were locked.

His scream to Lyla was lost in the warning wail of

the train horn as the engineer noticed the car splayed across the tracks. The cacophony was joined by the scream of steel-on-steel as the wheels locked, and the boom and crash of rail cars as they slammed together. There was little appreciable impact on the train's momentum.

Anderson kicked at the driver's side window, but his rubber-soled runners did no damage. He slammed a palm on the car roof. Lyla slumbered on. He scanned the trackside for a heavy rock but saw only gravel ballast. Then, twenty feet past the car, the train's headlights lit a stack of creosote-coated rail ties.

He grabbed one and charged to the car, smashing it into the rear passenger-side window. He stretched around the tie, popped the lock on Lyla's door and reached in, almost blinded by the brilliant lights of the train. She was seat-belted in, duct tape around the buckle. As a janitor, he'd loved duct tape. Tonight, with the train fifty yards out, it was a disaster.

He fumbled for the tape end, hampered by blood oozing from his shredded palms. Imprisonment left his nails long and unkempt. He worked one under the tape end. He focused entirely on the seat belt, the only thing in his power to control. He unwound the tape, popped the release and yanked a limp Lyla from the seat.

The train was upon them as he flung them trackside, covering her with his body. There was a horrific crash as the train slammed the car into a sideways spin. The rail tie, lodged halfway out the rear window, launched straight up.

Anderson braced for impact as the cartwheeling missile hurled back to earth.

Chapter Twenty-Seven

Aberdeen, Washington

Erik peered over his breakfast latté. "Before we were interrupted by our mystery guest—who, I'm disappointed to note isn't in evidence this morning—you mentioned a troublesome story you were working on?"

"She left by taxi last night. We're taking it slow. I don't want her caught up in my mess. That, and the idea of you in the neighboring bedroom cackling and rubbing your hands in glee, is a total buzzkill."

"I don't cackle. Admirable that you don't want to tie her to your troubles but don't tap the brakes. Untold damage is done by the parable of the *Tortoise and the Hare*. It's a celebration of mediocrity. It inspires successive generations of plodders to plod. Always bet on the hare. But I digress. What of this story?"

"Someone is trying to sell a Sedgewick medal at an insultingly low price. It belongs, or belonged, to a guy named Walter Meely, a mild-mannered choir director who risked his life pulling a guy out of a burning SUV. It's a case I investigated and verified. I attended the presentation. He was rightly proud of that medal. Why it's on the market begs many questions."

"Have you answers?"

"Yes and no. I had Jonathan Foley, a colleague at

the fund, look into it. We—they—don't like hero medals peddled on the open market. Walter has vanished, that much he knew. Jonathan says that kicked up a scandal at his very conservative evangelical church."

He gathered his thoughts as he finished the last of his smoked salmon omelette. "After his disappearance Walter's distraught lover, a young teacher and also a member of the church, went to his pastor seeking guidance and help. He got neither."

"He? Ah…messy."

" 'Fraid so. Until then, they were deep in the closet. The pastor, whose selective reading of the Bible missed all the stuff about compassion, excommunicated the young guy and demanded he speak of this to no one."

Erik bared his teeth. "Fuck that sanctimonious *sukin sin*."

"That's a new one."

"It means son of a prostitute."

"Anyway, the lover went to the cops, who opened a half-assed investigation."

"Let me guess, police theorized he fled in shame, or he killed himself. The latter happens all too often."

"It's possible Walter offed himself but…" Jake rubbed the back of his neck and closed his eyes. "Didn't know him well, I didn't even pick up on his gayness."

"You can be obtuse."

"Fair comment, but putting his mother through that grief?" Jake pursed his lips. "No. They were close. And crawling into a burning vehicle, that took guts. Walter's a little guy who was bullied as a kid. So, he endured that crap only to kill himself now that he's a bona fide hero in a loving relationship? Doesn't make sense."

"Obviously, no body's been found."

"Nope. And there's this douche who somehow got hold of his medal. He has a low opinion of heroes in general and Walter in particular. I want answers from this guy." With breakfast done, Jake reluctantly gathered the morning papers off the front stoop.

The *Aberdeen Daily News* ran an unflattering photo of himself on the front under the headline: *"Independent Editor Steps Down After Video Shows He Pushed 12-year-old In Path of Train."*

The story began with *"An investigation continues into what a police source calls 'a heartless, unprovoked assault' at Centralia's Amtrak Station that left 12-year-old honor student Summer Zhang hospitalized with head and back injuries.*

"Video obtained by The News appears to show Independent editor Jake Ockham pushing Miss Zhang in front of the incoming Amtrak Cascades Sunday afternoon. Ockham was initially hailed as a hero for pulling the girl out of the path of the train. Then a second disturbing video revealed Ockham's alleged role in what a source close to the investigation called 'a potentially life-threatening attack.'

"A statement released by Miss Zhang's distraught family demanded 'this callous assailant be brought to justice. It is only by God's will that our precious Summer wasn't killed during what had been an innocent outing with friends.'

"Centralia Police Det. Harry Brewster said, 'Witness interviews and the investigation into this serious incident are in their final stages.' While Brewster had no further comment, a source told The

News charges will be laid in a matter of days.

"Ockham, who refused repeated interview requests, claimed in a statement issued through Centralia lawyer Susan Price that he was violently pushed into Miss Zhang by an unknown person or persons. 'I welcome the investigation by the Centralia Police department and am confident it will support my version of events,' his statement said.

"Ockham has been 'temporarily' removed as editor by Independent publisher Clara Nufeld. Ramona Williams, a former digital editor for the Seattle Post-Intelligencer, has been named acting editor for the family-owned newspaper. (Cont. A 2)"

Jake didn't bother with turning the page for the rest. He pushed the paper across the table to Erik and flipped through the *Seattle Times*. It carried a shorter wire service version of the story on an inside page, linking, of course, to the second video on its website.

Jake rose from the table. "I'm heading to the office to meet Clara and my smarter, better-looking, and unindicted replacement. Coming?"

Erik patted his laptop. "I'm sticking here. Got digging to do. What was that gay chap's name again?

"Walter Meely, M-e-e-l-y. Worked at the Living Gospel Evangelical Church in Omaha."

Chapter Twenty-Eight

Jake arrived at the *Independent* to find receptionist Anna Mae looking more harassed than usual. He expected her to gloat, his current troubles confirming her low opinion of him.

Instead, she rose from her desk to give a brief, awkward hug. "I'm so sorry, Jake. I know you'll get through this, but it must be awful being dragged through the mud. It's hard on all of us. You wouldn't believe the calls, the cancellations, the insults I've had to deal with."

Jake smiled. She was back on familiar ground. "Thanks for holding the fort, Anna Mae. We couldn't do this without you."

She handed him a fat stack of pink phone messages. "All urgent, of course."

He flipped through them, plucked one from the pile and stuffed it in his jacket pocket. "I'll hand these off to my replacement when she arrives."

"Already here. In your office with Clara. She seems nice, I guess. She's quite tall, and, ah, she's black," she said, the last in a whisper.

Jake laughed. "So are you, Anna Mae."

"I am not!"

"Could have fooled me."

"I'm five-foot-one and shrinking by the year." She burst out laughing. "I'm messin' with you. Be good to

146

have a sister on the editorial side. Now get in there, they're waiting."

The two women rose, then turned as Jake knocked on his office door, which felt pretty damn weird.

"Jake," Clara said, "I'd like you to meet Ramona Williams."

Clara looked tired and stressed. Ramona, in her mid-thirties by Jake's estimation, looked exactly as advertised, though he'd add stunning and self-assured to the description.

"Welcome, and thank you for coming on such short notice," he said shaking her hand. In heels she was almost tall enough to look him in the eyes. He handed her the sheaf of phone messages. "You have my sympathy."

They gathered in chairs at the small conference table, Ramona too classy to take a seat behind Jake's desk. Or maybe she'd already tried his god-awful chair.

They started with small talk, studiously avoiding the smoking crater of Jake's career. He asked Ramona about her background, not only because he was curious, but because years of interviewing proved people are most comfortable talking about themselves.

She described growing up on an acreage outside Thomaston, Georgia. "My folks owned Williams Hardware and Paints, a small place on Thomaston's outskirts. It's not there anymore, not that I ever planned for a career selling screws, tools, and paint."

She smiled at a distant memory. "Seems like I grew up behind the oak counter where our brass cash register sat. Mom says I burst into tears the first time a white customer walked in. I guess I was about three. Gives you an idea who our clientele was back in the day. The city is named after General Thomas, a self-described 'Indian fighter' during the War of 1812, so political correctness isn't baked into its DNA. It was pretty enough, but a good place to be from, if you get my drift."

"Why journalism?"

Another smile. "Thomaston has the country's longest-running annual Emancipation Proclamation celebration. I wrote an essay about it in high school. Our local paper reprinted it. Boom, I was hooked."

He knew from Clara that Ramona had graduated from Columbia University's excellent journalism school with a Master of Science in Data Journalism. He often wondered where his career might have gone with that kind of specialized J-school education.

Talk turned to practicalities. Jake handed her the story list for the next issue, and passwords for his work computer and for various digital subscriptions. "There's an ideas file on the desktop and a recall list plugged into the laptop calendar for various events, court dates, council reports, and whatnot. Clara knows all—"

A crash of breaking glass and a piercing scream came from the front office. Jake and Ramona leapt from their chairs, almost colliding at the office door. Anna Mae was crouched behind her desk, sobbing. The front picture window, which for as long as Jake remembered proclaimed "*The Independent*" in an elegant arc of gold leaf script, was reduced to jagged shards on the floor and a nearby counter.

He scanned for further threats, but all he saw on the floor was a brick wrapped in white paper. He crouched beside Anna Mae, putting a protective arm around her shoulder. Ramona sprinted to the sidewalk, scanning for the culprit and looking for witnesses among the few passersby.

Clara joined Jake and they helped Anna Mae to her feet. "Jake will take you to my office," she said. "You can rest on my couch."

In an aside to Jake, she said, "A nip of Scotch might help. There's a bottle in my office."

"Wow, cliché alert. Let me guess, in your desk drawer under a half-finished novel?"

Clara glared. "Don't you take anything seriously? It's in the cabinet by the window—filed under S."

Jake dosed Anna Mae with a generous dollop of single malt, closing the door behind him. Clara handed him gloves, broom and dustpan. "You aren't recused from cleanup duty."

Ramona returned from the street, phone in hand. She looked at Jake. "Don't clean up yet. Cops are on their way, and I want photos."

"Beat me to it," Jake said. "Camera is in my bottom left drawer. Start with this brick so I can see what the note says."

She took shots of the brick and several wider interior shots. Jake put on rubber gloves and started to tease away the tape holding the paper around the brick.

Ramona looked concerned. "Shouldn't we wait for the police?"

"I have limited faith in law enforcement these days." He carefully unfolded the paper, handling it by the edges. "Get a photo of this."

The message was written in block letters in thick, black marker: "MUDERIS SCUM LIKE JAKE THE SNAKE OCHAM IS WHY HONEST CITIZENS HATE THE FAKE NEWS MEDIA."

"Interesting," Jake said. "Two spelling mistakes, an 'is' that should be an 'are," and an old high school nickname."

"Sounds like you were real popular," Ramona said.

"A segment of the student population was consumed with jealousy. What do you make of the note?"

"The writer was either semi-literate," she said, "or was trying to appear that way."

"I vote for the latter. The printing is awfully neat for someone uncomfortable with putting pen to paper."

An Aberdeen Police cruiser rolled up, and a young patrol officer emerged, hiking his utility belt. He stood on the sidewalk, taking in the scene, arms crossed. "Wow, that sucks," he said as Clara, Ramona and Jake gathered around.

He pulled out a notebook and wrote names, time and other particulars. "What's that window, about eight-feet-by-five? What's that gonna cost? Need an estimate for my report."

"No idea," Clara said. She gave him the particulars of their insurance agent. "He'll be arriving shortly."

"Thanks," he said. "Hey, shoulda asked off the jump, any idea who did this?"

There was a deep, derisive snort from behind Jake. "You can put most everyone from here to Centralia on your suspect list."

"Hi, Sheriff Shane," Jake said, not bothering to turn. "Out of your jurisdiction, aren't you?"

"Just happened by. Lucky for," he peered at the young cop's name tag, "Officer Turner, to have an experienced cop ready to assist. Two heads are better than one, right Turner?"

"I have this in hand," Turner said, his face reddening.

"The Sheriff's office always cooperates with the locals on the big cases: SWAT turnouts, drug cases..." Shane leered at Jake. "Attempted murders. Broken windows, not so much, but since I'm here, let's have a look."

He bulled in ahead of everyone, crunched across the broken glass and picked up the note, which Ramona had set beside the brick to photograph.

"Hey," Turner said, "there might be prints on that."

Shane unfolded the note with his bare hands, holding it up to the light. "My bad, left my gloves in the cruiser. Anyway, the Aberdeen cops won't waste resources running prints on a pissant case like this. Why, the *Independent* would write an angry editorial about wasting taxpayers' money. Right, Jake?"

Shane put hand to mouth in mock surprise. "Shucks, forgot, your writing days are over."

He set the note down, flattening the creases with a palm. "But we can do some good old deducing. See some spelling mistakes here, so either we have us a real dumb bunny, or a foreigner. Might be a Chinaman. They're plenty pissed at Jake for chucking one of their own on the tracks. Or maybe one of your oppressed minorities?" He looked pointedly at Ramona. "Say, we haven't been introduced."

She glared daggers and picked up the camera. "How about a photo, sheriff? Maybe one of you mauling the evidence with your big, ungloved mitts?"

"I'll pass," Shane said. "Gotta run. I'll leave it to Officer Turner to crack this case." He swaggered out the door.

"Asshole," Ramona and Turner muttered, in unison.

The insurance agent arrived. He took a series of photos and gave Clara the name of a glass company that would board up the window until a replacement was ready.

"Your claim should breeze through without an increase in your rates," he told them. "I'd suggest shelling out for anti-shatter film on all your windows."

He looked at Jake. "Not just because of your situation. Nothing personal, you understand. I recommend this for all my commercial clients. Keeps the rates low."

After he left, Clara headed out for a series of meetings. "To make nice with our advertisers. It'll give you two a chance to pass the torch."

"Have a seat, we can talk while I clean up," Jake told Ramona. He was surprised some of her earlier bravado had drained away. She looked tentative and troubled. "Helluva a way to start a new job," he added, "having to clean up my mess."

She gave a weak smile. "I knew what I was getting into. I really like Clara, and if she says you're innocent, I'm inclined to believe her."

"Appreciate that, Ramona. But take this story where it leads you. I'm too close to be objective. I don't expect—or want—you to pull your punches, if that's what's bothering you."

She gave a laugh, wholly lacking in mirth. "Oh, trust me, I won't. You can always write a letter to the editor if you don't like what we print."

"Fair enough. But something's bothering you. If it's my doing, let's make it right."

He turned to give her space, donned leather gloves and dumped glass shards into a garbage can. Behind him he heard a sigh. Jake said nothing as she worked toward her point.

"Ever more white folk were coming into my folks' store. Good for us, until we became a threat to our old-money competition. Mom and Dad had their windows smashed more than once. Didn't drive 'em off, but it hurt plenty." She gave the trash can a light kick, hearing the rattle of glass. "This raises ugly memories, but it won't scare me off."

She gave his arm a playful punch. "Welcome to my world, White Boy."

Chapter Twenty-Nine

Clearfield County, Pennsylvania, August

Lyla Watkins awoke and instantly regretted it.

She closed her eyes against the overhead light but it did nothing for the pain, like her brain had crashed down a flight of concrete stairs. A head-turn sent electric agony down neck and spine. Between her legs was a bucket reeking of vomit, though she had no memory of using it.

She tracked a random trajectory of spots floating behind her eyes. The last time she felt this bad was, when? When awful people dragged her out of a van and locked her in…Her hands explored her surroundings: a thin mattress, the metal frame of a cot. The last time she felt this bad was when they locked her…in here.

A recent memory swam to the surface: sipping coffee on a nighttime car ride, floating like a leaf on a journey from branch to…oblivion. Forcing her eyes open, she took inventory. She was naked, her torso a mess of welts, scabs and bruises. Her right wrist was bruised and swollen, reminding her of a hard crash during her basketball days. Not broken, but sprained. She'd been drugged, obviously, and then what? Had they beaten her? Raped her? Tentatively, she moved a hand between her legs. It was, to her relief, about the only part of her not bloodied or bruised.

She lifted the foul bucket and gingerly set it on the floor. That small act of housekeeping was excruciating. Tracking the floaters behind her eyes, she let herself drift away.

****

She heard the bolt click and the door creak. The headache, still throbbing with every heartbeat, had receded to tolerable levels. The young woman entered, setting panties, socks and a folded set of clean sweats on the plastic milk crate that served as a side table. She wrinkled her nose and set down a laptop case that had swung from her shoulder. She set the bucket outside the door. "You can deal with that when you have your shower."

She seemed cheerful, almost giddy as she squeezed onto the cot and opened the laptop. "You gotta see last night's adventure." Her eyes blazed. "You're gonna be famous, girl. In certain exclusive circles."

It was a video of the old car she'd been in, evoking memories of its stale, musty smell. There'd been a camera inside, though she hadn't noticed it, probably affixed to the inside rear-view mirror. It offered a wide-angle shot of a masked man at the wheel. And her, unconscious, head bouncing against the passenger window as a roaring engine carried them up a small hill.

The lighting was poor but the sound was crisp. The driver stopped and pulled the ignition key. He fumbled with her seatbelt, locked the doors and disappeared. All was still, then the laptop speakers played the faint throb of an engine, growing stronger and deeper with each passing second.

A face appeared at the driver's side window. It was

Anderson. He looked frantic. He screamed her name. He pulled at the door, gave the window a vicious kick and pounded the roof, achieving nothing. He looked around then disappeared. Lyla felt a wrench of abandonment.

The car's interior was cast in stark relief as light flooded the interior. The continuous blast of a train horn joined the thunder of diesels and the shriek of metal. Lyla's stomach clenched. She watched her unconscious self, still and unmoving. It was like she was trapped in a nightmare or cast in a horror movie. She hated horror movies.

She wanted to scream, *Get out of the car!* But she wouldn't give that smug bitch beside her the satisfaction. There was an explosion of glass as a heavy log or something smashed through a rear window. A hand reached through, pushed her roughly off the door and popped its lock.

It was Anderson. He was shouting but the sounds of the train drowned out all else. He bent over her lap— fumbling with her seatbelt, she supposed. She watched mesmerized as the car's driver-side window turned into a solid mass of dancing, blinding light. Anderson never let his focus stray from the seat belt.

Why was he taking so long?

Her captor paused the video. She clapped her hands in excitement. "You're gonna love this part. A few seconds left."

She played them in slow-motion.

Anderson flung off the seat belt, yanked her from the car and they disappeared from the view. Lyla slumped in relief. What happened next? What about Anderson? What a phenomenal act of will to ignore the train, to focus only on her.

The light show merged into four distinct headlights at the front of the train. And behind them, the locomotive loomed like a malevolent force. Even in slow motion, the car catapulted at remarkable speed. The camera spun off its moorings. All went dark.

"Anderson?" Lyla asked in a whisper.

"Oh, he streamed some great shit, too," she said. "And me, with my hand-held. I'm editing it all together tonight. Probably get it to our clients tomorrow."

"Anderson?" Lyla asked again.

"Kinda messed up. We're moving his cot in here. You being a teacher, we're hoping you know enough first-aid to patch him up."

Lyla swiped a shaking hand across her forehead. Her heart raced. The video triggered a reaction more visceral than anything she'd felt pulling that veteran off the streetcar tracks all those years ago.

And not for herself. Her anguish was for a guy she barely knew. A guy who put everything on the line. For her. For a woman just a few conversations short of a stranger.

Her captor packed away the laptop. Lyla wanted to dive across the cot, wrap her hands around that lily-white throat and strangle the life out of her. Could she kill? Crazy to think like that. But, yeah, she thought she could. Just not now. Anderson was her responsibility. She'd heal him.

Together, they'd make plans.

Chapter Thirty

Aberdeen, Washington, August

Jake left the *Independent* as glaziers hammered plywood over the gaping wound of the front window. He rounded the corner to his usual diner.

Two days ago, the manager wouldn't let him pay for his lunch. Today, he was treated as if he'd tracked in dog shit on his shoes. His request for a coffee was met with frosty disdain. There was a gap in the reading rack where copies of the *Independent* were usually on offer.

He passed on lunch. No way he'd trust the cook with his food. He asked for a takeout cup, tipped extravagantly and skulked out the door. Back home, he set the cooling coffee on the kitchen table and pulled the phone message from his pocket. It was from Sedgewick's Jonathan Foley, who never used three words when one would do. "Call."

Foley picked up on the second ring, the first thing that had gone right today. And made no pretense of small talk. "Remember Lyla Watkins?"

"Of course, one of my favorite heroes. The one who got me hired at your shop."

"She's missing. Big news here, but it probably never made it out your way."

His shoulders sagged. "Walter, now Lyla—and

poor Summer as collateral damage—all linked to me. This can't be a coincidence. What happened to Lyla?" he asked in a weary whisper. "And when?"

"Must be ten days ago. Was teaching summer students at a local high school. Finished classes for the day. Last seen getting into a van after a coffee date with a guy at a nearby shop."

Foley said both her mother and the high school principal reported her missing but it was days before the police took it seriously. Foley said coffee shop staff recalled her having a heart-to-heart with this guy on their patio. " 'A real hunk.' " according to one barista. "They left arm-in-arm." While the mother insisted her disappearance was totally out of character, police played the usual odds and initially read this as a lovers' tryst by consenting adults.

"By day four, Mom was in hysterics," Foley said. "She had access to Lyla's bank account, which showed a maximum three-hundred-dollar-withdrawal from a highway rest stop ATM the day after her disappearance. Police got a subpoena and pulled the security video. The withdrawal was made by a woman whose face was hidden under a wide-brimmed hat and sunglasses the size of hubcaps. A white woman."

"Not Lyla, obviously. If someone snatched her, then Walter—"

"Meely. Exactly. That's two missing medalists within the span of a few weeks. Something is wrong for damn sure."

"And both with ties to me."

"Yeah, that too."

Jake heaved a sigh and recounted to Foley the trackside incident, the phantom push, and the very real risk he was about to be charged with attempted murder.

"Not good. I knew about the rescue, but not the aftermath," Foley said. "Two people nominated you for a medal after it hit the news. That's pretty typical, as you know."

"Not to make this all about me, Jon, but somebody is intent on trashing my reputation. Is that linked in some tangential way to these disappearances? By targeting me, am I somehow putting the Sedgewick heroes at risk?"

"It seems farfetched," Foley said. "But I was a reporter, too, back in the day. Don't like coincidences any more than you do. Hey, did you ever buy Meely's medal?"

"Still working on that. The guy's gone silent, and I've been kind of preoccupied. I'll try getting back to him again. Assuming I'm not in jail."

"Strange times, my friend. Got to run, have a medal presentation to arrange."

Jake was about to cut the call. Then he shouted "Wait, Jon. Wait."

There was a pause. "Yeah?"

"You still have all my report files, right?"

"Sure. We're obsessive about record-keeping."

"This is a big ask, but could you folks contact the people I recommended for awards?"

"Ah, man. Half the staff is on summer holidays." He heaved a sigh. "But I see where you're going. Are others at risk? I'll have to bring this to our board. Our role is to recognize and assist our heroes, not put them at risk."

"There must be a way to do this without causing panic. Maybe say you're doing a follow-up study or something?"

Another sigh. "Gonna take time, but we'll get 'er done. Meanwhile, keep your ass out of jail, huh? Your reputation is tied to ours. Everything depends on resolving this quickly, and quietly."

"I'm on it."

Jake dumped the last of his coffee. He stared out the window, hands on either side of the sink, replaying memories of Lyla and Walter and other Sedgewick heroes.

It was a common refrain at every medal ceremony. People looking at the recipients, asking themselves, "What would I do? Would I go down that well, dive into those rapids, step in front of that bullet? Would I die for a stranger?"

As always, Jake wondered how he'd measure up.

This much I know, Walter and Lyla. For all my failings, I'll do all I can to save you.

Chapter Thirty-One

Clearfield County, Pennsylvania, August

"That went rather well," the professor said. "Five-star ratings across the board. I never thought our Mr. Wise had it in him. Do you forgive me now, Brad, for making you drag him across the country?"

They were having their nightly cognac, the professor ignoring Brad's desire for beer.

Brad slammed down his snifter. "You didn't have to change his diapers. Neither did Kristy. Disgusting. Forty hours of driving and the van reeked like an outhouse."

"Easy on the crystal, boy. Be grateful I had the foresight to give you enough drugs and diapers for the trip. Judging by his actions on the tracks three nights ago, a wide-awake Wise would have been trouble."

"It's not like Brad did all the work," his sister said. "I did most of the driving. He slept almost as much as Wise."

"Such bullshit," Brad muttered.

The professor swirled his snifter, taking an appreciative whiff. "Let's not lose sight of the big picture, children. Our audience loved the drama. Kristy, your mixing of the three points of view: streams from Wise's body cam, the car, and your own camera set a new standard in *cinéma verité*. Our audience is hungry for a sequel."

Kristy laughed. "Our Wise-guy is in rough shape."

"The good news is they'll live to fight another day," the professor said. "Saves the bother of sourcing fresh blood. The bad news, however, is the longer we keep them, the greater the risk." He leaned in. "That said, I've a plan to divert attention far from here."

His idea, as explained, was simple, cost effective and carried minimal risk.

"I like," said Kristy. "I showed Lyla her video from the other night. She'll do whatever we demand. Guaranteed."

"Quite right." He rubbed his hands as if before a fire. "It's a strategy to employ in all future endeavors."

"Speaking of the future," Kristy said, "when do we snatch Ockham?"

The older man steepled his fingers. "Patience, dear. Let him marinate in his sea of woes. Been tracking the local online media. The comment boards are incandescent with rage. Charges are imminent. Be a race to see what happens first, a lynching or an arrest."

"I don't want him in jail," Kristy said, alarm in her voice. "I want him here. I want him dead. Know what I really want, Daddy?"

"I'm all ears."

"I want him to watch a loved one die in front of him, just like I had to watch Mom while he did nothing. Then, we'll give him a nice messy death."

"Jesus," said Brad, his vague details of that tragedy largely shaped by Kristy's interpretation of events. "You are scary."

"What she is, Brad, is a woman who knows her audience."

Chapter Thirty-Two

Aberdeen, Washington

Clara was a good cook when she set her mind to it. Tonight, she whipped up a Marsala sauce for the finishing touch on pork tenderloins wrapped around prosciutto and asiago cheese.

The scents of dinner, the clatter of dishes, and her occasional muffled curses wafted into the living room where Jake and his father were banished. "Best you don't see the throes of creation," she'd said, handing them bottles of beer.

The aroma was familiar. It was one of his late mother's go-to recipes, featured in *Connie's Classics*, the booklet of photocopied family favorites she'd assembled as she battled cancer in her final months. Jake made it himself a couple of times with mixed success. It wasn't a dish to eat alone. Jake and his father had an amiable, if somewhat distant relationship. Roger was an introvert. Connie, the social gadfly, was the one to draw him out. It had been a good balance and a happy marriage.

Roger withdrew after his wife's death. He was supportive of Jake, always there to listen and sympathize as he vented his hurt and anguish. But it was a one-way street. Roger was loath to share his pain, though it was written clear enough on his face.

Clara had stepped into the breach. "Give him time," she'd advised Jake. "Your father processes things differently than you and me. He thinks he's protecting you from all that's churning inside. Never doubt he loves you and your mom with all his heart."

And Jake never did. That was evident tonight as he made Jake recount the events before, during and after "the accident" as he called it. He picked at the minutia with an accountant's eye, frustrated he couldn't tease out a motive as to why his son was targeted.

"It doesn't add up," he said several times. Jake smiled, such a dad thing to say.

Clara arrived with two more beers. "Fifteen minutes to dinner, boys. I'm going upstairs to change. When I return you will have moved on to other things, I won't have dinner ruined by talk of this mess. We've better things to discuss."

Roger watched her disappear up the stairs. "She's right, of course," he said with obvious fondness. "Usually is."

But didn't drop the subject just yet.

"I saw the videos, Jake. Both of them. I, ah…I'm proud of what you did to save that girl."

Tears pooled in Roger's eyes. So not a dad thing.

He continued. "I'm proud, and I wish to hell you hadn't done it. You can't imagine what it's like for a parent to watch his child almost throw away his life. What were you thinking?"

"If I'd had time to think, who knows? I probably wouldn't have done it. Don't honestly know."

"I expect you do. You don't have to prove anything. Not to me. Not to you. Not to anybody."

Jake laughed. "Tell that to the Centralia cops, to

the district attorney's office, and to my adoring public."

"How's your lawyer?"

"She's paid to believe me. Plus, she's whip-smart and delightfully ruthless. I've a lot of time for her."

"Billed, no doubt, in fifteen-minute increments. You send her legal bills to me."

"Not necessary, Dad."

"Please, I want to help you any way I can. And I—we—have selfish reasons for resolving this."

Jake opened his hands as if to say, go on.

Roger shook his head. "Later. That is a topic for the dinner table."

****

Or more accurately, for the dessert course.

Dinner was reserved for local gossip, a catch-up on the lives of distant relatives, and Clara's attempt to draw into the conversation news of the new doctor in town. She gifted Jake a sweet smile, and the heel of an excellent bottle of Oregon red. "Quite a move up from old Doc Wilson, both medically and aesthetically, wouldn't you agree?"

"Well, she's not my doctor. But she's a great benefit to the community."

Clara did an eye roll and turned to Roger. "He says 'benefit to the community.' "

She gave a derisive snort. "They've been dating. I happen to know she thinks quite highly of our Jake. And Jake, if he has a lick of common sense, should move things along."

"Well, well," Roger said. "Great news."

"Ah, jeez, only a couple or three dates. It's unfair to tangle her in my problems. I'm not exactly a catch at the moment."

"Let her be the judge of that."

Clara nipped into the kitchen, returning with a pavlova, all sugar and air, bowls of whipped cream and fresh blueberries. She handed Jake a cake knife. "You serve."

He bent to the task but didn't miss an unspoken high sign she sent Roger.

Roger took a deep breath and began. "Jake, I'm getting married. I will always love your mother, but it's time to move on. I'll be retiring in a few years, and I want to share that time with someone special."

Jake froze momentarily, wondering when a woman had entered his father's life and resumed dishing out the dessert. "Congratulations are in order," he said, warming to the idea. "Don't think you need to justify this to me. You've been alone way too long. Who's the lucky woman?"

"Here's where it gets a little weird," Clara said. "It's me."

Jake almost dropped his fork. He groped for the right words. Clara was blushing, which had to be a first. She looked radiant and a bit tentative as she searched his face for a reaction. She looked so much like his mother Jake wanted to weep.

Clara tugged at her earlobe, a nervous mannerism she'd shared with her twin. "Well?"

Jake gave his head a shake. "Well, I'm surprised. Please don't take that awkward silence as disapproval. I'm stunned. But, no, not weird, Clara. It seems…right."

"Well, a little weird, marrying Connie's identical twin," Roger said. "When we first started seeing each other—romantically, I mean—Clara accused me of a failure of imagination."

Clara reached across the table for Roger's hand. "I said he was trying to complete the matching set."

"I think my problem was too much imagination," Roger said. "For way too long, I saw Connie when I looked at Clara, and I kept my distance. When I finally saw Clara as, well, Clara, I realized I was falling in love with a unique individual. They're quite different, you know."

Jake burst out laughing. "No kidding. Clara is so not Mom. And bonus points, Dad, she loves to golf. Mom always called it an excuse to award trophies for wasting time."

"He proposed after putting out on the eighth green at Widgi Creek," Clara said. "Pulled the ball and a ring out of the hole. What could I do but say yes?"

"I promised myself I'd propose on the first hole I parred that day. Took me until the eighth, I was that nervous."

"Had I known," Jake said, "I would have brought bubbly."

"It's already on ice," Clara said. "Be right back. Rog, can you set out the glasses?"

Clara returned with a bottle of France's best rattling in an ice bucket. She waggled her left hand under Jake's nose, displaying a fat blue sapphire ringed with small diamonds. "Now I can show this off."

Jake knew sapphire was his mother's birthstone. *Both* mothers' birthstone. Something to get used to. They raised glasses in a toast and discussed possible wedding dates. Then Roger pulled a large envelope from under his chair and slid it to Jake. "Have a look," he said, casting a nervous look at Clara.

Jake slogged through the first couple of pages of lawyerly lingo before realizing he now shared equal ownership of the *Independent* with Clara. "Really? Are you guys crazy?"

"Connie willed her half to me, but it was always her wish it go to you when, and if, you joined the business," Roger said. "Keep reading."

Turned out he was also half-owner of four buildings bracketing the newspaper.

"Your grandfather gradually acquired the entire block," Roger said. "He wanted the potential to expand if the *Independent* went daily. Didn't happen, but the properties generate a nice cash flow."

"Basically, they keep the paper alive," Clara said, "as you'll learn six months from now when I retire to Bend, and you take over as publisher."

Jake stuffed the deeds back in the envelope with fumbling fingers. "This is crazy, suddenly I'm a newspaper publisher and owner, and a landlord and—"

"And you're stuck in Grays Harbor," Clara said. "We worry how you may feel about that. Oh, and it's half-owner, Bucko, don't get delusions of grandeur."

"I don't know anything about running the business side of things."

"You will after six months under my thumb. That is, if you're committed to staying," Clara said. "As for the landlord part, we've always farmed that out to a real estate management company. Oh, and you'll need a permanent replacement as editor. I'm hoping Ramona fills the bill. Lord knows I'm paying her enough."

"My plan was always to stay. I had my shot at a big city daily, I like running my own show. But I'm toxic now. I don't want to drag the business down with me."

"That's a mess we'll have to straighten out before this goes public," Clara said.

Jake pulled out his phone. "I hadn't wanted to ruin dinner, but I got a text from Sue, my lawyer, as I was getting ready tonight."

He called up her message and held up the phone.

—*Bad news, Jake. That sumbitch Brewster demands you 'surrender yourself' tomorrow at 2 p.m. for interrogation at Centralia PD. Be at my office at 12:30 for a strategy session. But prepare for a probable arrest. Sorry—*

He'd already forwarded the text to Erik.

—*Working on it, Moi Horoshiy*—was his cryptic reply. He might be a "good boy" in Erik's eyes, but that was definitely a minority opinion.

Clara and Roger looked crestfallen.

Jake attempted a grin. "Cheer up. Let's see how this plays out. Don't let this ruin tonight's great news."

He slid the envelope back to his father—deeds that would have made a comfortable life until he became the most hated man in town.

Chapter Thirty-Three

Clearfield County, Pennsylvania

After three days, Lyla became increasingly more uncomfortable with her role as nurse. She was concerned over the potential for fractured ribs due to the massive bruising on Anderson's lower chest and abdomen. From her days on the basketball court, she was certain he had a dislocated shoulder.

Their bitch captor ignored Lyla's pleas to get him to hospital and told Lyla her video showed a flying railway tie had crashed into the ground beside them, then slammed into Anderson. "Lucky it hit the ground first, or he'd be dead for sure. Probably you, too."

There were other logistics to consider after he regained consciousness.

Anderson pulled a towel over his face to give Lyla the illusion of privacy when she used the bucket, a humiliating experience for both of them.

His ribs made it impossible to squat. This necessitated calling the big guy to thump down the stairs to haul him to the toilet. He complied with much grumbling. "Better than changing your fuckin' diaper."

Anderson gasped in agony the first few times she and the big guy shifted him into an ancient looking wheelchair, the size of which looked like it was designed for a child. Now he merely grunted, swore, and staggered to the toilet gripping the young guy's shoulder. Lyla credited modest advances in his recovery to a liberal dosing of pills the woman said she'd obtained by telling her doctor she had debilitating period cramps.

None of the captors used names in their presence, denying Lyla a focus for her hatred.

"You have a name?" Lyla asked the woman. "Something besides hey you?"

She smirked. "Bet there's a bunch of names you want to call me."

"I'm trying to keep it civil."

"Daddy sometimes calls me Pele, after a Hawaiian fire goddess. That's personal." She thought for a moment. "Blaze. Call me Blaze."

Lyla nodded. So that's her father. Interesting, their body language when they hauled them outside for their trip to the train tracks suggested something else.

What's with this fire fixation?

Chapter Thirty-Four

Aberdeen, Washington

Jake was on his second Americano the morning after the engagement announcement. He'd miss his espresso machine in jail. Wondered what to pack for Centralia today. Socks and underwear, maybe an electric razor? Or, hell, grow a beard, make him look tougher. Can he bring books? Should he pack jeans, or does the well-dressed felon wear orange?

Last night was a gerbil wheel of worry and senseless questions. Totally sucked the joy out of his father and Clara's big reveal. He worried about them worrying about him. And 'round and 'round it went. All freakin' night.

An anonymous email arrived at seven a.m. The subject line: *"Views you can use."*

Jake opened the email hoping it wasn't a virus. *"Click on these attachments, asap."* It was signed *"329Anonymous."* Jake smiled, 329A was the address of the shitty apartment he and Erik shared their final two years at university.

The first was low-rez security video of the Amtrak platform at Centralia. The wide-angle view showed him and Tina entering the frame. He handed her the shopping bags and pointed her to a bench. He made his way to the platform edge, found a spot behind the three schoolgirls and slipped off his backpack.

The camera, which must be mounted on a pole, offered a partial side view of the crowd. The video had no sound, but heads turned in unison as the train approached. He wondered at the dubious quality of the video. By showing most of the platform crowd it sacrificed useful detail. Amtrak cheaped out on its security contract.

He was easy enough to spot, though, being the tallest guy in the frame. Until a man of equal height edged in tight behind him. Jake paused the video. The guy was partially obscured by Jake's body. He wore sunglasses and a ball cap with an improbably large bill.

Jake pressed play, hoping for a better view. But the guy never looked up, never looked toward the camera even as the train approached. Then, he seemed to brace his body, and with both hands palm-out, he slammed his arms into Jake's back. The powerful push was done with such minimal movement no one near the guy seemed to notice.

Jake's head snapped back as he crashed into Summer who launched onto the tracks. Heads turned; mouths opened in silent screams as the drama on the tracks drew the crowd's attention.

Jake replayed the video, focusing on the man behind him. He turned immediately after the push and, head down, moved calmly through the surging crowd and disappeared.

The second video was of even worse quality. It was a view of the opposite side of the tracks from a security camera primarily focused on a loading dock and parking lot.

Still, it caught a peripheral view of the tracks. The

video began as Jake followed Summer onto the tracks. It showed him throwing her out of the train's path, and him being knocked airborne by the train and flung down the tracks, out of camera-range.

Jake reflexively touched his side where the injury was painfully apparent.

Seconds later, he stumbled back into camera view to kneel beside Summer's inert body. He wondered why Erik bothered sending this blurred, indistinct video. The version leaked all over social media was way clearer.

Then it became apparent.

A slight figure dressed in black edged into view, stopping well short of Jake and Summer. Man or woman? Impossible to tell. He or she also wore a ridiculously broad-billed cap. Something was held to the person's face.

Others who rushed around the stopped train clustered around the trackside drama. The person made no move to join them.

Jake pressed pause, then thought back to the leaked video. It would have been shot about where that person stood. Erik found the shooter, for all the good that indistinct image would do.

He picked up the phone. Erik answered on the second ring with a hello that morphed into a yawn. "Sorry, was up all night, strip-mining Amtrak's servers."

"This is amazing, Erik. It shows I was pushed. And you caught a glimpse of the mystery videographer, though the images of him or her are about as clear as your typical Sasquatch sighting."

"Look closely, my friend, it's a her."

"How do you figure?"

"She's also in the first video. Look twelve seconds in. Upper right, along the platform. Same hat, same black t-shirt, a camera pressed to the face. Impossible to identify but blessed with what you heteros would call a major-league set of knockers."

"Ah, yeah, see what you mean. How did you get this?"

"A total hack-job. Utterly illegal, which is why this can't be tied to me or BitBust when you send them to your lawyer. Which you should do, posthaste. Here's a more relevant question: why don't the cops have them?"

"An excellent point. Maybe Brewster is stalling his investigation. Or maybe he has them, but he wants to twist my nuts at the request of his good buddy Trent Shane?"

"I'm off to bed. Good luck today. Have your lawyer legally subpoena the videos before they disappear. Somebody's got a real hate-on for you."

Chapter Thirty-Five

Centralia, Washington

Attorney Sue Price was a vision in red this afternoon, from pumps through pantsuit, to an artful application of lipstick.

"Wow," said Jake, when they met at her office for sandwiches and strategy, "you're some politician's wet dream."

"I'm agnostic. Red or Blue, I'm there for you." She rubbed her palms in anticipation. "Let's take another run through those videos. Here's how we'll play it…"

****

They arrived at Centralia Police Headquarters at two-ten that afternoon, tardy enough to annoy Brewster, by Price's calculation, but not so late he'd issue an arrest warrant.

Jake held the door as Price breezed through. "There will be blood," she muttered.

Brewster looked meaningfully at his watch as he led them into an interview room where they declined his offer of coffee.

He turned to Jake. "Let's chat before proceeding with the legalities. Hope you packed your toothbrush."

Jake smiled and, per his lawyer's instructions, held his tongue. With difficulty.

"An excellent idea," Price said. "We welcome a

free exchange of information before we're fettered by those annoying legalities." She set her briefcase on the table, popped the latches but kept it closed. She batted her eyelashes. "You show us yours, and we'll show you ours."

Brewster reared back. "To be clear, counselor, while we're dispensing with the arrest and Mirandizing for the moment, anything said during this discussion will surely be revisited later."

"I certainly hope so, should it come to that," she said. "How be you go first?"

He looked unsettled, as if she'd thrown off his game plan. "I'm not handing you our full investigation on a platter, but I see no harm in sharing the bare bones of the formal complaint we'll file with the magistrate."

Price turned to Jake. "That will be the poor dear's attempt to establish probable cause for your arrest."

Jake smiled. Price smiled. Brewster didn't.

The detective opened a buff-colored file, scanned the contents as if to refresh his memory, then smiled. "It really boils down to those damning viral videos, and several corroborating witness statements obtained during our extensive investigation. They all point to a callous attempt by Mr. Ockham to kill an innocent schoolgirl by throwing her in front of that train. Really, what else is there to say?"

"Did you establish a motive for this heinous assault?"

"I'm sure that will come clear during our interrogation. Let's just say we're considering this attack may be racially motivated, what with Miss Zhang being Chinese."

"Third-generation American, I believe. Of Chinese

origin to be sure. A hate crime, huh?" Price turned to Jake. "Dear me, that's serious." She looked at Brewster's thin file. "I assume that's the sum total of your *extensive* investigation? It looks rather anorexic."

"All we need. Your turn to spill."

She opened her briefcase. It was covered in rich burgundy leather, the color of drying blood. She roused her laptop from sleep. "Just the two 'damning' videos, you say?"

"All we need."

She positioned the laptop so it was visible to all, punched a key, and the crowd scene at the platform played out, including the shadowy figure who shoved Jake.

By the time it ran through its full length, Brewster's face had gone beet red. "Play it again."

She complied.

"Where did you get this?"

"No idea. It was leaked anonymously to my client. There's a lot of leaking in this investigation, don't you think? Or do you mean where was the camera located? I think that would be obvious, even to you."

"Anonymous, huh? This could be doctored. There's all kinds of fake video on the Internet."

"Really, detective? You're grasping at straws. But just to put your mind at ease, an hour ago, I issued a *Subpoena Duces Tecum* to the Amtrak station manager demanding the production of any and all surveillance video from the relevant period." She turned to Jake. "*Subpoena Duces Tecum* roughly translates from the Latin as 'this case stinks like week-old herring.' "

Brewster looked like he was in the midst of passing a kidney stone.

Price pulled back the laptop, hit a few more keys. "Here's another for you. I apologize for its poor quality. Appropriate, considering this so-called investigation." She paused it as the blurred figure in black came into view. "Hard to tell, but she's holding a camera. I'm sure your tech people will be able to confirm by her position she's the one who shot that second *damning* video."

Brewster snorted. "Proves nothing, can't even tell it's a woman."

"Oh, she's all woman, detective. She makes an appearance at the twelve-second mark in that first video we showed you. I'll let you discover that yourself. Why should we do all your work? She's what you folks call a suspect. Her, and that big lug who shoved my very innocent client."

"I'll be the judge of his innocence," Brewster said, though his bravado was unconvincing.

"That's a judge's job, as I recall. Pray it doesn't get that far or I'll barbecue you on cross-exam like a county-fair back rib."

She made no pretense of smiling now. "The court would learn that your inept investigation failed to uncover evidence so obvious a rookie beat cop would have found it, blindfolded. Or worse," and now her voice was a snarl, "you had this video and you withheld exculpatory evidence for God-knows what reason."

Palms-out, he pushed back on her verbal assault. "I did no such thing. And we would have found that video, the investigation is on-going. That's why Mr. Ockham hasn't been charged."

"Here's what's going to happen, detective. You have forty-eight hours to get your head out of your ass and get a real investigation underway—or we go public. That will give you more than enough time, and the grounds, to issue a statement exonerating my client. It will include a full and complete apology for the leaks insinuating Mr. Ockham was guilty and about to be arrested."

"Nothing leaked from here."

"Right," she said again. "Maybe you just whispered it to Deputy Shane, your fellow Pussy Patroler. Same difference. I will review it before it is released, and it had better grovel."

Brewster waved his hand, not bothering to rise. "Get out, I got work to do."

Jake followed her out the door, finally uttering his first words. "You were magnificent."

"God," she said. "Haven't had this much fun since the gals of Alpha Delta Pi's lost weekend in Vegas."

She leaned in and got serious. "Their only way out of this mess is another attack on your credibility. Watch your back."

Chapter Thirty-Six

Clearfield County, Pennsylvania, August

"Blaze made me write a letter yesterday," Lyla said, "when she hauled me out for a shower."

Although their close quarters and shared fears imposed an unaccustomed intimacy on the two people, Lyla had held back this latest bad news. But he seemed stronger today.

Anderson looked up, didn't seem surprised. "And?"

"And…I think I signed my death warrant."

"Why did you do it then?"

"She didn't give me much choice."

"Let me guess," he said, biting his lip. "If you didn't, they'd tie me to their van and drag me down the gravel lane. Guess I owe you one."

She gave a start. "How did you know?"

"The professor made me write one, too. With the same threat."

"Bastards." She gave her pillow a vicious punch, sending dust mites flying. "Thanks for sparing me the exfoliation. They're malicious, in a smart sort of way. Instead of playing us against each other, they gambled we'd have each other's backs."

"Mine's not much of a prize these days."

He gave a painful stretch. "They played me, that's

for sure. He'd visited me a couple of months ago, that professor guy." He shifted uncomfortably on his cot. "Flew out to Spokane to interview me for his 'research.' Even took me to dinner. I was flattered at first, but it got weird."

"Weird how?" Lyla Watkins hiked up his sweatshirt to change the dressings on his gravel-shredded left side. "As weird as this?"

"No, this is evil. Back then, he was fixated on analyzing my motives. Like did I stop that school shooter to increase my potential for sexual gratification? Kept talking about 'the subconscious calculous of risk-reward ratio.' Bullshit like that."

Lyla peeled off a soiled bandage. "Well?"

Anderson jerked. "Ow! Fuckin' hell."

"Sorry. Got to get an antibiotic cream on this mess, the last thing you need is an infection. Focus on my question, or was 'fuckin' hell' your answer?"

"Ah, jeeze, my ribs. Don't make me laugh. I'd be lying if I said I wasn't amply rewarded by the ladies of Spokane. Too much, really. Started seeing myself as a total fraud. But it wasn't some grand plan."

"Who had the time?"

"Exactly. You just act, right? That's what bugged him the most, my 'lack of analysis and self-awareness' as he put it. I'm not putting myself out there as some comic-book hero, but he used a lot of big words to suggest I was too stupid to be brave. Got up my nose."

Lyla opened the pack of bandages Blaze provided. "I got the same thing during my interrogation. Said I was a useful addition to his latest research paper. The title was something like, um…"

She searched her memory. " *Selfless or Selfish?*

The False Narrative of the Heroic Act.' Something like that. I told him he was a pretentious jerk."

"Nice." He stiffened as Lyla applied the new dressings but didn't cry out. "I asked why the subject interested him so much."

"I wondered about that, too. Why study a subject you think is bogus?"

"That night I told you about started at Sharkey's, my favorite bar. Then cocktails and wine at a fancy restaurant. We were well lubricated. He started talking about his father and ordered another round of Manhattans. It was early in the dinner. It might have been his way of getting me to open up, but he got pretty loose, too."

Anderson sat up with difficulty. Lyla tucked a pillow between his back and the wall.

He continued. "Seems his dad was some kind of war hero, a sergeant. In Korea, I think. Came home to a big job with a petrochemical company. He'd saved the life of his captain over there and the captain's very grateful father was this company's CEO. Got him the job and a pile of shares. Trouble is, he was seriously messed up, what they call PTSD now. Drank like a fish. Beat his wife, beat his kid—the kid being our crazy professor. His old man walked out of a bar one night and saw two guys drag a teenage girl into a dark alley and start ripping at her clothes. They had knives. He picked scrap rebar from a construction site and charged in after them."

"That took courage."

"That took alcohol, according to our professor. Reason his dad was walking is he was too drunk to find his car. Too drunk to feel the pain when one of the guys slashed his arm. Not so drunk he couldn't lay out those punks and save the girl. He'd been a soldier, remember. Months later he was awarded a Sedgewick medal, just like us."

"Let me guess," Lyla said. "Our professor thinks his dad was too drunk to form a heroic intent."

"Something like that. So, the old man cleans up for the awards ceremony. He goes home, hits the bottle hard, and his wife harder. Our professor who is fourteen at the time tries to intervene, but he's no match for dad, who slams him to the kitchen floor. He's holding his medal. They're pretty heavy, right? Uses it to whale on his son until he loses consciousness. The kid wakes up in his mother's arms. She's a mess. He's a mess. The father's gone, the bloody medal is on the floor.

"Our guy takes it, and all his father's war medals, limps outside, and chucks them down a sewer grate. Puffed out his chest when he told me that."

"I'm trying to feel sympathy for the guy, growing up with a monster like that."

"For the mother, sure. But the son became everything he hated in his father. I asked what happened to his dad. He smiled and shook his head. Wouldn't say how that ended."

Lyla gently patted his uninjured shoulder and held his gaze. "It hasn't ended."

"But it will." He squeezed her hand. "It ends here."

Chapter Thirty-Seven

Aberdeen, Washington

Erik arrived the next afternoon, having caught up on his "paying work," and his sleep. "I suggest you call your lady doctor and we go for a celebratory dinner. Then, back to work. We have the missing Mr. Meely and Ms. Watkins to find, and that gruesome duo who set you up."

"Might be premature, word of my exoneration is a day away."

That was semi-true. Jake worked the phones as soon as he got back from Centralia. His father and Clara were the first to learn of his reversal of fortune. Clara cried. As for Tina, he heard a sniffle when he gave her the news, but it might be seasonal allergies. And finally, acting editor Ramona Williams, who was all business.

"Congratulations," she said. "The glass company will be devastated. Those bloodsuckers charged a thousand bucks to replace our window, they were hoping for repeat business. I want the videos, and an exclusive interview."

"As I told my folks, this stays under the dome until the Centralia cops issue their apology. I'll give you a statement, vetted by my lawyer, but it's strictly under embargo until I'm cleared by the cops. Deal?"

"Yeah, yeah, okay." No tears from Ramona, just a weary sigh. "And the videos?"

"Sue, my lawyer, says no way. They're evidence before the court."

"Really? Such bullshit. Sue your lawyer? It may come to that."

"Hang on. I said *I* can't give it to you. But those videos were anonymously leaked to me. Who's to say they won't be anonymously leaked to you at the appropriate time?"

"You work in mysterious ways, Jake, like a news ninja. Mr. Anonymous better appreciate the need for an *Independent* exclusive on those vids, or there'll be hell to pay."

"News ninja, I like it. Might put that on my business cards. Speaking of which, have some printed as editor, not acting editor. I'm chasing whoever set me up, no time to fill the editor's chair."

"Thanks." She didn't sound surprised. "Ergonomically speaking, one doesn't fill this editor's chair, one endures it."

He laughed. "Use the money we'll save on windows and buy a new one. Just don't trash that wooden monster. I'm strangely attached to it."

"Yes, boss."

****

Jake needed some convincing before agreeing to show his face at a restaurant.

"No good comes from hiding in a closet," Erik advised.

"Were you ever in a closet?"

"You've seen my extensive wardrobe, there's simply no room. Now, phone your doctor."

Tina took no convincing at all. "You betcha, pick me up at eight."

Erik made reservations at Wally's Winery, a short hop west of Aberdeen on Highway 105. He and Jake scanned the parking lot, making a point of ignoring a car that trailed them from Aberdeen and was now parked in a distant corner of the restaurant lot. The two occupants inside showed no inclination to leave their idling vehicle.

Erik excused himself on their arrival for a quiet word with the manager.

The service was impeccable. They shared two appetizers, a Dungeness crab dip and something called Seahorses, which looked suspiciously like bacon-wrapped prawns.

The mood was light. Erik was his usual amusing self. Tina pretended to give Jake hell for avoiding her in recent days. Jake tried to stammer out an excuse, but she squeezed his hand and smiled. "You did it to protect me. Very sweet, don't let it happen again."

A hovering waiter took their wine order, a bottle of Wally's Wheely Wonderful White. Jake, the designated driver, battled to keep the guy from topping up his glass.

Still another waiter took their dinner order: line-caught fish and chips for Jake and Erik. Tina asked for something called Hamtastic Quiche. "Brilliant choices," he gushed. "Madam will love the quiche."

The food was outstanding. The service, almost too attentive. The waiter, in fact both waiters, were crushed when they said no to dessert, having decided to head into Aberdeen for ice cream.

"But our Dream Puffs are homemade." Waiter One

pulled a sad face, like they'd just backed over his grandmother. "Everyone adores our Dream Puffs."

"Next time," Jake assured him.

As they were leaving, Tina had a quick consult with Waiter One and emerged with a bottle of Wally's Rockin' Red. She settled in beside Jake. "Someone there is in charge of silly names. Wasn't that service amazing?"

"Suspiciously so," said Jake, eying Erik sprawled in the backseat. "Makes me wonder what you said to the manager?"

"Moi?" He shrugged. "I may have let slip that the travel section of *The New York Times* is considering the region for one of its most popular features. How does *'36 Hours in Grays Harbor'* sound to you?"

"It sounds like I'll never be able to go back there."

"It guaranteed no one spit in your soup. You're welcome. Besides, I know a, um, dream puff of a sub-editor in their travel section. I'll put in a word. By the way, check your mirrors."

Jake nodded. "Yeah, I noticed. I think Sue Price was right."

They were on Boone Street in South Aberdeen when Jake said, "There's a convenience store, reminds me I need milk." He turned left on MacFarlane and into the lot. "Won't be a minute."

He lingered at the dairy cooler, noting a guy who bee-lined to the slushie machine after following him inside.

Jake returned to the car with the milk.

"They're still with us," Erik said.

"Yup," said Jake. "One of them is riding a sugar high."

Chapter Thirty-Eight

Jake took the bridge over the Chehalis River into downtown Aberdeen, stopping for ice cream at the Happy Cow. It was a cheery modern take on an old-fashioned ice cream parlor, right down to the row of stools along a marble-topped counter, and booths padded in shiny red vinyl. Equally important, it was very public.

He peered through the plate glass window at the customers inside. "No Archie. No Jughead. Disappointing."

Erik pointed to a security camera pointing through the window to the street. "Have you considered one of these for the *Independent*?"

"Not a bad idea. Why don't you commandeer that sidewalk bench out front? I'll bring out whatever you want."

They settled on the bench, Erik with a root-beer float, Tina spooning a banana split, Jake with a cone scooped with raspberry and dark chocolate. Erik pulled a pen from an inside pocket of his sport coat and moved it in front of the artfully folded handkerchief in his breast pocket.

Car doors slammed down the street, and two men emerged, one working on a slushee, the other tucking a phone into his jacket pocket.

"Ten o'clock and closing," Erik said.

Tina glanced at her watch, frowned, and returned her attention to her split.

Jake said, "I got this."

The two men, mid-twenties and burly, both wore nylon warm-up jackets. Black jeans on one, blue on the other. They passed the bench as if to enter the Happy Cow, when Black Jeans fumbled his drink and dumped it on Tina's lap.

She jumped up, crying "What the hell?" Her dress was stained with florescent green drink, and the remains of her banana split.

"So-ree," Black Jeans said, giving an indifferent shrug.

Blue Jeans nudged his partner as if in surprise. "Will ya look at that, it's the dirtbag who pushed that Chink in front of a train."

"Need to teach the boy a lesson," Black Jeans said.

Jake rose from the bench. Black Jeans shoved him back. Jake rose again, side-stepped the man's block and jammed the remains of his cone in the guy's face. "So-ree."

Black Jeans threw a sucker punch, a direct hit on Jake's stitched and bruised left side, almost like he knew his vulnerability. Jake groaned and stepped back, shaking his head and retreating to the grass boulevard. Without looking back at the bench, he swept an open hand down, a signal for Erik not to intervene.

"As you wish," Erik said in a low voice. He turned to Tina with a calming smile. "Has Jake told you about The Gay Horsemen of the Apocalypse?"

"What?"

"One of our early adventures," Erik said, nodding with approval as Jake blocked a second punch with a forearm. "We'll share it once we're done here."

The men closed in, ready to brawl, Black Jeans swearing and wiping ice cream off his face and jacket.

Tina looked wildly at Jake then back to Erik. "Aren't you going to help?"

Erik crossed his legs, adjusting the crease of his pants. "If it comes to that. But there's only two of these mutts, and Jake could use the practice."

By now Blue Jeans was rolling in agony in a fetal position, hands between his legs.

"Jake's go-to move," Erik told Tina.

Black Jeans pulled out a switchblade, flicked it open, waving and thrusting like a maniac.

"Big mistake," Erik said.

Jake seemed to relax, his body loose and free like he was about to dance. Rather than avoiding Black Jeans, he moved toward his knife, blocking the thrust, using the momentum to steer it behind the man's back. Simultaneously, his free arm dealt a brutal elbow to the guy's exposed throat. He gave an anguished grunt and his knife clattered to the sidewalk.

"Well played," said Erik.

The enraged man flailed with his fists and Jake danced on, delivering three devastating punches to ear, nose and kidney before sweeping his feet out from under him.

Jake loomed over him awaiting his next move when a siren chirped and a Sheriff's Department cruiser skidded to a stop, its lightbar flashing red and blue. "Enough," the uniformed officer shouted. "Stand away from the victim."

Jake grinned. "Why if it isn't Deputy Shane, one of Gray Harbor's finest. Happened to be in the neighborhood, I suppose?"

"Damn lucky I was, Ockham. Attempt murder not enough for ya?" He looked at the two men on the ground. Black Jean's nose gushed blood. "Now you can tack assault causing bodily harm to your charge-list."

He scanned the ground. "Whoa! Is that a switchblade? Let's add a prohibited weapons charge."

"It's not his," Tina shouted. "These men attacked him, they—"

"Sit down and shut up."

Erik uncrossed his legs and handed Tina his pen. "Would you keep this pointed in their general direction, please." He gave her a smile and mouthed the words "video camera."

She nodded and thrust out hand and pen as if wielding the sword of justice.

"Discreetly, Tina." Erik said. "We don't want the bad sheriff taking away our toys."

Erik walked over to Blue Jeans, still curled on the ground.

"Get away from him," Shane shouted.

"I'm an expert in first-aid, just checking his injuries."

Erik knelt, made a show of taking his pulse, while pulling a phone from the guy's jacket pocket. Shielded from the sheriff's view he tried the phone, but the screen was locked.

"May I borrow your thumb?" he asked in a whisper. He got a groan in response. He pried the guy's right hand from between his legs and held the thumb to the phone's screen. "I do hope you've no immediate plans to start a family."

He pulled up the recent-calls list. The last three

were to the same number. Erik pressed redial—and somewhere inside Shane's ballistic vest, a phone warbled.

Erik straightened and smiled at Shane. "You don't wish to answer?"

Erik pressed the speaker option and cranked the volume as the call went to voice mail. "You have reached Deputy Sheriff Trent Shane. If this is an emergency, dial 911…"

"Happened to be in the neighborhood, huh?" said Jake. "What do you think, Trent, should we dial 911? Does Internal Affairs respond to emergencies?"

Trent Shane, face flushed and hands clenched, spit out, "Fuck you."

Erik turned to the two thugs, now slumped on the grass and casting worried looks at Shane.

"Gentlemen," said Erik, "are you as eager as we are to put this unpleasantness behind us? Specifically, do you wish to press charges against my friend?"

Both shook their heads and mumbled "no" in unison.

Erik smiled. "There you have it, deputy, the matter has been handled extrajudicially. Spares you all that paperwork. We'll take our leave."

"Fuck off," Shane muttered, making no move to stop them.

****

"Where were we?" Erik said from the back seat as they were enroute to Tina's apartment. "Ah, yes, the Gay Horsemen."

"Really?" Jake gave a snort then clutched his side. "You tell her, it hurts too much to laugh."

"It was early days in our friendship, must be

fourteen years back. We'd exited Lefty's, a dive bar in Pittsburgh's Strip district. I bade good night to Allan, my date of the moment, with a chaste kiss."

Jake snorted.

Erik continued. "Down the block two bruisers, not unlike tonight, pushed us into an alley, a fetid place, reeking of garbage and urine. Two more thugs emerged from behind a dumpster boxing us in. Jake—so straight, so naïve—wanted to surrender his wallet."

Jake made another snorting sound.

"I knew from sad experience we were to be gay-bashed. I told them: 'My friend thinks you're after our money,' The alpha dog of the group replied, 'That, too. Call it a fag tax.' I suggested these fellows had issues of repressed homosexuality, which disturbed them."

"To put it mildly."

"Since there were only four—and I'm a master of Systema, a particularly nasty martial art passed down from the Cossacks to Russia's special forces—I urged Jake to dispatch one assailant with a solid kick to the gonads. You'll note he performed a similar nutting tonight before employing some of the Systema moves he's since acquired under my tutelage."

"Thank you, sensei."

"You did well, Grasshopper. Anyway," Erik continued, "I put two of them down in the alley, and the fourth fellow fled into the night. They were in no position to resist as we gathered their wallets. I warned their identities would be turned over to the Gay Horsemen of the Apocalypse, a fearsome organization bent on vengeance."

"I've never heard of them," Tina said.

Jake snorted yet again.

"The Horsemen don't exist, but perhaps they should," Erik said. "Not being common thieves, we dumped their wallets down a grate. One hopes they spent months quaking in fear."

The story ended as Jake pulled up to Tina's apartment. "Sorry again for the drama," he said.

Tina gave a weak smile and looked at her trashed dress. "Why expect anything less on a date with you? Do you think they'll be back, those guys?"

"Doubtful," said Jake, "but I think we should stay with you."

"An excellent idea," Erik said. "Unfortunately, I've overseas calls to make for my real job. I'll borrow your car, Jake, and head for your place."

Jake nodded. He and Tina headed for the apartment door. There was a light tap on the horn and Jake turned back.

Erik handed him a bottle. "Tina's wine. I expect the poor dear could use a stiff…drink."

Chapter Thirty-Nine

Mid-afternoon, the day after the ice-cream parlor assault, Erik and Jake were taking their coffee on the deck. Jake was taking joy in evading Erik's demands to "tell all" about his night with Tina, his initial reply— "The wine was excellent, thank you for your interest"— having failed to slake Erik's curiosity.

"Sedgewick Trust" popped up on Jake's vibrating phone.

Jonathan Foley dispensed with the preliminaries: "Another of your heroes is missing."

Jake closed his eyes and sighed. "Who this time?"

"Anderson Wise."

"Ah, man, I was at his presentation ceremony. When did this happen?"

"Early August, about ten days ago."

"And we're just hearing now?"

"He gave notice to quit his job at the school board and told his friends he planned a temporary move to Mexico or Costa Rica," Foley reported. "Given that he's a free spirit, people assumed he'd buggered off early. His landlady raised the alarm. She'd arrived to inspect the place before returning his damage deposit. His furniture remained, and all his personal items: clothes, suitcases, toiletries, even his passport."

"Oh, oh."

"Have to ask, when were you last in Spokane?"

"Not since the presentation. Ah, shit, you think I'm a suspect?"

Foley sighed. "Not me, but our board is alarmed. That's three missing heroes all tied to you. And, hate to say it, you're linked, tangentially, to the suicide of another."

"Christ, really. Who?"

"Remember Zaki al-Jafari, the well guy?"

Jake buried his face in his hands. "Oh, no."

"Hikers found his body, what the animals left of it, at the bottom of a ravine, impaled on the branch of a deadfall. Judging by a trail of broken limbs he plowed through the forest in a panic and hit the ravine at a dead run. A search dog backtracked his scent to a nearby cave. His wallet was jammed in a crevice at the back."

"Where exactly was he found?" Jake asked.

"Sproul State Forest in northern Pennsylvania," Foley said.

"Zaki in a cave?" said Jake. "He wouldn't even use an elevator."

"Well, the coroner ruled suicide," Foley said. "You of all people know how the rescue messed him up. He had more than three years of counseling, paid by us. Then, this spring, he simply walked away. No one's blaming you."

For that one was left unsaid.

Vetting Zaki's heroics had stirred up Jake's inner claustrophobe.

Four years earlier, a two-year-old girl fell into an abandoned well in Pennsylvania's rural Bedford County. Rescuers heard her cries, but none could fit down the narrow opening. Zaki—a nineteen-year-old farm laborer, all of five-foot-two and one hundred five pounds—was among the bystanders. Rain threatened and the well was known to flood. Zaki swallowed his fears and was roped head-down into the opening, carrying a rescue harness and flashlight.

He reached the girl, banged up and terrified. For three hours they dangled twenty-five feet down after the rope snagged on a turn in the shaft. The flashlight dimmed and died as Zaki struggled with cold-numbed hands to attach a cable that rescuers had snaked down.

Months later, Jake tracked down a CNN camera operator who'd been at the wellhead. "My microphone captured this Zaki guy singing the same song over and over. Then the kid joined in. I wasn't long back from Afghanistan, and, man, I lost it. They were singing the *Bismillah Song,* I sing it to my girl, too." I doubt the kid knew they were invoking 'God, the merciful and compassionate.' But, hey, it worked."

When the two were hauled to the surface, blinking and shivering, Zaki was already an international star. A hero with a crippling fear of enclosed spaces, wholly unprepared for his unbidden role as America's *good* Muslim. He spiraled into depression. Jake sat with him for hours, and helped the Trust arrange psychiatric counseling. His Sacrifice Medallion was announced in a brief news release and awarded in a private ceremony, the girl holding his hand.

"Ah, man, Zaki," Jake murmured. "And three others missing. There are too many coincidences, Jon."

"Agreed."

"I'm a regular shit magnet. If it's any consolation, when Anderson vanished, I was pushing an innocent schoolgirl in front of a train over here in Washington State. Haven't been able to leave since."

"Yeah, and there's that."

"Look, somebody is setting me up. I have no idea why. The only semi-good news is that I'll soon be cleared of that attack."

Jake fumbled with his phone. "I sent you video proving I was pushed."

There was the clatter of a keyboard, a pause and a low whistle. "Somebody hates your guts."

"Show this to the Sedgewick board, but no one else until the legalities are cleared up."

"It may placate them." Foley sounded skeptical. "Hate to say this, I've orders not to give you more freelance investigations. We have our reputation to consider."

"Wouldn't take any. I have to sort this out, good people are getting hurt."

Foley lowered his voice. "Totally off the record, the Spokane cops are doing SFA on Wise's case. They say there's no evidence of foul play, and the guy did plan to bug-off. They've opened a file, that's it. My board would be real upset if you were to go to Spokane and poke around. So, I am formally asking you *not* to go to Spokane in some misguided attempt to find our missing hero—*whom no one else is looking for*. Do I make myself clear?"

"Very. Bye, Jon."

Jake turned to Erik. "Fancy a road trip?"

Chapter Forty

Detective Harry Brewster's mood was thunderous. He glared across the interview table at Jake and his lawyer. "This is absolute fucking blackmail."

"I agree," Sue Price said with eloquent indifference. "Inept blackmail at that."

"What the fuck you mean?"

"Well, Har-ree," she said, drawing out his name. "It's obvious you drafted this pathetic attempt at an apology for Mr. Ockham, confident he'd soon face assault charges in Aberdeen. Didn't happen. As this video shows," she tapped her laptop, "your buddy Deputy Shane shit the sheets."

A vein pulsed on Brewster's forehead. "I had nothing to do with that."

"A nudge here, a wink there, and Deputy Dawg did your bidding. Trouble is that the man's as subtle as a falling anvil. I'd warned my client to watch for such shenanigans. Honestly, though, we'd expected something more…artful."

"You can't prove a thing."

"Don't need to." She looked at her watch. "In two hours, the Battle of Happy Cow will be sent to the Grays Harbor Sheriff, the Aberdeen Police Chief, and hell, everybody down to the janitors. Shane will be under investigation by dinnertime. By breakfast, he'll be singing your name to Internal Affairs, hoping to save that big ole star on his shirt."

She turned to Jake with a smile. "My client is now going to buy me a nice lunch. We'll be back in an hour forty-five. By then, you'll have added a shit-ton of grovel to this apology. We'll press delete on the video and leave this unpleasantness behind."

She turned at the door, clearing her throat, and Jake realized there's always one more thing, like she's the Lieutenant Columbo of the legal world.

Brewster jerked out of his chair, fists on the table.

"Get that blood pressure checked," Price advised. "Your face is as red as a whorehouse lightbulb."

****

Prior to the confrontation with Brewster, it was a busy morning for Jake. He'd packed a week's worth of clothes and submitted to a brief embargoed interview with Ramona Williams, who'd asked such great questions, he had to guard against oversharing. He'd also jumped the line in Tina's busy waiting room for a private consult.

"Really," she said, "you're leaving for Spokane just after we started to, ah, get to know each other?"

He smiled. "I hope that particular project will take many years."

He said he was optimistic that he'd soon be "detoxified" by a Centralia police statement. And he described the disappearance of Anderson Wise, another of his heroes. "I have to find him. Things are getting ugly."

"Shouldn't the police handle this?"

"Yes, but they aren't."

"Somebody has already shoved you in front of a train. This is dangerous stuff."

"It's why Erik is coming along. He's the most lethal guy I know."

"That's hard to believe. He didn't even help when those guys attacked you at the ice cream shop, like he didn't want to mess his hair."

"I'm flattered he left it to me. He'd have waded in if things got dicey. Lucky for those two he didn't."

She cocked her head. "I was shocked you had a violent streak. I hadn't seen that before."

"Systema is a handy skill to have, I can teach you a few moves some time."

"Thought you already had. Be careful, okay?"

"Agreed, no more drama."

She hugged him, teasing open his mouth with her tongue. "Some drama I quite enjoy. Now get, before my patients start an insurrection. And don't take the train."

Erik joined Jake and Price for lunch. Just after two o'clock they headed north on the I-5, Erik at the wheel of his Japanese SUV. Shortly after, they'd skirted Seattle and worked their way onto the I-90 east.

Sue Price texted from her office:

—The grovel is posted. A thing of beauty, total vindication—

Jake texted back:

—Thanx Sue. Release my statement, pls. Say I'll have no further comment—

—Had so much fun I should be paying you—

—Fine by me—

—Won't happen, I've an avaricious reputation to uphold. Safe travels—

Next, he texted Ramona:

—Embargo lifted. Release the hounds—

It was a straight shot on the I-90 to Spokane,

elapsed time from Centralia: five hours, twenty-five minutes. Coffees: two. Pee breaks: one. Speeding tickets: zero. They checked into their rooms at a downtown hotel, had a late dinner and planned their strategy for tomorrow.

Chapter Forty-One

Spokane, Washington, August

Their first stop was Spokane Police headquarters. Jake flashed a business card from Sedgewick Trust, saying they were following up on reports of their missing hero. He hoped the cops wouldn't check with the Pittsburgh office to confirm. That, he soon realized, would take more effort than the department was investing in Anderson Wise. He'd requested a meet with the relevant investigator. After an annoying wait, it was the department's public affairs officer who trundled out. Never a good sign.

He was a fiftyish guy named McNab, with a bad comb-over, a rumpled brown suit, and the hang-dog energy of a tranquilized sloth. Think Willy Loman as a cop. McNab didn't carry Wise's file. If it even existed, Jake expected it was thinner than motel toilet paper.

"Got nothing for you, gents," he said. "There's no evidence of foul play. And the guy, ah, Mr. Wise, told friends he was quitting his job and heading down Mexico way."

"With everything still in his apartment, even his passport?"

"What can I say? He's free, white, and over twenty-one. A guy has the right to go walkabout. It's not as if we haven't worked the file. Checked his bank records and everything. Made a three-hundred-dollar cash machine withdrawal in Montana, outside Bozeman, and another in Bismarck, North Dakota. Heading east. Guess Mexico didn't appeal."

"Did the machine's video show he made the withdrawals?" Erik asked.

McNab shrugged. "That requires a subpoena. Didn't have grounds to apply."

Jake considered and rejected telling McNab about the other missing medalists. The idea of serial disappearances would make his head explode. He pulled out a notebook. "Can you give me the contact info of the person who filed the missing-persons report, heard it was the landlady?"

"No can do. Privacy issues and all. You could file an access-to-information request, there's a form online. Takes a while."

They rose to leave. Jake asked: "Your first name wouldn't be Willy, by chance?"

McNab looked puzzled. "Nope, Hector. Folks call me Heck."

"Bet they do," said Erik.

They regrouped for "ethical" coffees at a nearby café. Jake broke a sugar cube in half and stirred it in. "Keeps me awake nights, all the unethical coffee I used to drink."

"What now?"

"Around the corner to Mayfair Street. Anderson's favorite hangout is a bar called Sharkey's. It's almost eleven now, it should open soon for the lunch crowd."

It was closed, but a pounding on the door caught the attention of a kid wielding a broom. It opened a crack. "Sorry, we open at 11:30."

Jake figured him for thirteen, his cheeks carrying a spray of adolescent acne. Too young to be working at a bar. He handed the kid another of his Sedgewick cards. "Could you give this to Sharon Key when she arrives, please?"

He nodded. "Please wait, sir, I'll see if she's about." He locked the door behind him.

A minute later, Key peered out, clutching his card. She was a familiar face, early sixties, big and blonde; blowsy was the term that sprang to mind. But with bloom still clinging to the rose.

She looked him over, hands on hips. "I remember you from that Sedgewick bash."

"And I remember an epic hangover. You throw a fine party, Ms. Key."

"It's Sharon, darlin'. Come on in, you and your handsome friend."

She led the way, pulling off an apron as she went. She pointed to a table. Her face clouded. "Please tell me you're here about Anderson."

"Absolutely. This is my friend, Erik. We're hunting for answers."

"Glad someone is. But first things first, coffee's on. Or"—she nodded toward the bar— "I can fix you an eye-opener?"

"Coffee's fine."

Jake helped carry mugs and fixings to the table and they settled in.

She ran her fingers delicately across the tabletop. "This is where he conducted his business affairs."

Jake looked puzzled. "Business? I thought he was a janitor?"

As if summoning a memory, she smiled. "I mean

of the monkey kind. And by affairs, well, I mean exactly that. Let's just say he was an enthusiastic heterosexual." She winked at Erik, as if, by some barkeep's sixth sense, she had his orientation dialed in.

She explained that her concerns for Andy, as she called him, were raised more than a week after his last visit. "We knew he was leaving but no way he wouldn't say good-bye. This was his second home." She looked around the bar, cupped her hands and called out. "Toby dear, come here, please?"

He arrived from what Jake assumed was the kitchen. He'd traded his broom for a dish towel slung over a shoulder.

"This is my grandson, Toby," Key said. "He's working here for the summer, learning the business from the ground up. Someday, he'll run the joint."

Toby smiled and blushed.

"He and Andy were…are…very close."

Toby's smile evaporated. He looked down and nodded.

"These gentlemen are going to find Andy, dear."

He looked at them, guileless and trusting. "Thanks, I miss him a lot."

Jake looked at Key, who nodded her permission. "When did you see him last, Toby?"

"Don't know the date, but it was like a Wednesday night. I used to go to a lot of his ball games. Hardball. He's a really good shortstop."

Toby puffed out his chest. "I was like the first person he told he was going away to someplace warm and sunny. Even before Grandma. Said he'd be back when he ran out of money. He was going to stop by before he left to give me his ball glove. He said it was just for safekeeping, but I think he was going to let me keep it."

"Did you get the glove?" Jake asked, his voice soft.

"No. Never said goodbye, either." He looked to both men, eyes pooling with tears. "Please find him, tell him I don't care about the glove."

Key kissed her grandson's forehead and turned him toward the kitchen with a gentle push. "Now get those bar glasses ready."

She turned to Jake and Erik when Toby was out of earshot. "They really did have a special bond. Do have a special bond. Did? Do? I don't know what to think."

She buried her face in her hands. She looked up after a time, cheeks wet, and swept her index finger to the framed accolades on the wall.

"See, Toby was in that classroom when that crazy bastard came in with a shotgun. Andy saved his life. A lot of lives. Not a day goes by that I don't thank the good Lord for Andy Wise."

Erik reached across to rest a hand on hers. "We'll move heaven and earth to get him back. Can you tell us everything about the last time you saw him?"

"It was the first of August maybe. He was at this table. I brought him his usual, a Jack and ginger. It usually took one to prime the pump, then people lined up to buy him drinks. Mostly ladies, but guys, too."

Erik sipped his coffee, let her fill the silence.

"This young gal came in early that afternoon, asking after Andy. Like, what days does he usually come in? What times? She seemed pretty enough, near as I could tell under her big ole ball cap, a bulky sweater and no make-up. Well, she comes in that night, not long after Andy arrived. Lordy! Hair piled up, her face a work of art, and a body all legs and boobs squeezing out of a little silver dress."

She refilled their coffees from a thermal carafe. "Now we get some hotties here, but this gal was a whole 'nuther level. She homed in on Andy like a cruise missile. Thought the poor boy was going to swallow his tongue. She leaned over this table, giving him a close-up of those puppies. Don't know what she said, but they left within a minute. That's it. Last time I saw him he was following that epic ass out the door."

At Jake's request, Key scribbled down the contact information for Wise's landlady. She promised to call her to clear the way. "I paid Andy's next month's rent to keep his things safe."

The early lunch crowd was filing in. Wait staff took drink orders, and regulars tossed cheery waves at Key. She looked down at her smock. "I've got to change, boys, get my warpaint on. Can't run a swank joint like this looking like an unmade bed. Come by for dinner, hear? We'll talk more."

Chapter Forty-Two

The landlady, a Mrs. Struthers, waited in an ancient VW Bug outside Wise's apartment building. Windows down, the idling engine stuttering like a flatulent sewing machine, her fingers tapped the steering wheel to Charley Pride on the AM radio.

She waved them over, not getting out, and waggled a key. "Unit five, second floor. Sharon says you're good people, an' she's payin' the bills. Thank God for that, don't know what I'll do if Andy don't come back to clear out his stuff."

She checked an oddly delicate watch sunk in the flesh of her meaty wrist. "Gotta run, leave the key with Sharon, huh?" She stomped the accelerator and wheezed down the street to attend to more urgent matters. A daytime soap, Jake guessed, and a bag of chips.

The apartment had the hot, stale smell of abandonment. While Erik cracked open some windows, Jake checked the fridge with trepidation. It was empty, mercifully, save for a six-pack of beer. Mrs. Struthers had probably emptied it of anything edible.

Apart from that, the apartment seemed untouched, a light layer of dust on counters and tables was undisturbed. Two glasses stood on a coffee table, any liquid long since evaporated. A desiccated wedge of lime, an open plastic bottle of store-brand tonic, and a fifth of bargain-priced gin rested on the kitchen counter.

Erik shook his head. "The boy is no cocktail connoisseur." He stopped Jake's attempt to pick up a glass. "Treat this as a crime scene, sad to say. The glasses and bottles may be the last things he and a guest touched."

Jake thrust his hands into his pant pockets and nodded.

They started with a cursory walk-through, ending in Wise's bedroom. It was surprisingly tidy for a single guy. The queen-sized bed was crisply made with good quality linens. "Wants to impress the ladies," Erik said. He eased open a nightstand drawer to find an economy-sized box of condoms. "Neatness and a commitment to safe sex, sure to earn him points."

He reached into a dresser drawer and pulled out two balled-up pairs of socks, tossing one set to Jake. "Put these on your hands."

Erik dropped to his knees, peered under the bed, checked between box-spring and mattress, pulled out every drawer, inspecting the contents and ensuring nothing was taped to their backs and bottoms. All of it done with a practised ease. They moved to what would be euphemistically described as a den, though it wasn't much larger than a walk-in closet. This had more guy-clutter and was obviously not intended for female inspection.

There was a folding rack for drying clothes, a cheap dresser containing sports gear, and a backpack holding sunscreen, water bottles, and a lined workbook probably pinched from his school's supply cupboard. Jake flipped through its first pages, a meticulous record of league standings, team statistics, and batting lineups.

A bit of a nerd was Anderson Wise.

There was a metal two-drawer file cabinet tucked under a table repurposed as a desk. The tabletop held three file folders, a couple of unpaid bills, his passport, and a laptop wired to a printer.

Erik's eyes lit up at the electronics. He slipped off a sock and was mildly disappointed to find the laptop password protected. He peered under the laptop and table. No luck. He nodded toward the file cabinet. "Look for a password."

Jake sifted through files for bills, income tax, work-related school and union notices. There was a fat file of news clips of the school shooting filed under A for "Asshole." Under S was correspondence from Sedgewick Trust.

He turned to the tabletop and struck gold with the top folder, not-so-cryptically labelled "PW."

A printout inside listed eight passwords for credit and bank cards, various apps, and his laptop. "Try sparkyadams289, a baseball name if ever I heard one."

He typed the name into his phone's search engine. "Yup, a Pennsylvania-born shortstop from the twenties and thirties; .289 was his career batting average."

"And we're in," Erik said. "I'll ransack his hard drive. You scope out the rest of the apartment; see if you can scare up some paper bags for the glasses and bottles."

Jake returned with nothing to show for his efforts but empty supermarket bags. Erik was equally frustrated. "Somebody wiped the search memory and the hard drive. Maybe my people can restore some. Maybe not. This will take time."

Jake, being a paper-loving guy, sifted through the

remaining folders on the tabletop. One held travel information for Mexico and Costa Rica. The last, titled "Hero Research," contained only a paystub. "Hero research, wonder what that was about? There's nothing heroic about his payrate."

Jake turned over the paystub and found barely legible pencil scrawls. "Okay, this is weird. Why would a meat-and-potatoes guy like Anderson be interested in stuff like 'extreme altruist stimuli,' or 'empirical perspectives on the duty to rescue?' And maybe something that reads 'Bionic and Lily Heroes?' "

"Who knows?" Erik said. "Even you must wonder why heroes do what they do."

"An unanswerable question."

Erik, bent over the keyboard, made no reply. The printer sprang to life and began pumping out pages. Erik beamed. "Whoever file-killed the laptop, forgot to clear the memory cache in the printer."

"Didn't even know they had one."

"Which is why it pays to hang with a genius."

Erik gathered eighty-odd pages from the printer and elected to leave the laptop behind for now. Jake pulled on the socks again and placed the glasses and bottles in bags. He returned to the den with a last empty bag and opened the cupboard for a final sweep. He rooted past two pairs of cleats—and smiled.

Chapter Forty-Three

Clearfield County, Pennsylvania, August

The item hit like a thunderbolt as they listened to a news break on the Top 40 station they'd finally agreed on, lousy reception and all.

Days earlier, the professor, beaming with magnanimity, rewarded them with an ancient battery-powered transistor radio to "while away the hours." Like they were on a cruise or something, instead of locked together for a week now in what Lyla called their Plywood Palace.

"The reviews are in," he'd said. "The audience can't wait for your next adventure. In the meantime, music is a great balm for convalescence."

The nursing duties were dumped on Lyla. Anderson was more ambulatory, though he relapsed into painful immobility whenever his captors arrived to haul one or the other across the basement for toileting or showers. It wouldn't be long before he was deemed well enough to move to his old cell, something Lyla realized she'd regret. Their close quarters imposed a forced intimacy, like they were an old married couple.

There was nothing sexual about it, just acceptance that occasional flashes of nudity or visits to the honey-bucket were unavoidable, and the least of their worries. Besides, his move would presage the next "adventure."

Whatever that was, it would likely kill one or the other. Or both.

The news reader said: *"Investigators in nearby Armstrong County have a mystery on their hands after a failed attempt to derail a Buffalo and Pittsburgh Railroad freight last Wednesday turned into a missing-persons case."*

Lyla dove for the radio and cranked the volume.

"As previously reported, an empty automobile was deliberately left on an isolated stretch of B&P track in what a company spokesman initially said was 'a dangerously misguided prank with potentially fatal results.' Now, an investigation by state and local police in the Armstrong County seat of Kittanning have uncovered disturbing new details. Here's State Police spokeswoman Allison Canfield with an update: 'Upon extensive examination of the mangled wreckage, a bloody handprint was found on the vehicle roof.' "

Wise grinned and nodded as if enjoying a private joke.

Canfield continued: *"We had no hits from an initial search of local and national data bases. After delays due to privacy issues, a match was found in the U.S. Army archives. Fortunately, the military fingerprint all personnel. The prints are a match for Anderson K. Wise, who served a three-year stint as an Army private. Mr. Wise was employed until recently as a custodian with the Spokane Public Schools system. A spokesman for the Spokane Police Department said there was an unconfirmed report Mr. Wise had gone missing.*

"Canfield said: 'We don't know when he arrived in Armstrong County—or how or why he came in contact

with the suspect vehicle. There's no evidence anyone was in the vehicle at the time of the collision. We're appealing to Mr. Wise, or anyone who knows him, to contact us.'

"In other news, a two-vehicle crash near Du Bois claimed the life of—"

Lyla turned to Wise. "You look rather pleased with yourself."

He shrugged, and then winced.

"My uncle Eddy on my mom's side was a cop in Wyoming. I loved when he talked shop. He used to say traffic stops were the worst, you never knew what kind of lunatic you'd pulled over. Eddy had this trick where he'd put his bare hand on any vehicle he stopped. 'Dead-handing,' he called it. He learned it the hard way when an old-timer on his force was shot and killed during a traffic stop. The suspect they eventually found denied any dealings with police, but the old cop had left his prints on the car. It nailed a conviction."

"You owe Uncle Eddy a nice bottle if we ever get out of here."

"It would have to be flowers on his grave. He's long dead, went two years after my mother."

"Folks would be fools to underestimate you," Lyla said, admitting to herself she'd been among them. "A train barrelling at you and you think of a dead uncle? Amazing."

"Crazy, huh? I was sure I'd die on those tracks. No time for a will, best I could do was leave a mark. Say, hey, world, I was here, find the fuckers who did this."

Lyla patted his knee. "We're not dead yet. I'm worried our jailers will freak when they hear this news."

"It's not as if my prints can tell the cops where we are. But our hosts may speed things along. We better make a move before they do. And before they separate us."

"I want to leave a mark, too," Lyla said. "Even if that means dying on my terms, not theirs."

He instinctively lowered his voice and leaned forward. "I've been thinking…"

Chapter Forty-Four

Spokane, Washington

Back at the hotel, they left the glasses and bottles in Erik's car, undecided when, if, or how they'd get them dusted for fingerprints. They carried the other items from the den to Erik's room.

It was close to five when Erik divided the printouts and gave half to Jake. They budgeted a couple of hours before walking to Sharkey's for dinner and, they hoped, more answers to nagging questions. The top few pages were airline timetables for Mexico City and San José, Costa Rica. Clearly, he was still undecided on a destination.

"So, why milk an ATM in Bismarck, North Dakota?" Jake thought out loud. "What would draw anyone to North Dakota? Or South Dakota, for that matter? Why are there two Dakotas? Seems excessive."

Focus, Jake. Focus.

He turned to the rest of his pile, studies exploring courage, altruism, and heroism. Hero or not, what possessed a school janitor to explore the academic esoterica of his actions? Jake worked for Sedgewick, and he'd never read this stuff.

Stuff like, *"Risking Your Life Without a Second Thought: Intuitive Decision-Making and Extreme Altruism"*.

Stuff like, *"An Empirical Perspective on the Duty To Rescue."* It began: *"Intelligent human action is goal-directed, but when pain, fear, or danger intrude, it is difficult to sustain the mental equilibrium to follow through, even if the goal is very important and the action critical. Hence, the need for courage."*

"Well, duh."

Another study quoted old Philip Sedgewick's simple explanation. *"Heroic action is impulsive."* That said it all, in Jake's view.

The last study in his pile was: *"An Existential Alliance of Byronic and 'Lilithian' Heroes."*

"Hey, wait a minute."

He dug out Wise's payslip. That sounded a lot like his pencil-scratched *"Bionic and Lily Heroes."* It's likely someone fed Wise a pile of ivory tower analysis and he'd misunderstood a citation. Couldn't blame him, Jake was stupefied after wading through all this learned crap. He turned over the stub. It was for a pay period ending a month before Wise's last sighting at Sharkey's. Interesting.

Erik finished the last of his printouts and rubbed his eyes. "What have you got, aside from a headache?"

"A heavy-duty analysis of heroism."

"Positive or negative?"

"Humm? Windy explanations for why people do what they do, but ultimately positive."

"Paralysis by analysis," Erik said. "By the time a potential hero explored his motivational ramifications the victim would be dead and buried."

He swung off the bed. "As for me, I'm motivated by hunger."

****

Sharon Key pulled the reserved sign off Wise's favorite table and handed menus to Jake and Erik. "Eat first, we'll talk later."

The place was bumping. A one-man band arranged his instruments in a corner: a tin whistle sticking out of his pocket. He arranged a fiddle, a mandolin, and accordion around a percussion box he'd use as a seat.

"He'll have to be an octopus to pull this off," Erik said.

"The Irish have great dexterity," said Jake. "Think I'll start with an Irish ale."

"It was prime rib night, and Sharon allowed nothing less than inch-and-a-half-thick slabs on their plates, house-made Yorkshire puds, garden-fresh veggies, mashed potatoes, and lashings of gravy. It was perfect.

By now Connor Murphy, the one-man band, had worked through a few teary ballads, livened the pace with *Black Velvet Band,* and launched into the U2 songbook.

Key sidled over and leaned in. "You boys are causing quite the stir. Do the ladies a favor and dance off your dinner, I'll be clear in a half hour or so."

It was another forty-five minutes before their backsides returned to their chairs. They danced with the young, and the old, with fat ones, thin ones, and pretty maids all in a row. Jake sent over an ale to Connor. He took the pint, and mercifully, a freakin' break.

Key nodded toward her back office. She set a top-shelf Irish whiskey on her desk, three glasses, a pitcher of water and an ice bucket. The men drained the water in one go.

She grinned at Jake. "I feared you'd be carried into

the night by big Sissy Hanes, the human bouncy castle. Poor Andy had it right about Sissy. 'The odds are good. But the goods are odd.' " She sighed. "God, I miss him so much."

She waved to the whiskey. "Serve yourselves, I'm off duty. What else do you need to know?"

"Dangerous to assume he was done in by the fox in the silver dress without checking other possibilities," said Jake. "Who else did he interact with?"

"I wondered about that," Key said. "Andy was tiring of the chase. He'd taken a break, was really only back in the game three weeks before he disappeared. Mostly women he'd previously, ah, *interacted* with. Kind of his greatest-hits package."

"None of them presented a risk?" Erik asked.

"No. Well…there was *Mrs.* Eleanor Mayfield, a semi-regular despite my efforts to steer Andy away, the damn fool. Thing is, she's married to Bruce Mayfield— Captain Bruce Mayfield of the Spokane PD."

"Oh, shit," said Jake. "That may explain why his missing-persons investigation is being slow-walked. Could he have disappeared Andy?"

She shook her head.

"No way. He probably suspected Andy was mowin' his grass—hard to keep a secret in this town. But Bruce had problems with his ticker. He was in the shop for a quadruple bypass at the time. That may explain why Eleanor needed servicing, but not why Andy disappeared. Expect your first guess is right, though, the cops aren't inclined to bust a gut for Andy, not with Bruce laid up."

Jake showed the cryptic paystub to Key. "Any idea what would have inspired his academic interest?"

She looked at the pay date and nodded. "Sure do. Would have been the time a professor paid a visit. He and Andy started the night here, then swanned off to a fancy restaurant. Our menu wasn't good enough, apparently. Looked every bit the professor, right down to the elbow patches on his tweed jacket."

"Did Andy say what the visit was about?" Jake asked.

"Apart from a whole lot of drinking, Andy said the guy asked a lot of damn fool questions. Left him feeling pretty stupid."

Erik leaned in. "Do you have a name or at least a description?"

"He introduced himself, but I can't recall the name. A white guy, mid-sixties I'd say, said he flew in from out east. Didn't say which state. A good head of hair and a neatly trimmed goatee. Central casting's idea of a professor, and he sure wanted you to know it. Why your interest in him?"

They explained Wise's fixation with obscure studies on heroism. They walked her through their search of his apartment and said his laptop hard drive was wiped.

"Creepy," she said. "Wasn't me, and I doubt his landlady has the brains to work anything more complicated than her TV remote. Far as I know no one but Vera had a copy of Andy's key. Not even me."

"You do now." Jake set it on her desk. "Mrs. Struthers asked me to leave it with you."

She swept it into her top desk drawer.

Erik fished out his phone. "This is a longshot, Sharon, but think back to the first time the mystery woman came in asking about Andy. Have a look at these surveillance videos, see if they ring any bells."

She watched them, gasping with shock. "Good heavens, Jake! Is that you, hit by the train and rescuing that girl?"

He cringed. "A story for another day. Take another look please, see if our mystery woman pops up."

She replayed both videos. "That one's pretty useless. Too blurry. But this one…hmm…the woman in black in the corner there." She poked the screen. "Can't see her face, but the hat looks familiar, and it's pretty obvious there's an exceptional pair of titties under that shirt. It could be her. Where was this taken?"

"Centralia," Erik said. "July 29."

Key looked at her desk calendar. "That's three days before our girl swanned out of here with Andy. Doesn't make any sense."

"Actually, Sharon," Jake said. "It kinda does."

He reached down for a paper bag he'd carried with him tonight. "I have something Andy left for Toby." He set a ball glove on her desk. It was closed around a hard ball and tied with an old shoelace. "Read the note under the lace."

"*Dear Toby,*" she read aloud. "*Can't think of a better man to have this glove than the Wildcats' biggest fan. It's—*" She couldn't choke out the rest and shoved the note to Jake.

" '*It's a bit scuffed up,*' Jake read on, '*but it caught a whole lot of happy memories for me. I hope it will for you, too. Your BFF, Andy.*' "

"Guess that means Best Friend Forever," Jake said. "There's a PS: '*I have a new glove on order, I'm packing it on my trip, so it's broken in for the Wildcats' next season. And for us to play catch.*' "

Jake choked up, too. "Gotta find this guy."

He reached into the bag and pulled out Wise's workbook. "Andy was meticulous about tracking the Wildcats. I thought Toby might want to take over as statistician until Andy gets back?"

Key nodded, struggling for composure as she flipped through the pages. A business card fell out, landing face down.

Jake and Erik drained their glasses. "We'll take our leave," Erik said. "Thank you for your help and hospitality. You have our contact information if anything pops up."

Jake said: "Best dinner, ever, Sharon. We'll let you know how our search goes. Give my regards to Toby. And don't you dare give Sissy Whatshername my phone number."

They were almost out the office door when Key gave an excited whoop. She waved the fallen business card. "It's him," she said, handing it over. "Dr. Barclay Dawes. He's that professor guy."

Out on the sidewalk, a stunned Jake turned to Erik. "Dawes is the guy selling Walter Meely's medal. This stinks."

Chapter Forty-Five

Aberdeen, Washington

Erik spent the night at Jake's after the drive back from Spokane. He'd make the trip to Seattle today to handle pressing matters at the BitBust offices. "Plus, all that dancing churned up my hormones. I've a new gentleman friend who's adept at pushing my buttons. He's a wonderfully dangerous techie, pretty much a genius—possibly smarter than me, hard as that is to believe."

Jake snatched the last croissant. "Can't wait to meet him. Could this be: The One?"

"You are so quaint. I hope it works out with your doctor, I truly do. But be strategic in matters of the heart and related organs. Do you have an exit strategy? Do you have a plan B?"

Erik got no answer, Jake was absorbed in his emails. "Well, do you?"

"Yes," Jake said with growing excitement.

"Really," Erik said, surprised. "Who's this?"

"Who's what?"

"Never mind, keep gazing at your laptop, pretend I'm not here."

Jake slid the device across the table. "A Google News Alert I set just bore strange fruit."

Such alerts seem archaic in the rapidly evolving

virtual world and yet Jake found they often delivered. He'd set up a key-word search for "Sedgewick," "hero," and "missing," then set the search engine trolling news sites for stories containing all three words.

"You reel in plenty of junk that way, but this morning there were two variations of the Anderson Wise train derailment mystery. Both were from Spokane news outlets, the *Spokesman-Review* and *KREM* television. Both tacked local angles to a Pennsylvania-based wire story about the missing Wise—noting he was a beloved Spokane 'Sedgewick Hero.' "

"*Much* beloved, according to Sharon Key," Erik said. "Don't know how he ended up in Pennsylvania, but I can't imagine derailing trains was high on his bucket list."

"Read on. Google coughed up another weird one."

Erik clicked the link from the *Pittsburgh Post-Gazette*. The headline read *"Missing Pittsburgh-area Welder Was Awarded Sedgewick Hero Medallion Ten Years Ago."*

"This Obergon guy," Erik asked, "is he one of yours?"

"No, before my time. This is nuts. There's Andy, Lyla Watkins, Walter Meely, and Reggie Obergon. I now have serious doubts about Zaki al-Jafari's supposed suicide. That's five Sedgewick heroes. Who knows, maybe more?"

The story began: *"Friends in Pittsburgh and Michigan are alarmed by the disappearance of local welder Reginald (Reggie) Obergon, 26, who failed to return after a two-week vacation..."*

The rest of the story recounted the awarding of the

hero medallion and linked to an archived story about the boy he saved from drowning going on to become a Rhodes Scholar.

Jake slapped the tabletop. "Stupid. Do you know what we didn't find in Andy's apartment?"

Erik lowered his head in shame. "His medal. So bloody obvious. Or not, in this case."

Jake pulled back his laptop. The story mentions Evie Meyer, a friend of Obergon. I'll track her down. Want to bet his medal is missing? And I better phone Jonathan at Sedgewick. They need a deep dive into past recipients. Someone is hunting heroes."

Erik headed home, promising to stay in touch. "There's some longshot possibilities I want to look into."

Jake was about to call Sedgewick when his cell warbled. It was Clara, sounding stressed. "Are you back, can you get to the office?"

"Sure, what's up?"

"I've put Amanda Shane in my office with her little boy," she said, her voice almost a whisper. "She showed up here, looking for you, said she had nowhere else to turn. She's in a bad way, Jake. When the boy wasn't looking, the poor thing hiked up her sweater. The bruises are pretty bad."

"Trent fucking Shane," Jake muttered.

"Yes. Apparently, he's been spiraling ever since you humiliated him at the ice cream shop. What was that about? Never mind, tell me later. Get down here. She left with the clothes on her back and she's scared to go home."

"On my way."

Chapter Forty-Six

Clearfield County, Pennsylvania

"He's not breathing," Lyla Watkins screamed and pounded the walls. "He's not breathing."

Anderson—Andy after these many days—lay still, the blanket pulled to his chin.

All was quiet in the house above.

Lyla screamed and pounded some more. She was sure the young guy was away. It was an old house and the two had come to identify the footfalls of their captors by their signature thumps and squeaks on the floor overhead.

They knew the young guy—who does not walk lightly upon the Earth—was up early today because they heard him *ka-thumping* above. They knew him now as Brad, their captors were getting sloppy about hiding identities. More reason to worry. Brad had part-time work schlepping boxes at an e-commerce fulfilment center. He returned home mid-afternoon on workdays, bitching loud and often about the job. He complained his sister—the name Kristy slipped out several times—escaped such drudgery.

She was the house videographer. Lyla suspected she had secondary duties servicing "Daddy."

Lyla tried to read their power dynamic. Had control shifted at some point from him to her? Had the groomer become the groomed? Blaze/Kristy was ruthless enough. Lyla could glean an entire PhD thesis on family dysfunction out of this, should she survive.

She pounded the walls again. "He's dying. He's dying."

There was the creak of the cellar door, and tentative footfalls on the wooden stairs. Finally.

The deadbolt slid back. Kristy, her hair dishevelled, cautiously peered inside. "Back on your cot," she snapped. "Sit on your hands."

"Hurry. He needs help."

She pointed a taser at her. "Shut it, bitch."

She leaned over Andy as Lyla heard other footsteps. Andy whispered, "Now or never."

His good arm flashed out, jamming an aluminium rod into Kristy's stomach. Lyla simultaneously pounded both feet into her ass, adding thrust and velocity to Andy's gut-punch.

She and Andy had rehearsed for hours until the moves were as ingrained as anything Andy learned on the ball diamond or Lyla on the gym floor.

Air woofed from Kristy as she groaned and crumpled. The taser went flying.

Lyla's cot buckled from the force of her kick. The rod, painstakingly unscrewed with purloined nail clippers, had been an integral part of her cot. She dove for the taser, scooped it up and fired 50,000 volts into Kristy's back. She shuddered and collapsed on Andy's cot.

Among the sad realities of modern education are the innumerable lockdowns, active-shooter and self-defence drills teachers endure. Tasing was a skill she'd hoped never to use in the real world, but there you go.

By the time the professor reached the door, gun in one hand, first-aid kit in the other, Andy had the bar jammed across Kristy's throat, her limp body between him and the professor. Lyla sheltered behind Andy, safe from the professor's pistol unless he was one hell of a shot.

They'd choreographed this, too.

Andy pressed hard. Kristy was in distress.

Lyla had worried Andy—more lover than fighter—was too squeamish to hurt a woman. Clearly, near-death on the train tracks offered sufficient motivation. And his ribs must hurt like hell. That had to make him mean.

"Drop the gun" Andy snarled. "A crushed larynx is fatal. I learned that in the Army." He heaved harder. Kristy made macabre gurgling sounds.

"Jesus, stop," the professor said. His gun and first-aid kit dropped to the floor.

Andy eased up. "Smart move. Kick the pistol across the floor. Slowly."

Lyla snatched it up. She tried to look deadly. "Do up your fly," she said. "You're creeping me out."

Daddy looked down and fumbled with the zipper. He'd dressed in a hurry, probably explaining their delayed response.

"Flat on the floor." Lyla ordered, waving the pistol for emphasis. "And slide over your handcuffs."

"Too bad you didn't bring your camera," Andy said. "We'd make you a star."

Chapter Forty-Seven

Aberdeen, Washington

"I'm sorry, Jake. I didn't know what else to do, where else to go." Amanda slumped in a chair in Jake's former office, head down, hands pressed between her jean-clad legs. Sam, her four-year-old son, was asleep on the couch in Clara's office. Ramona had the day off.

"He never hits me. Well, hardly ever. Trent has a temper, but he keeps a lid on things. Usually."

Amanda stared at the floor. "Do you know what's really sad? Realizing I've lost touch with all my friends. Trent used to diss them as fat or ugly or boring. Except for Jann—remember her? He tried to hit on her."

Jann was high school president in their senior year. Jake remembered her as kind and smart and self-assured. She's a lawyer in private practice now, down the road in Montesano. "I can't imagine her putting up with that."

"Oh, she didn't." Amanda gave a weak smile. "Chucked her drink in his face and walked out of our house. I sent her a card apologizing, but I was too embarrassed to keep in touch. Maybe she was, too. Now, all our friends are cops, so I can't go to them. So here I am, your pathetic old girlfriend."

She was crying now. And kept saying "I'm sorry. So sorry."

"I'm here for you," Jake said. "Always."

Clara looked over Amanda's head and gave Jake a nod. "Stay here, dear, drink your tea. I want a word with Jake."

They slipped into the former darkroom, now storage for office supplies and back-issues of the paper. "It's your call, but we have a place for Amanda and the boy. If you agree, and she goes for it, that is."

"Where?"

She smiled. "Next door. You forget, you're a landlord now. The Eyeglass Center and Foote's Jewelers have apartments above them. Not fancy but nice enough—and fully furnished. I know one is vacant. We could slip them in there, tuck Amanda's car in the old press building."

"It won't take long before Trent learns she's here," Jake said. "I've never seen the apartments, but let's get a locksmith in to install deadbolts or whatever is needed to beef up security."

Clara kissed his forehead. "I'm on it. You tell Amanda."

Jake knocked on his former office door, it was getting to be a habit. Amanda had composed herself and was peering in a compact mirror, applying lipstick. "God, I'm a mess."

"Where's Trent this morning?"

"He pulled courtroom security duty this week, another reason he's in a bad mood."

"Good. I don't want to control your life, but for what it's worth, you need to get away before he comes home with wine, roses and an *it'll-never-happen-again* apology. Give yourself time and space to think things through."

She nodded. "I've seen that movie before. But where can we go?"

"We've got a place for you two, nice and safe and quiet. Let's go to your house and pack up whatever you and Sam need."

"Trent will be pissed."

An added bonus, Jake thought. "We'll get your car off the street and take the paper's van. It's new, doesn't have our logo on it yet. Clara will stay with Sam until we're back. You tell him while I make a call."

He was supposed to have lunch with Tina. He hadn't seen her since Spokane and missed her terribly. His call went to her voicemail. He begged off, said something had come up. He didn't want to launch into the sad details in a message. He'd fill her in later, sure she'd understand.

****

They were in and out of Amanda's house in an hour. A force of nature, she tossed clothes, toiletries, towels, sheets and pillows, kitchen essentials, photo albums, and Sam's favorite books into boxes that Jake pillaged from the *Independent*. He hauled them to the van, keeping a nervous watch for Trent. Court trials would soon break for lunch. The last thing they needed was an ugly confrontation.

They unloaded in the lane behind her new, and probably temporary, apartment. She professed to be happy with the two-bedroom flat, which was clean and bright, even if the furniture and appliances were careworn. They set up Sam's room first, arranging his bedding, toys and books in hopes of making the transition less fraught.

Jake unpacked the kitchen, knowing Amanda was

certain to rearrange things. He looked in the fridge and smiled. It was already stocked with juices, milk, eggs, butter, fruit and other essentials. Tea and a can of ground coffee sat on the counter. Clara's doing, or more likely she handed the task to the receptionist Anna Mae.

Amanda surveyed "my little kingdom," brushed an errant lock of hair from her face and managed the first smile Jake had seen all day.

"Before we pick up Sam and I get out of your hair, there's something we need to discuss," he said. "I want you to consider filing a police report."

Her face clouded. She shook her head violently. "Half our friends—Trent's friends—are on the Aberdeen Police force and the rest are with the Sheriff's Office. What chance would I have? Even if they acted on the complaint, do I want to tell Sam I had his father thrown in jail? God, what a mess."

"Clara said he hurt you."

"Only in places others can't see."

"We need to record this, Amanda. Please."

She nodded and pulled off her sweater, unzipped and lowered her jeans, standing, hands on hips, in bra and panties. "Nothing you haven't seen before," she said, a sob punctuating the sentence.

Jake hid his gasp. "Not like this. Never like this."

There were welts and bruises on her stomach and side, on her buttocks and thighs. He took a copy of the morning newspaper and set it on the table beside her, the date prominent. Using his phone, he photographed the bruises, apologizing all the while as tears streamed down her face.

"It's up to you what you do with these," he said.

"I know." She pulled on her clothes, walked over

to Jake, wrapped her arms around him and rested her head on his chest. "I should have hung onto you. I didn't appreciate how much rowing meant to you. I was jealous of all that time on the water, all that time with your crew."

Jake said nothing, remembering those arguments, and how his rowing scholarship across the country allowed for a clean break.

She looked up. "Time to get Sam. The poor kid must wonder what's going on."

Chapter Forty-Eight

With Amanda and Sam safely installed in the apartment, Jake called Tina. It went to voicemail. She was probably already at lunch.

The move had left him famished. He considered bypassing his regular diner, still pissed at the rude treatment during his last visit. But they did make a great Cobb salad. Decided to give it a last chance. They could take his money or screw off.

It was like the staff had a convenient case of amnesia. He was again the local hero. The *Independent* was back on display, Ramona's front-page story trumpeting his vindication. He was shown to his regular table. His coffee arrived fast and hot. The cook threw everything but the kitchen sink into his salad.

There were friendly nods on his walk back to the office. He was out of purgatory.

He caught Tina on the phone before her afternoon office hours. She was mildly annoyed but accepted Jake's apology and his promise to explain all that night over heaping plates of his "world-class" *linguine alle vongole*. "I'll pick you up at seven, pack a toothbrush."

He mailed a get-well card and apology to Summer Zhang now that he wasn't bound by a non-contact order. She was out of hospital and headed to a full recovery, to his great relief.

Next up was a call to Sedgewick. He filled Foley in

on his concerns over the five medalists, and the possible risk to others.

Foley reported that while the videos showed Jake was "the pushee, not the pusher," he remained under a cloud in the eyes of some board members. "Too bad, we could use your help. We're checking the last ten years of cases, hoping to hell no one else is missing."

"Don't tell the board, Jon, but I'm working this from my end. I've got connections to four of them: Watkins, Meely, Wise, and Zaki's dubious suicide. I'm not letting this go."

"I'm apt to forget this conversation."

"Also, I got a Twitter direct message today from Evie Meyer, a friend of Reggie Obergon. Asked her to check his apartment for his medallion. She said there's an empty space where it was mounted in a display frame. Wise's is missing, too."

"So, they're connected. Not that there was much doubt. I'm at a loss. Do I recommend a temporary halt on the awards program? I can't put lives at risk."

"When's your next award list due?"

"A month-and-a-half."

"That buys time before there are fresh targets, but the list of living past recipients is in the thousands. Are you calling in the police?"

"It's a possible kidnapping and a jurisdictional nightmare, so it has to be the FBI. The Pittsburgh field office is all about counter terrorism these days, but it's impossible to ignore all these missing heroes. I expect they'll be ransacking our files any time now. They promise a discreet investigation—the Sedgewick name carries a lot of weight here—but word will leak eventually. Then what? A reputation built over a century goes in the tank."

"I feel for you. An FBI investigation is as subtle as a troupe of elephants dancing *Swan Lake*. I'll keep from underfoot but pass along anything I find. Appreciate if you do the same."

"That's strictly *verboten*. Don't you dare check my encrypted and informative WhatsApp messages."

"Received and understood."

The next call was to Erik. They bounced around several strategies that showed promise.

"I've convinced BitBust to take this on *pro bono*," Erik said. "If we crack this sucker and find those people, the publicity is priceless. That's a secondary consideration, of course."

"Naturally. Who wouldn't want box seats at the Elephant Ballet?"

"What?"

"Never mind. Talk soon."

He checked his watch, time for one more call before he went on the hunt for clams and the makings for his Caesar salad, also world renowned. He wondered how he'd ever had time to edit a newspaper.

He called an office number in Montesano and reached a legal secretary. "It's Jake Ockham calling for Jann Maxwell. She owes me, I voted for her during our senior year."

The puzzled secretary put him through.

"President Maxwell? I'm calling on behalf of one of your loyal subjects."

Her laugh sounded the same now as it did in high school. "I heard you were back in town, big guy. I've been expecting your call for months, but I suppose you've been too busy jumping in front of trains."

They spent a few minutes catching up. Jake and Amanda used to double-date with Jann and her now ex-husband. "I'm calling about Amanda Shane," he said.

Her voice got wary. "What about her? Is she still married to that jerk? He makes my ex look like a superhero in comparison."

He filled her in on a redacted version of Amanda's problems. "She's hurt, Jann, she's embarrassed and regrets losing touch. She could use a friend. And maybe a lawyer."

"Give me her number," she said with a sigh. "I fucking hate bullies. And take this down." She read off another ten-digit number. "That's my cell number. It's open season on eligible Grays Harbor males, so watch yourself."

"Thanks President Jann. I want you to know I voted for you."

"Yeah, so my secretary tells me."

Chapter Forty-Nine

Clearfield County, Pennsylvania

They locked the professor in their cell, hands cuffed behind his back and ratcheted tight. Andy took control of the pistol, his ribs screaming as they prodded a still wobbly Kristy up the stairs. He sat her on a kitchen chair while Lyla scouted the ground floor. She couldn't find rope or a telephone. They must have left their phones upstairs in their rush to reach the cellar.

They'd find one soon and call 911.

Maybe there was rope in the basement, but neither wanted to see their prison again. Lyla knotted together dish towels and tied Kristy's hands behind her as best she could. They wanted answers, starting with their location.

"Wouldn't you like to know," she said, the reversal of fortune doing nothing to moderate her rage and defiance.

"We'll find out soon enough," Andy said. How had he ever found her attractive? It was like she'd shed a mask to reveal that cruel mouth and those dead eyes. He lowered the gun, more comfortable in his army days with a socket wrench.

Lyla pulled a knife out of a wooden block on the counter but kept her distance. "Why do you hate us?"

"As if you'd use that," Kristy said with a sneer.

"Wouldn't be heroic, would it? Stabbing an unarmed girl. Come closer, let's have a go."

Lyla stood her ground.

"Fucking coward." Kristy spat on the floor. "Fucking fraud. Wasn't for your boyfriend over there you'd be a grease spot on the front of a train."

"Shut it, Kristy," Andy said, figuring it was safe to dump Blaze, her ridiculous pseudonym.

"You are so dead." Kristy looked at Lyla. "He fucked you yet? If he did, he was thinking of me." She thrust out her pelvis. "Wanted this so bad he could barely walk out of the bar." Her lips curled. "As if."

Lyla glared back. "Saving it for Daddy?"

Muffled thumps and curses came from the cellar.

Kristy raised her voice to a shout. "Big talk with him locked in the basement. We get out of this, I'll let him take a run at you. Brad, too. The boy's had a case of blue balls since he scooped you off the street. Gonna be open season on little Lyla. Maybe I'll throw that on the web, too."

"Enough." Andy looked to Lyla. "See if you can find a cell phone upstairs. I'll keep watch on Little Miss Sunshine."

"Thought you wanted to know why we're doing this," Kristy said, unruffled, seeming to revel in their attention. "It's about the Dark Web, see? Sickos pay big bucks for our *Hero Hatr* channel. They get off knowing you're no better than them just because you've got a shiny medal. They pay to watch you scream and piss your panties. And die."

"You're all crazy," Lyla said.

"Getting crazy rich. You know about Incels, right? Involuntary celibates who couldn't get laid if they walked into a whorehouse with written instructions and a roll of cash. We call our audience Inwards: Involuntary cowards. They want to see how average you are. They want to think they'd be heroes, too, with a bit of luck."

The kitchen door was ajar, and Andy felt a welcome breeze. It was time to call the cops. He was eager to feel the sun, and impatient to reset his priorities.

He and Lyla had passed the time talking, her passionate about all she wanted to accomplish in the classroom, and eventually in school administration. "It's kind of a superpower," she'd said, "to change a young life."

No way he was as smart, or as driven. But how many times had he leaned on his mop at the side of the gym, watching a phys-ed teacher run the kids through practice drills. *I could do that.*

That Sedgewick money could go for tuition. Get a teaching degree and his own whistle. Why not?

He saw a blur in his peripheral vision.

He turned, slowed by his injury, and was raising the pistol when a heavy object slammed into his damaged ribs. He screamed in agony and crashed to the floor. The gun flew from his hand, his world reduced to sheets of hot, white pain.

Lyla glimpsed Brad inside the open door, hefting a heavy wrench. She wheeled back, but Kristy, who'd surreptitiously freed her arms, was poised for Brad's arrival. She spun with surprising speed, hurling the wooden chair with brutal accuracy. The knife clattered to the floor as Lyla crashed on her backside.

Kristy kicked away the knife and retrieved the gun.

"Some heroes," she said with a snort.

"Blue balls, huh? Thanks a bunch, sis. Was in the garage, changing the van's oil. Was heading in to use the can when I heard your little sermon. Went back for a wrench. Lucky I quit that damn job, huh?"

"Not for them."

Brad looked at Lyla on the floor, blood streaming from a cut forehead. "Guess you've had worse ideas, if I cleaned her up some. Shouldn't be the only one here not getting laid."

"How be you point your dick to the cellar and free Daddy?"

Kristy walked to Andy, still sprawled on the floor. She reared back her foot and gave a vicious kick to his broken ribs.

Screaming worsened the pain until, mercifully, he lost consciousness.

Chapter Fifty

Aberdeen, Washington

Tina looked at a brass plaque hung above the kitchen window while Jake assembled pre-dinner drinks on the counter nearby. She made an attempt to read it. "*Numquam ponenda est pluralitas sine necessitate.*"

"Not bad," Jake said. "Hand me that bottle of bitters, will ya? As for your question, it translates roughly as "Plurality must never be posited without necessity."

"Sounds familiar."

"It's a family conceit that we think it was written by a distant relative. Fourteenth century distant. William of Ockham, a Franciscan friar. It's his law of parsimony: the simpler of two competing theories is to be preferred. Or as we say in the news biz: Keep it simple, stupid."

"Of course, Occam's Razor. I apply it in my diagnoses. Odds are my patient's sore head is just a headache or a hangover and not a brain tumor. That sort of thing."

Jake nodded. "Or a well-known example: if you hear hoof beats, think horses not zebras."

"My medical texts always spell it O-c-c-a-m so I never thought to connect it with you."

"Our spelling—O-c-k-h-a-m—is the same as the

Ken MacQueen

village in Surrey where old Bill was born. Dad gave me that plaque for my thirteenth birthday. It's followed me around ever since."

She accepted his cocktail and they toasted. "Here I am, little Tina Doctorow, basking in your reflected greatness."

"Probably not. There are many missing limbs in our family tree. But we prefer to apply the Razor to our thinking: the coolest theory is likely the right one."

A light rain carried on a chill breeze. They ate inside, the sliding door cracked open to hear the buzz and hum of insects, the calls of night birds, and once, the crash of something in the underbrush. This was followed by the overpowering scent of skunk spray.

Jake slid the door shut. "Somewhere out there is an unhappy racoon."

With the antipasto done, they tucked into the linguini and salad, and Jake launched into his explanation of why he'd stood up Tina for lunch. "I missed our date because I was installing an ex-girlfriend and her son in an apartment beside the *Independent*. I've recently been informed I own—co-own with Clara—a bunch of buildings on that street. Imagine my surprise."

"Imagine mine," said Tina, who arched her eyebrows but didn't seem too perturbed. "How ex is this ex?"

"Very ex. Remember the high-school sweetie I told you about?" Jake saw no need to mention that one misguided night of sex with the ex, well before Tina was in his life.

He described Amanda's abuse at the hands of her husband, Trent Shane.

246

"That asshole deputy from the night at the ice cream shop? Knew he was trouble."

"Ever since high school."

"Why isn't he in jail?"

He explained her refusal to press charges. "I don't agree, but I can't fault her logic."

"Tell me she's at least had a medical exam?"

He shook his head. "She doesn't want the news spread all over town."

Tina looked offended. "Doctors wouldn't do that."

"As I told her. Even suggested she go to you. No dice. She's always had a stubborn streak. I documented the injuries as best I could."

He wouldn't share details of the photos as he didn't want to violate Amanda's privacy, nor spoil the evening. "I got her in touch with a lawyer, but it's up to her, obviously, what she does with that. There's a kid in the mix to consider. A cute little guy named Sam. He's trying to be brave, but he's deer-in-the-headlights confused. It rips me up." He stood to clear the plates. "Can we change subjects?"

"Please."

She opened the door and sniffed. "Rain stopped. How about coffee on the deck?"

They wiped dry adjoining Adirondack chairs, wrapped themselves in throw-rugs and sipped decaf in insulated mugs resting on the wide arms of the chairs. "I've got something I want to bounce off you," he said.

She smiled. "I'll bet you do."

"That, too. But hear me out. It's about Spokane, and the train, and a bunch of heroes…"

He ran through what he'd learned so far. Tina stared into the distance, quiet except to interject with a few clarifying questions. Finally, she said, "Tell me more about those missing people, and their ties to you."

He gave her everything he had on Lyla, Anderson, Walter and Zaki.

She wasn't satisfied. "What about this Reggie guy? Reggie Obergon?"

"He's the exception. I had nothing to do with him. He was from someplace in Michigan, got his medal more than a decade ago."

"There's a link somewhere," she said. "He went missing in Pittsburgh, and so did his medal. Other medals are missing, too. This Watkins gal is from Pittsburgh, is her medal missing?"

"The Sedgewick folks are checking into that."

"No matter. She's from Pittsburgh, from your time in Pittsburgh. The medals, of course, originate in Pittsburgh. Your medal recommendations for Mr. Wise and Mr. Meely were approved where, Mr. Ockham?"

"Pittsburgh, of course."

Her head bobbed. "And don't forget Mr. Wise's bloody handprint popped up on a wrecked car somewhere in rural Pennsylvania. Where exactly?"

"Outside a burgh called Kittanning, which is about an hour north of—"

"Pittsburgh?"

"Yup."

More head bobbing. "Let's cut out the extraneous stuff. Finish this sentence for me: All roads lead to—"

"Pittsburgh."

"Exactly. Call that Razor 1.0. But we've got to cut deeper. Somebody hates you a lot. Enough to push you in front of a train. So much hate. Let's broaden the thinking beyond Pittsburgh to the whole darn state—

and to all of your time there. Who did you piss off?"

He pulled on his coffee and tapped his fingers on the chair arm.

"A bunch of our competitors at regattas, and some guys who didn't make our eight-boat. But rowers don't do shit like this. There was this reporter I sort of got fired from the *Post-Gazette*. Well, technically, I filed an ethics complaint, and he wasn't kept on after his summer job."

"A complaint about what?"

"He wrote a story about something I did. He obtained it in a dubious way and torqued it beyond all reason. A guy named Travis Barnes who I thought was a friend. He drove me home from hospital when I was stoned on painkillers and splashed my ramblings all over the front page."

She reached across, grabbed both of his hands. "Could the story 'about something I did' have a headline that goes something like: burns kill rower's Olympic dreams after saving teen from tragic fire?"

"How in hell?"

"Come on, Jake, I saw your file. Plug your name into a search engine and up pops every story you wrote, and every story about you. Fascinating stuff. You can't expect a girl to hook up with any random Tom, Dick or Jake. The sensible woman exercises due diligence. You might be a mass murderer for all I knew. Lord knows I've one in my family tree."

"I passed the audition?"

She waggled an upright palm, indicating a firm maybe. "Would this Barnes fellow hate you enough to toss you in front of a train?"

"Doubtful. And it's not as if I killed his career. He

ended up in television, last I heard. I consider that punishment enough."

"Who else then? Think back. Fire and death, that has to be a seminal moment."

He closed his eyes and replayed the horror of that day in Washington County, hauling an unconscious Brad Nichol out of the burning house. The terror on his mother Shannon's face in the window as he watched helpless from the lawn. Him, whaling on Brad's chest. Her little daughter, Kristy, screaming and swearing and pounding his back as Shannon burned, bled, and died. No child should have to witness such horror.

He remembered Kristy's rage and how that morphed to hatred during their encounter days later in Brad's hospital room. "Well, there was this girl," Jake said after an interminable pause. "Kristy, a skinny little thing, eleven years old. She watched as I chose between a futile attempt to rescue her mom, or the safer—and I thought at the time—equally futile option of performing CPR on her brother."

"He lived, as I recall the story."

"Yeah, came alive in the ambulance. I'm pretty certain Kristy thought I chose wrong. Maybe I did. She hates me for sure, but she was just a kid."

"It's never fun playing God, Jake. Trust me on that. That was what, eleven years ago? Consider this: a skinny girl in 2008 is a full-grown woman in 2019. Where was this fire?"

"Ah, Washington County. South of Pittsburgh."

"So, Mr. Ockham, what does Razor 2.0 tell us?"

He buried his face in his hands, then looked up. "That somewhere out there, maybe in the wilds of Pennsylvania, is a woman named Kristy Nichol who hates my guts. Jesus, that's depressing. Can we change the subject?"

"Please," she said. "But first, a note of caution. Your ancient relative isn't infallible. Sometimes *it is* zebras, not horses. And sometimes, unfortunately, it is a brain tumor. Bear that in mind."

Maybe, but not this time. He'll talk to Erik and book a trip to Pennsylvania, a state with very few zebras.

She'd sat the last several minutes with the throw rug wrapped around her shoulders, her arms underneath. She stood and turned to Jake. "The amazing thing about girls is how they grow into women. It's a natural fact."

She cocked a hip and slowly parted the throw rug. She'd managed to unbutton her blouse as well. It opened, revealing hardened nipples poking at a bra so tiny and translucent it might have been spun by silkworms with very little work ethic.

"Take me inside. I'll demonstrate."

Chapter Fifty-One

On her third day in the apartment, Amanda phoned, asking a favor. She asked Jake to drop Sam at his preschool. Desperate to see his friends, he was driving her crazy. She wanted to return some stability to his life.

Jake agreed, though what did he know about kids?

After an awkward pause she said she'd had a call last night from Jann Maxwell. "We had a catch-up and a cry and a grand old time trashing Trent. She booked me an appointment today to talk about, ah, next steps. If, you know, I don't stay in this marriage. I went to bed thinking I'd cancel this morning. But what the hell, can't hurt to talk. Right?"

"Jann's a smart woman with a good heart," he reminded her. "It sounds like she's moved on quite happily from her own marriage." Her phone number in his wallet was proof of that.

After another pause, Amanda asked, "Could you go with me? We could drop Sam at preschool, then go straight to her office. Just for an hour or so?"

Jake cringed. He had much to do. With Erik in hot pursuit of leads, they'd planned to speak this morning. But…

"I'll drive you, but I won't sit in on that meeting. You know my opinions about Trent and it's not my place to meddle in your marriage."

Her hollow laugh lacked the music he remembered. "You made that clear on your one and only overnight. I won't air more dirty laundry in front of you. It's bad enough Jann has to hear it. I could use a friend, just for the drive. So I don't lose my nerve."

"I'll swing by and pick you up."

Jake phoned Erik, and they postponed their talk until the afternoon. "It's gonna blow your mind," Erik promised.

Sam marched from Jake's car and into preschool, carrying his lunch in a backpack almost as big as him. He walked with a self-assurance that reminded him of a younger Amanda. He saw nothing of Trent in his sweet demeanor. *Pray it stays that way.*

He then dropped Amanda at Jann's law office and used his free hour to zip up the road to the Lake Sylvia State Park. He hadn't been here since his return from Pennsylvania. The park was cut with trails converted from old logging roads. He'd run them often during his training days. Had he thought ahead, never his strong suit, he'd have packed running gear. Still, time enough for a five-mile circuit of the lake.

He delayed the start to take a quick call from the office. He felt guilty Ramona had been thrown into the deep end with little preparation, not that she needed it. She had great instincts and deft writing chops. She had the potential to be better than he ever was. That may already be true, but he wasn't prepared to admit that. Not yet. Leave a guy his pride, huh?

"Quick question," Ramona said, all business. "An out-of-town TV guy popped in this morning. He's researching a feature piece on Grays Harbor and was hoping for a look through our morgue. I said he should call back after I checked with you."

"A TV guy doing actual research? Amazing," Jake replied. "I've used many newspaper libraries in my travels. But you're running the ship, what are your thoughts?"

"I'm cool with it. It's standard practice to toss a lifeline to traveling journos."

"Fine by me. Just make sure he doesn't walk away with any files." It struck him after ending the call he should have asked what the story was. Not his worry.

He upped his pace, heading by the dam used a century ago to power the former lumber camp. He breezed past gangs of Canada geese lazing on the grass, fat and incontinent, like they'd arrived on Harleys instead of wings.

With school out, watchful parents lounged at picnic tables while the lake boiled with children. He'd remind Amanda of this place, it could be a great diversion for Sam. Whatever their future held, there'd be bleak days for the little guy. He could only imagine the guilt she must feel.

He was back in the parking lot when Amanda finished her session. "Jann gave me a lot to think about," she said. "If it's all right with you I don't want to discuss it yet."

"I understand," he said. *Was there a guy in the history of the world who'd say, 'No, please share those feelings in minute detail?'*

He stopped in front of the apartment and popped the trunk. "I found an old reading light and a drip coffeemaker I don't use, better than the antique that came with the place."

"Thanks," she said. "Another way to lose sleep."

He carried them upstairs and set them on the kitchen counter.

She stifled a yawn. "Could you put the lamp on my nightstand, please?"

Jake carried it into her street-facing bedroom, fumbling on his knees for an electrical socket.

She stood by the window, looking defeated. "Two hours 'til I pick up Sam."

Jake looked at the bed. "Time for a nap, you look exhausted."

"You always knew how to sweet talk a girl."

She stepped close and wrapped her arms around him. She stretched up and kissed him, her mouth warm and open. He lingered a second longer than he should have, then lifted his face away.

She sighed. "Time was, you'd have me on my back by now."

"Wonderful memories, Amanda. That's where they stay."

"Someone else?"

"Early days, but yes."

He closed her curtains, darkening the room. "Get some rest."

****

His phone held three texts from Erik, each one increasing in urgency They accelerated from—*Where are u?*—to—*Must talk*—to—*Haul ass to my house, we're on the red-eye to Pittsburgh.*—

Jake threw clothes, shaving gear, assorted electronics and a rats-nest of chargers into a roller bag. He chucked it in his car, called Tina and got her voicemail. No surprise, she was going straight from her practice to her weekly shift in the ER.

He left a message: "Hello, dear doctor: Phoning to say tomorrow's dinner is off, sorry. I'm heading for Seattle. Erik found something big and booked us on an overnighter to Pittsburgh. You were right about Pennsylvania. Hope your shift goes well. Break a leg. Or set a leg. Or however doctors wish one luck. Will update you when I can. Ah, bye."

He'd almost ended the call with something romantic. Somewhere on the spectrum between "bye" and "love" there had to be an appropriate expression. He'd work on that.

He phoned Erik using the hands-free option.

"Tell me you're in your car."

"Yup. Be at your place in a couple of hours if Otto, God of Traffic, smiles upon me. What-cha got?"

"You'll have to see it yourself. I'm not letting these electronic files out of my house. Let's just say I've found the mysterious doctor. Interesting we've both homed in on Pennsylvania. Tell me what you've got, that should be safe enough for the phone."

Jake described the theory he and Tina worked through two nights before, all of it led to one angry girl. Woman, actually, had to start thinking of her that way.

"Your doctor is very creative."

"You don't know the half of it," he said with a secret smile. "I've just merged onto I-5. See you soon."

Chapter Fifty-Two

Clearfield County, Pennsylvania

On her knees on the kitchen floor, a frantic Lyla bent over Andy's body. "He'll die unless you get him to a hospital."

"He's dying. He's dying," mimicked Kristy, gun in hand. "Where have I heard that before?"

"You jammed broken ribs into his lungs, bitch. He needs a hospital."

"Needs, needs, needs. He's been damaged goods for a week, I'm sick of his neediness." She hiked her sweater and ran a hand over a developing bruise on her abdomen. "And yet he managed this. You seriously think I give a fuck about his needs?"

Andy was on the edge of consciousness now, moaning in pain. His face was pale, almost blue, his breathing was tortured and Lyla's hand on his neck found a racing pulse. From her rudimentary first-aid knowledge she feared this was fatal without medical intervention.

"Look, just leave him outside a hospital somewhere. He'll never know where to find you. Even if he could, he'd never tell. He knows I'm still a hostage here."

"You think we're stupid?" Kristy said. She was across the kitchen now, huddling with the two men, her eyes and her gun never straying from Lyla. "Sit still and shut up. We're going to turn this mess into something beautiful."

****

Kristy stood watch while Brad and the professor hauled Andy to his feet, set him in a wooden armchair and carried him roughly out the door. He moaned in pain but was awake enough to gasp out a string of expletives.

Brad returned to take over guard duty. Kristy threw a wink to Lyla before heading outside. "This will be epic." She hummed a happy tune, as if planning a birthday party, a picnic, or a beheading.

After what seemed like an eternity, Brad led her outside next to a garage, settling her in an armchair. He taped her arms and legs to the chair. She was immobile, save for the fingers of her right hand.

A video camera swung from Kristy's neck as she pinched Lyla's cheek. "You messed up my morning. And. You. Tased. Me." She punctuated the last four words with face slaps: Left. Right. Left. Right.

"But, hey, when life gives you lemons, the smart play is to monetize the living fuck out of them. Our clients are hungry for another instalment."

"They're insatiable." The professor's voice came from behind. "In retrospect, it was a fortuitous twist of fate that prevented me shooting you both this morning."

Even if she'd had the inclination, Lyla couldn't turn far enough to see him. She looked instead at Andy in a chair ten feet in front of her, head slumped, arms and legs similarly bound.

Video cameras on stands stood beside both of them. The one near Andy was pointed at her, and she assumed the other focused on Andy.

"Anderson performed heroically on the railroad tracks, quite a surprise," Kristy said. "Now it's your shot at glory."

"Literally," the professor said.

He reached from behind and placed a pistol in her hand. "Don't try anything foolish now, I'm sure you appreciate you have a very limited range of motion."

Kristy, standing safely to the side, gently placed Lyla's finger on the trigger and taped gun and hand together.

The barrel pointed at Andy. Lyla willed her shaking hand to be still, afraid the slightest twitch would send a bullet smashing into his chest.

Brad flung a bucket of water in Andy's face. His head jerked up and he croaked a subdued "Piss off."

Brad activated the camera beside him, and the professor did likewise with the other unit. Kristy turned on her video camera. The captors stayed out of camera range.

Kristy pulled on a ski mask. "Here are the rules. In our last episode, Anderson Wise pulled Lyla Watkins from the path of a speeding train.

"Today, the life-or-death decision rests in Lyla's hands. Quite literally," she said, stealing Daddy's line as her camera focused on the pistol.

"Mr. Wise, as you can see, hasn't recovered from injuries suffered in the train accident."

"Despite our medical intervention," the professor added.

"Yeah," said Kristy. "He's a mess. Probably on his last legs. It's up to Lyla to end his suffering."

Her worst fears realized, Lyla groaned.

"Frankly, it's an act of compassion," the professor said. "One might even call her a heroic instrument of assisted death."

"Kill or be killed, those are the rules," said Kristy. "If she doesn't shoot Anderson, we shoot her. Simple as that. She has five minutes to decide, starting...now."

After a long silence Andy fixed his gaze on Lyla. "Do it," he said quietly.

She shook her head a violent no. "Can't. Won't. We've gone through too much together."

"Can't face...your snoring." He spoke in tortured gasps "Put me out of...misery."

"No way. It's your turn to empty the honey buckets."

Both hung their heads as Kristy announced the passing minutes.

At minute three, Andy said: "Not going to make it...chest busted up...can't breathe for shit."

"Not happening."

At minute four, Andy said in a weakening voice: "Remember your superpower...kids need you."

"No."

At minute five, Andy said. "Do this...my friend. Please."

Lyla was crying. Crying and shaking her head no.

At five minutes, thirty seconds, Kristy pressed her pistol to Lyla's head. She felt Kristy's breath as she whispered in her ear. "You're shaking like a leaf, you fucking coward."

At five minutes, forty-five seconds, Andy said: "No."

A second later, two pistol blasts launched birds roosting in a nearby sugar maple.

Chapter Fifty-Three

Seattle, Washington

"We have ways of trolling the Dark Web, not unlike those news alerts you use, but several generations advanced," Erik said, bare feet tucked beneath him on a leather couch, sounding a bit smug. Well, a lot smug.

He swirled a vodka martini while Jake nursed a pale ale. "BitBust doesn't advertise this," Erik said of their clandestine search engine. "We're hardly unique, it's just that ours is better, and unlike the Stealth-e browser on the Dark Web, we know its anonymity hasn't been compromised by one government agency or another."

"Stealth-e? You've already lost me."

Erik checked his watch. "No time to dive down that mineshaft, we've a flight to catch tonight. You do know much of the Dark Web is a toxic waste site, right?"

Jake nodded.

"BitBust jealously guards our ability to hunt there in anonymity. Don't want to alert the site's resident vermin, they'd find better ways to hide. Nothing more creative than cornered rats. That said, it's not all bad down there. Some of our clients arc government or corporate whistleblowers or dissidents in oppressive regimes. We facilitate their ability to share information in complete safety.

"Anyway," Erik gave a dramatic arm-sweep, spilling nary a drop of his martini, "I've found our professor."

****

Erik's skillset afforded a comfortable life. Home was a top-floor condo conversion in a century-old warehouse in Seattle's Capitol Hill neighborhood. Twelve-foot ceilings, plank floors artfully refinished to retain the stains and divots of old, two loft bedrooms, multi-pane windows offering hilltop views of the downtown. One spacious corner was a dedicated Systema workout area/dance floor complete with weight racks, wrestling and yoga mats, an exercise bike, a kick-ass sound system, and, improbably, an overhead disco ball.

Erik had come a long way from the bare-bones residence quarters they'd been assigned fourteen years ago, though even then, he'd strolled into their shared space like he'd owned the university.

Though Jake was half a head taller—with wavey brown hair, hazel eyes, cleft chin, and what one casual date called a "handsome-ish smile"—Erik was in another league.

He moved with leonine grace, confident—make that haughty—blue eyes in a face at once hard, delicate and aristocratic. It lacked only a dueling scar to achieve perfection. Tolstoy would have wept. Anna Karenina would have said, 'Count Vronsky, who?'

That first day, they took each other's measure at a nearby dive bar. A flirtatious waitress served Erik's drink with a side-order of cleavage. "Gosh, you could be that famous ballet dancer." Erik smiled, accepting cleavage and compliment as his due.

"Poor dear must be an Arts major," Jake said, feeling ignored.

"I've seen videos of him in his prime," Erik said, knowing well whom she meant. "Pity he dances for the wrong team."

That took a moment to process, Jake pretty sure that dancer was married with children.

"Ah, the penny dropped," Erik said. "Thought I'd get it out of the way. That going to be a problem?"

"Naw, we English majors are terribly liberal."

Both grew up without siblings. They became the brothers they hadn't known they needed.

Today, they sat in Erik's library: brown leather couch and armchairs on an Afghan carpet. Jake lingered over two signed photographic art prints of, yes, that famous ballet *danseur*, and Erik's favorite rock star.

"What are you smiling at?" Erik asked.

"Aw, nothing. About this mysterious professor?"

"Ah yes, I believe Dr. Barclay Dawes, who is peddling the medal, is actually one Stafford Crabtree."

"And he is?"

"A citation in one of the hero studies we printed."

Erik checked his notes. "The monograph derisively mentioned two papers published in the 1980s by Stafford Crabtree, PhD, a lecturer at something called the Elmdale Christian Women's College in New Bethlehem, Pennsylvania."

He read out the titles:

" *'No Courage Required: Lack of Impulse Control as the Primary Factor in Heroic Acts.'* And, *'Feet of Clay: Sometimes a Hero is Just a Sandwich.'* "

"Never heard of the school."

"It's many notches below the Ivy League. As for Crabtree, he vanished into obscurity after those two studies, which I've downloaded and read. To my great regret. If he ever taught at this little college, he's been expunged from its website."

"That reference to hero sandwiches rings a bell."

"It's a reference to a book and film about the downward spiral of a teen traumatized by the desertion of his father. Sad stuff."

"Seems Crabtree lacks originality."

"He's moved to the Dark Web as this Dr. Dawes, a pseudo academic nutbar and champion of the anti-hero."

"What links them as the same person?"

"Apart from the subject matter, the writing has the same word choice, sentence rhythm, and convoluted style. I ran both through an artificial intelligence program we sell to universities as an anti-plagiarism tool. Dawes and Crabtree are an eighty-eight percent match. Trust me, no other academic would willingly emulate Crabtree's assault on the English language."

"Assuming Dawes is a pseudonym—real name Crabtree—that's another link to Pennsylvania."

"A populous state," said Erik, "with Crabtrees thither and yon among a population of thirteen million."

"So, what have we got?" Jake counted off on his fingers. "We know the *who*, probably. We know the *what*, a fixation with Sedgewick's medalists. We know the *where*—the entire friggin' state of Pennsylvania. As for the *when*, the rescues stretch over at least a decade. That leaves the *why*, always my favorite question. What is his motivation?"

"While you're cogitating, look at this." He led Jake to an antique partners' desk holding two oversized screens, a keyboard, and a laptop hardwired to a modem. He tapped rather a lot of keys. The screen darkened and the graphics reverted at least two decades.

"So, this is where Pac-Man went to die," said Jake.

"And where, with sufficient cryptocurrency, you can hire hitmen, or buy drugs, guns, stolen credit cards, kiddie porn, and believe it or not, human body parts for transplant."

Several more keystrokes brought Erik to the portal of something called *Hero Hatr*.

"I've a feeling this holds the answers. It bills itself as the ultimate reality show: *'Watch as we challenge so-called heroes to prove themselves in ordeals so extreme failure isn't an option.'* It's invitation-only, with a five-thousand-dollar initiation fee. BitBust will pay, with some grumbling, should I pass the vetting process."

"What does your vetting entail?"

"Therein lies the challenge. I'm in the midst of creating the false persona of a very nasty man sitting on a pile of Bitcoin."

"Must be a stretch for a saint like you."

"Too true. My guy is only slightly wacko in his public social media posts. He gets rather ugly on the deep web. And he's a full-time resident of the local cuckoo's nest when he descends to the Dark Web. It's time consuming, but perversely fun."

He waved toward the kitchen. "Grab another beer while I pack. We'll eat at the airport."

"First get me on a sane web browser. I've just suffered a brainwave."

As Erik headed to his loft, Jake typed "sedgewickheroes.com" selected the "Search Heroes" option and filled in the criteria.

When Erik returned with his carry-all, it was Jake's turn to be smug.

"Randal S. Crabtree," he said.

"And who would that be?"

"That would be Stafford's father. Found him on the Sedgewick website, awarded a medal in 1968." He pointed to one of Erik's monitors displaying a description of the act, written in the stilted, facts-only style Jake knew so well.

"Randal S. Crabtree rescued a 16-year-old high school student from a violent assault, Borough of Monaca, Pennsylvania, March 29, 1968. The girl was pulled into a dark alley on the fringe of the commercial district by two men armed with knives. They pushed her to the ground and tore at her clothing. Her screams attracted the attention of Crabtree, 43, petrochemical executive. He ran 80 feet into the alley, and realizing the assailants were armed, acquired a four-foot length of scrap rebar from an adjoining construction site. Hearing Crabtree's shouts, the attackers leapt to their feet brandishing their knives. Crabtree used the bar to smash the eight-inch blade from one assailant's hand before striking a blow to his knee, sending him to the ground. The other lunged at Crabtree, slashing his left arm and striking a glancing blow to his side. Though bleeding heavily, Crabtree struck the assailant's face with the bar, breaking his jaw. The fight drew the attention of passersby who separated the combatants and summoned police. The traumatized girl suffered scrapes and bruises. Crabtree received twenty-one

stitches and missed two weeks of work. His assailants, who were also hospitalized, were convicted of aggravated assault and sentenced to prison."

"Quite the tale," Erik said. "Are you sure he's Stafford's father?"

Jake pointed to the second screen where he'd downloaded two stories from the *newspapers.com* website. One was from the local *Beaver County Times* and the other from the *Post-Gazette* in Pittsburgh, about twenty-five miles southeast of Monaca.

Both were stories and photos of the resulting medal ceremony in 1969. Crabtree, a handsome, powerfully built man in a well-cut suit, stood beside his diminutive wife, Beatrice, and his "proud, 14-year-old son Stafford." The photo put the lie to the cutline. Stafford stood apart from his father, head lowered, hands clasped in front. He was a foot shorter than his father, slightly built and overdue for an adolescent growth spurt.

Erik slapped Jake on the back. "So, it's off to Monaca, dig up the parents and see what their little boy is up to."

Jake scrolled down the screen. "Better pack a shovel."

He pointed to a story in the *Beaver County Times* in 1970. It began: *"The Beaver County Sheriff's office has launched a murder investigation after the body of Monaca resident Randal (Randy) Crabtree was pulled from the Ohio River Friday. Crabtree, 45, a petrochemical executive, was beaten to death, possibly with a metal bar, before the body was dumped in the river," said Sheriff's Department investigator Lt. Charles Gordon. "We're not ruling out robbery as the motive, but the savagery of the attack is troubling." Crabtree was a highly regarded community member. In 1968, he courageously..."*

Erik packed his laptop. "When we locate Crabtree," he said, "we'll also find a worm-can of daddy issues."

Chapter Fifty-Four

Monaca, Pennsylvania

A red-eye flight and a rented car brought them to Monaca's City Center Inn. They shaved, showered, and traded the temptation of a morning nap for the drama and excitement of the local public library. It was a former elementary school, two blocks from the Ohio River. It was less than a mile from where, years ago, Randal Crabtree's body was pinned by the current against the footings of a railroad bridge.

The interior was bright and modern, still having that new-library smell after its recent move exorcized the scholastic demons of its past. In comparison, Jake considered his own elementary school education a sad waste. He'd have happily spent those years at the Aberdeen Public Library. He loved books. He loved libraries. And librarians.

And, wow, the one helping an old gent navigate the Internet was a knockout. Tall, slim, a classic beauty with artfully unruly auburn hair, flawless skin and a radiant smile; a ten-plus on the Dewey Decimal scale of hotness…

"Hello, sir. Hello? What can I do for you?"

She'd finished with the old fellow and was attempting to rouse Jake from his reverie. Her name was Cathy, so said the nameplate pinned to her snug cardigan. And those eyes: warm green pools of wisdom and compassion.

"Sorry, got into town on an overnight flight. Still dopey, I guess."

Erik snorted. She smiled. "How may I help?"

"Actually, I'm looking for someone older, ah, Cathy," Jake said, careful not to let eyes stray further south than her nametag.

"That," she said, barely holding back a laugh, "is not something I often hear."

"What I mean, Cathy, is someone who knows the town's history from the 1960s and '70s."

"I was born here, third generation," she said. "I could put my hair in a bun, and my glasses on a chain if that gives you comfort?"

His face flushed. "My name is Jake, and I'm an idiot. May I start over?"

"Please do." She checked her watch. "I'm ten seconds older now, and that much wiser."

"And I'm Erik, his faithful manservant."

"Um, sorry," Jake mumbled. "Yes, this is Erik. Actually—"

"We're investigating a murder," Erik said.

Cathy's eyes widened. "You're police?"

"Um, no. A murder from 1970." Jake gave her one of his Sedgewick cards. He wrote Foley's direct line on the back, the only person there who might vouch for his semi-legitimacy.

"The victim is Randal Crabtree, a Sedgewick Trust hero. We're investigating the circumstances of his death, hoping there's surviving family here."

"Fifty years later?" She shrugged. "We'll probably have a clip file. It's pretty peaceful here, not too many of those, especially back then."

She pointed to a study carrel. "I'll bring what materials we have."

Cathy returned twenty minutes later with a slim file, a long enough wait Jake feared she'd fled the building. "I hope you don't mind, Mr. Ockham, I Googled your name, I like to know who I'm dealing with."

Jake gave an uncomfortable smile. "You're not the first woman to tell me that. And it's Jake, please."

"Anyway, Jake, the search engine coughed up pages and pages. From your rowing days at Carnegie Mellon—my alma mater, too—through your reporting career, your work at the hero fund and, ah, that mess at the Centralia train station."

Jake felt himself blush. "I stand before you naked."

"Please, no. Someone stripped in the biology section last month. Not a pretty sight."

Erik glanced at the file. "Thanks, Cathy. Not much here. But it's a start."

"I know, rather thin, that's why I phoned my nana. She taught high school here back in the day. She remembers the murder, and the family—the only time one of her students had a parent murdered, she said. Not something you're apt to forget."

Jake brightened. "Do you think she'd—"

"Speak with you?" She laughed. "Try to stop her. I was taking her to lunch anyway, I'm off this afternoon. You'll like her, Jake. She's old."

****

Gertrude Evanston was probably in her eighties, though she'd aged with grace and style. They lunched across the river at the Tomahawk Chophouse, a family restaurant in the tiny community of Beaver.

"The food's good, even if the name is politically incorrect," Gertrude said. "Of course, when your town is named Beaver, the bar's set low."

Jake almost spit out his coffee.

"Oh, Nana." Cathy giggled and patted her grandmother's hand.

"I'm sure these boys have heard worse." Gertrude pecked at her fish sandwich and turned to Cathy. "How be you order me a glass of wine, dear? Not that sweet swill they pass off as a house white. I'll tell these fellows the sad story of the Crabtree family."

The waitress delivered Gertrude's wine and topped up coffees for the other three.

She took a delicate sip, leaned in and lowered her voice. "That Randal Crabtree was a lout in my not-very-humble opinion. He was big and handsome, and quite the lady's man if the rumors were true. He liked his drink. Don't know how Beatrice, that's his poor wife, tolerated it. She put on a brave face, we went to the same church, but it had to be a humiliation."

"Was his murder solved?" Erik asked.

She took another sip. "No, sad to say. It put the town on edge, folks started locking their doors. If you ask me, and I guess you have, there were too many suspects. Jilted husbands, one of his secretaries put in the family way—and he was a bully when he was drinking."

She shook her head, conjuring a memory. "He showed up drunk at one parent-teacher meeting for his son and gave me what-for. Apparently, a B wasn't good enough for Stafford, as his father let me know at full volume. It was scary. Our physical education director heard the commotion and led him out of the school. Like most bullies, Randal was a coward at heart."

"Tell me about Stafford," Jake said. "He became a professor from what I hear."

"That was a surprise. He was certainly no genius. Of course, the girls' college where he taught wasn't much more than a veal pen for virgins."

"Huh?" Jake asked, his hand hiding his open-mouthed surprise.

"A place to keep their knickers on," Gertrude explained, "until they hit marriageable age."

"Nana!"

Gertrude grinned, seeming to enjoy her granddaughter's embarrassment. "What can I tell you about Stafford? He was a skinny wee thing until puberty hit round about eleventh grade. He was a loner with anger issues. A product of his home life, I suspect." After another sip, she said, "Understandable with a father like that. A hero both locally and in Korea, and a big cheese at our chemical plant. Why in this town, Randal Crabtree could get away with murder."

She set down her glass, rippling the wine. "Surely you're not suggesting that Stafford…" She left the rest unspoken.

"We're not suggesting anything, Mrs. Evanston," Erik said, his voice a calming purr. "We merely have some unfinished business, and we can't seem to locate him."

Gertrude was nobody's fool. Far from horrified, this unexpected twist set her eyes ablaze. Or perhaps it was the wine. "Stafford graduated two years after his father's demise, leaving here with enough sympathy marks to qualify for university. Penn State, his mother told me. By then, several suitors were sniffing around Beatrice and her juicy life insurance settlement. Double indemnity from what I hear, due to Randal's murder."

"Is she still in the area?" Jake asked.

She shook her head. "Oh, no. She was swept off her feet by a traveling farm implement salesman. He was at least ten years her senior, a wee slip of a man, quiet and kind. Everything Randal wasn't. They married and moved across the state."

Both men leaned in.

"And, no, I can't remember his name or where they moved. Some rural county, I think."

Gertrude stifled a yawn.

Cathy rose from the table. "Let me freshen up, Nana, and I'll take you home."

Jake waved down the waitress for the bill.

"Cathy's such a dear," Gertrude said. "Don't see rings on those hands, boys. Pity you're from out of state."

"Truly a pity," Erik said. "How does the saying go? The good ones are either taken or gay."

She nodded. "Or conservative."

Cathy arrived in time to hear her grandmother's final comment. "Dear Lord, have to get her out of here before she starts on politics. Thank you for an entertaining lunch."

She graced them with a dazzling smile. "You must let me know how this plays out."

"Absolutely," Jake said.

Erik watched them out the door. He dabbed his mouth with his napkin, failing to hide his smirk. "Like I said. In matters of the heart, always have a Plan B."

Chapter Fifty-Five

Clearfield County, Pennsylvania

"Crazy bitch went at me like a mad dog." Kristy set down her breakfast coffee and lowered a stylish scarf from her neck, revealing a ring of livid bruises and ugly scratches. I got Brad to throw her down some breakfast before he went out. I would have fucking killed her."

"Can't have that," Crabtree said. "She's our bait."

"Not sure she has to be live bait."

"Disposing of one body was challenge enough. They had an interesting dynamic, a bond of loyalty that could only be severed in death. How was it forged?"

"Who cares?"

"Oh, I do. I'll explore this in my next monograph. Can't have been sexual, he was too banged up. Was it born of mutual fear, or anger? Did they feel compelled to live up to their past heroic narrative, about the only characteristic they shared? Did they, in other words, come to believe their own press clippings?"

Such ramblings bored her. It was his way of rationalizing murder, burying bodies in academic bullshit to keep them at a safe distance. She didn't see the need. Keep it simple.

She loved how the bitch jumped when she shifted her pistol and blasted two holes in Wise's chest. The gun was so close to Lyla's head it probably ruptured her eardrum. And then her crying and screaming and swearing, like that would bring him back.

Dead is dead. Enjoyed cutting the bullets out of Wise's body with Lyla watching. A little lesson in who's boss. That's when Lyla came at her, Brad too stupid to leave her taped to the chair until she finished.

Apart from that bit of excitement, it was no different from field-dressing a deer, about the only useful thing a late, unlamented foster father taught her.

"Remember your first kill?" Crabtree asked, pushing away his breakfast plate.

Kristy gave a wry smile. "My first was before your time. But you mean Richard, right?"

Amazing how sympatico they were, both thinking of her first foster placement after the fire. She hadn't hit puberty yet, not that it stopped Richard Frost in his island cabin in the middle of nowhere.

"It'll clear her head, get her in touch with nature," Richard had told his wife, Beth, as he packed rifles, fishing gear, and bourbon in his pickup. Beth stayed home to mind Brad.

And they did hunt. And they did fish. And at day's end, Richard got in touch with…her.

The first time was a blur with all that bourbon sloshing inside. She remembered throwing up and him making her clean up the sick. After that, Richard saved the bourbon for himself.

Finally, she and Brad went on a rampage, trashing Richard and Beth's house. That got them out of there and into a series of foster homes. Crabtree came along with Nancy, his wife at the time, presenting themselves as prosperous and caring. Social services couldn't push through the adoption fast enough.

She was fourteen when they moved into Crabtree's mother's big farm home. This very place. Granny Beatrice was a frail widow by then. She joined Norm Morrison, her beloved second husband, in the family plot six months later. Crabtree's wife filed for divorce shortly after, about the time of his "retirement" from Elmdale College.

Crabtree made a half-assed attempt at gentleman farming, though Granny's inheritance left him comfortable. "Where there's a will," he'd told Kristy with a wink, "there's a way."

She loved that he treated her like an adult. "Kindred spirits from the first time we met," he said. He confided in her and she in him. She even told him about Richard.

And they made plans for Richard. Revenge was like a drug for Kristy, it energized and inspired her.

Kristy rubbed her raw throat, refilled their coffees, and they strolled down memory lane. "Richard couldn't believe his luck when you got in touch, said you wanted to go fishing again." Crabtree looked over his mug, gave her an appraising gaze. "You were on the cusp of sixteen and all woman."

She laughed. "I said, 'I'm only fifteen, Richard, it has to be our little secret.' That got his motor revving faster than his outboard as we headed for that damn cabin."

"Then you came upon me in my *broken-down* boat. I could tell he didn't want to stop."

Kristy mimicked a little-girl voice. "Oh, Richard, *pleeeze,* won't take a minute to help. I'll make it up to you at the cabin."

"He leaned way over the gunwale to look at my

outboard," Crabtree said.

"A smack on the head with an oar, my boot in his ass, and he was in the water."

"He came to, sputtering and swearing. No life jacket and a gut full of booze. Just another boating fatality. You hopped in with me, and we sent his boat putt-putting away. Had the whole lake to ourselves that time of night."

"It had just turned midnight and you sang *Happy Birthday*. Even pulled out a cupcake and lit a candle. I cried."

"Sweet sixteen."

"Old enough to marry in Pennsylvania, if we'd had a mind to."

"But only with parental consent."

"Oh, you consented, Daddy. You were still consenting when the sun came up."

Chapter Fifty-Six

Monaca, Pennsylvania

It was two in the afternoon when Jake and Erik returned to the hotel. They had no particular place to go and no need to break camp. Both had an avalanche of texts and messages to dig through.

There'd been no response to several messages Jake sent Tina. With her busy job that wasn't unusual. What surprised him was the FBI's silence. He'd expected to be among the first interviewed if they were serious about their investigation into missing heroes.

A partial answer to that came when he opened a voicemail from Sharon Key. "Hey, Jake, great news." In the background, he heard Sharkey's lunch-hour buzz, and the clink and ping of glassware. He pictured Sharon behind the bar doing three things at once.

"Got a letter from Andy two days ago. Really. Said he's on his way to Mexico. Said he figured I'd be worried about that thing with the train and the car. No shit, huh? Seems he had nothing to do with that. He was putting away extra cash working at a used-car lot in Pennsylvania. He cut himself changing the belts on an old beater and didn't realize he'd left his prints on it. The plan was to buy it and drive south, so he left his phone in the glovebox. He figures punks stole it overnight and left it on the tracks. He took that as a sign

279

to get moving. A buddy was heading to Mexico, and he was hitching a ride as soon as he mailed this letter."

Her message ended. Andy tying up those loose threads seemed rather…convenient.

There was a second briefer message from Sharon. "Sorry, Jake, had to click off. Table of eight all wanted something from the tap. Damn things take forever to pour. Anyway, reason I didn't tell you sooner is the FBI grabbed the letter and told me to keep it on the down low. They ran some tests, prints and DNA, I guess. Got back to me today, confirming Andy actually wrote it. They said he made a five-hundred-dollar ATM withdrawal in Birmingham, Alabama, which is sort of on the way. The bank video was broken but they're sure enough it was him to 'stand down,' as they put it. Once he gets a new cell, I'll give him holy hell for putting us through this worry. Gotta run, bye."

Jake had serious doubts, but he wasn't about to bust Sharon's bubble.

He gave Jonathan a call to see how the other investigations were proceeding.

"Going nowhere," Jon said. "Lyla Watkins' mom heard from her daughter yesterday. Seems she ran off with this guy she met at a coffee shop. They're planning to get married, details to follow. Was too embarrassed to tell mommy until now."

"Let me guess. She said this in a letter, and the feds confirmed it with her fingerprints."

"How did you know?"

"Wise wrote a letter, too. Quaint, this sudden reliance on old-school correspondence. Might want the Pittsburgh Feds to contact their Spokane field office."

"My marching orders are to leave this be. If it ain't

broke…etcetera, etcetera. That's the FBI's philosophy, too. No interest in blowing their budget sinking a dry well. By the way, our boy Walter Meely is working his credit card in San Francisco. A couple of gay bars, a bath house, and an ATM withdrawal. So, there's that."

"There's too much *there-and-that* going on, you ask me."

"Um, you didn't hear this from me, but—"

"I know, Jon. I'll plug away."

Still no response from Tina.

There was an email from Ramona. Ever organized, she'd listed three "action items" requiring a publisher's approval. That fell to Jake. Clara was preoccupied with wedding preparations, the event just ten days away. *Note to self: rent a tux, write a toast for the happy couple, get Tina on the guestlist.*

His publisher's duties burned through two hours. Then, finally, an email from Tina, titled: *"Enough."*

What?

She wrote: *"Stop bombarding me with messages. Our relationship (I thought we had one) is not something I'll argue from a distance. We can discuss on your return if you wish to bother. We talked early on about the value I place on fidelity. I will not be hurt like that again."*

He tried her personal cell, but it seemed out of service, like she'd yanked its SIM card. No way he'd poke the bear by phoning her work number and sharing this soap opera with her office.

Had she magically known about his mild flirtation with a librarian named Cathy? Ridiculous. All he did was buy her lunch—with her grandmother, for gawd's sake.

What. The. Hell?

He took a breath and replied: *"Dear Tina: I have no idea what prompted your message. I very much believe we have a relationship, one that means the world to me. There is no infidelity, you have my word. Erik and I are closing in on our missing medalists. I honestly believe their lives are at risk or I'd return home now to clear the air. I will reluctantly honor your wish to break contact until I am back. I see a future for us, Tina. There's nothing I want more. If I've done anything to jeopardize that I am sorry.*

"Jake."

He slammed his laptop shut and stormed out of the hotel. The damn place had a fitness center but no bar. He wouldn't make that mistake again.

Chapter Fifty-Seven

Clearfield County, Pennsylvania

They'd hatched the plan while clearing the breakfast dishes, Stafford realizing there'd be no peace until they acted on Kristy's primary target: Jake Fucking Ockham.

They headed to the cellar. She carried a phone, a notebook, and Lyla's lunch, a bowl of canned chili. With added spit. Kristy's ravaged neck still hurt like a motherfucker. Crabtree carried the gun.

Lyla stared at the ceiling, not acknowledging their arrival. Her cot tilted at a crazy angle because of the missing strut. Kristy's bruise was fading, the memory wasn't.

They'd moved out Andy's cot—he rested in pieces elsewhere—leaving her with this busted piece of crap. Kristy took her joys where she found them. "Remember Jake Ockham?" She detected a subtle eye twitch. "Guy who wrote a story about you pulling that old cripple off the tracks?"

Lyla looked away.

"Sure you do," Crabtree said. "He's the genesis of your heroic myth. You owe him big."

"And now you're going to send him a WhatsApp voice message," Kristy said. "I see on your phone you two still keep in touch. That's so sweet."

"No."

"Wrong answer."

"You're inviting him to your forthcoming nuptials," Crabtree said, raising his voice an octave. *"It's really important to me, and it will help get Mom on side. She just loved your story. Please, Jake, it's short notice, but it means the world to share this day with you."*

"Blah-de-blah blah. Just like that," Kristy said. "We wrote you a script."

"No fucking way. You two are insane."

"Ouch," said Crabtree. "If you prick us, do we not bleed?"

Kristy ripped a page out of her notebook and dropped it on Lyla's chest. "Have a look."

Lyla swept the unread page to the floor. "You murdered Andy. You get nothing from me."

Kristy read out a street address in Pittsburgh.

Lyla jerked upright.

"Of course, we kept mommy's address when we made you write her that letter. Bet your ass we'll pay a visit if you don't cooperate," Kristy said. "My face will be the last thing she sees."

She dropped the notebook on the cot. "Here's what you're going to say."

"And while you're thinking about that, you may wish to reflect on Andy's *suicide*," Crabtree said. "You shared a strange attraction to rolling stock so we created a fitting coda to his altogether unremarkable life."

"Andy was a hero, something you'll never be."

His voice went cold. "That word means nothing."

"We drove his damned body twenty miles up the tracks that night," Kristy said. "Dragged him through the woods to a nice downhill stretch where trains go full-tilt."

"Waited until the last second then the three of us heaved him in front of a Genesee & Wyoming freight," Crabtree said. "It's doubtful the engineer even noticed Andy being masticated by a mile long chain of rail cars. Be a miracle if there's enough left for a DNA swab."

"You callous bastards."

"Keep that in mind," Kristy said, "while you rehearse the message to your pal Jake."

Chapter Fifty-Eight

Monaca, Pennsylvania

Jake sweated out an epic hangover on the hotel's rowing machine: chest heaving, thighs screaming, hands afire. An unsympathetic Erik Demidov loped beside him on a treadmill. They were the only two in the fitness center at ten in the morning, still undecided on a plan of attack. He stopped long enough to chug a second bottle of water.

"By the time I caught up with you at bar number three you were beyond redemption," Erik said. "Kept ranting 'You an' your fuckin' Plan B.'" He mimicked a slurred, drunken voice, his steady breathing gave little indication the treadmill was set at maximum speed on an intense incline. "You quite hurt my feelings."

Jake wound down his workout. "Never tried boilermakers before. Never again."

"It seemed the beverage of choice in that dive. I will say it had a great jukebox."

Jake covered his face with a towel and groaned. "If I ever press play on *Sweet Home Alabama* again, shoot me dead."

"Three times was quite enough. Judging by the audience reaction, your extended analysis of the song's backstory amused more than it enlightened."

Another groan from under the towel.

"She got under your skin, this doctor of yours. I'm happy to intercede on your behalf."

"That would piss her off even more. Can I have my phone back now?"

Erik fumbled in his gym bag and handed it over. "Be grateful I stopped your attempts at contact last night. Wouldn't have gone well."

Jake swiped the screen. "Battery's dead."

"Plug it in. Have a shower." Erik waved a hand in front of his nose. "A long shower. Then we'll make another attempt at breakfast. Plans must be made."

****

Jake was on his fourth coffee, feeling almost human after a breakfast of sausages, home fries and a bacon-cheddar omelet. Grease therapy. He filled in Erik on the letters from Lyla and Andy conveniently grinding further investigation to a halt. And Walter Meely's alleged bacchanal in gay old San Francisco.

"Interesting, all this happening at once," Erik said. "I hope for Walter's sake it's true, but the idea of him bursting out of the choir stall and into a steam bath is a bit hard to swallow…Let's strike that image."

"Please."

"Meanwhile, I'm happy to report I've provisional acceptance to join the *Hero Hatr* channel. I have to endure a final phone interview with the founder but they've already grabbed my entry fee so I'm optimistic. I'll dazzle them with venality and hope they don't expect me to roast a baby or something to prove my worth."

"Ah, man, I just ate."

"I'm thinking of Walter's credit card binge, and Andy's ATM withdrawal in Birmingham. The Dark

Web is ideal for trafficking in stolen credit and bank cards. Don't need the physical cards, just the numbers, verification codes and some personal info. Find willing buyers in, say, Birmingham and San Francisco, and you're off to the races. Offer them the bank card money gratis, on condition they make a few credit card purchases to establish location. Their reward, after a week's delay, is to go nuts with the card until it hits its limit."

Jake checked the screen on his vibrating phone. It was an incoming WhatsApp voice message. "O-kaay, this is weird. It's from Lyla Watkins. Let's find a quiet spot."

They paid the bill and reconvened in Erik's room. Jake played the message:

"Hey Jake, been a long time. I've a huge favor to ask."

Jake hit pause. "Lyla's voice for sure."

He hit play:

"I'm getting married, it's a love-at-first-sight thing. I dropped everything to be with him. Moved out and left my job. I guess Mom is pretty bummed at my disappearing act. I wrote her a letter explaining this is the most exciting thing that's ever happened to me. It's huge, Jake, bigger even than pulling Robert off those streetcar tracks. Anyway, I know it's short notice, we're getting married next Monday, but I really need you to come to Pittsburgh. I want you to meet my guy and give away the bride. And help make things right with Mom. You know how much she loved talking to you for that interview. She went on and on and on. Please say yes, it'll make my big day perfect. I'll text you the details when you reply. Bye, hope to see you soon."

"What does this tell us?" Erik asked.

Jake closed his eyes, processing what he'd heard. "The tone and substance are diametrically opposed. The words are gushy. But they don't match the tone, which is stilted and wooden."

"Agree, like she was reading a script."

"A script for sure, but with improvisation. She didn't pull any Robert off the tracks. His name was Michael Crumley. No way she'd forget, they became quite close."

"Interesting."

"And interviewing her mother was a trial. She was so traumatized by the risk Lyla took she fretted the publicity would inspire more rash acts. I had to take her to dinner—twice—to coax out an interview. And it sure didn't go 'on and on and on.' Lyla and I joked about it. There was an Egyptian exhibit in the city at the time and I complained I'd have more luck prying quotes out of one of those mummies. Lyla and I took to calling her Mummy Dearest."

"She's under duress," Erik said. "Saying she's in 'huge' trouble. And warning, I'd guess, you're being lured into a trap."

"Right on all counts. Yet there's nothing here to raise a red flag with the cops."

"What to do?"

"I love a good wedding. And I'm one hell of a dancer, as you witnessed last night."

"Yes, but shotgun weddings are the worst. If you go through with this—and I'd rather you not—preparations must be made. Our only advantage, apart from our suspicions, is they think you're still in Washington State. That gives us an extra day or two here to plan."

"And to pick out a present."

Jake tapped a message on his phone:

—*Congratulations, Lyla! I'm honored to give away the bride. Please send me the details, I plan to fly in Sunday night. My best to Mummy.*"

Chapter Fifty-Nine

Pittsburgh, Pennsylvania

They checked out of the hotel and made the forty-five-minute drive to Pittsburgh. Jake booked rooms at a moderately priced chain hotel, which offered a fitness center *and* a bar, the latter should he waver on his temporary vow of abstinence.

"Lots of shopping to do." Erik said, annoyed by Jake's refusal to be talked out of his plan. "Timing is tight, who gets married on a Monday?"

"I'm sure folks do," Jake said, "but we can agree Lyla isn't among them."

They made several stops as Erik filled his shopping list: a medical supply store, a costume shop, a shoe store, a tux rental chain, and a spy shop catering to the nation's rising level of conspiracy and paranoia.

"On the plus side, I can return my tux to their Seattle location after Dad and Clara's wedding," Jake said. "But is all this necessary? My credit card is exhausted."

"A man in your terrible condition can't be too careful," Erik said.

"I feel okay."

"Not when I'm through with you."

****

Lyla responded via WhatsApp as they finished a

late sushi dinner.

Jake looked in envy at nearby tables where the Friday night crowd toasted the weekend with craft beers, elaborate cocktails, and carafes of warm sake. His soda water did nothing to settle his nerves, despite two lime wedges to double the fun.

No voice message this time, just a text.

—*Thank you, Jake!! So excited you're coming. I don't know when you arrive Sunday, but I've booked you a room at the Pittsburgh Airport Marriott, our treat. No arguments, big guy! My hubby-to-be is loaded. He says its the least he can do after dragging you across the country on short notice. You'll love him. We'll pick you up Monday morning at 10:30 for the big event. See you then, you've made me so happy, Lyla—*

The message ended with three red hearts and a smiley face.

"The emojis are a nice touch," Erik said. "So profound. What are the odds she wrote this?"

"Lyla is not a two-exclamation-mark, four-emoji gal. And she knows to apostrophize it's."

Erik picked up the phone and started to type. "Here's your reply."

He typed, erased, retyped and frowned. "Sorry, couldn't find an appropriate emoji."

The text read,

—*Dear Lyla: Don't be alarmed when you see me. I was in a car crash the other day. A damn fool ran a stop sign and t-boned my car. I'm a bit banged up, but in high spirits and ready, willing and able to fulfill the honor you've bestowed upon me. Do you have an online wedding registry? I'm bereft of ideas for an appropriate gift. Love and hugs, Jake—*

Jake shrugged. "Rather florid, and kind of gay. A gift registry, really?" He hit send.

"A mere thank you would suffice. But your ingratitude makes tomorrow's task easier."

"Easier for what?"

"To hit you. I'm thinking the face. Has to be the face."

"What?"

"Surely you haven't forgotten you were in a car crash. 'A bit banged up' you wrote not five minutes ago. Can't have you looking hale and hearty. Your very life depends on authenticity."

Jake signalled a passing waiter. "A double scotch, please. No, a triple."

They left the restaurant and, at Erik's insistence, stopped for a nightcap at their hotel bar. Saturday would be full-on. Much to prepare before Sunday's fake arrival from Washington State. Friday night was ending in a Scotch-infused glow.

Jake fumbled with his key card, didn't really need that nightcap. He got it open and turned to Erik. "You're kidding about hitting me, right? We have makeup for that."

"Of course. I don't want you going to bed tonight dreading, 'oh he's going to hit me tomorrow.' What kind of friend would—"

Erik lashed out with an open-handed left slap to Jake's face, and a right cross to his cheek.

Jake reeled into his room. "What the fuck? You lying son of a bitch!"

"I promised not to hit you Saturday." He checked his watch. "It's eleven forty-nine Friday night, just under the wire."

Jake dabbed blood from the cut on his mouth. "You hit me."

"Two splendid surgical strikes. You'll awaken tomorrow with the worst behind you—and a nicely bruised cheek and genuine black eye. This hurt me more than it hurt you. Such are the sacrifices I make for a friend."

"Some friend."

"Night, Jake. Catch you at breakfast."

Chapter Sixty

Pittsburgh, Pennsylvania

Jake taxied to the airport well in advance of the first logical arrival from Seattle. He had his roller bag, his tux and a three-hundred-dollar necklace for Lyla's alleged wedding.

"Your quest for verisimilitude is bankrupting me."

"Look on the bright side," Erik said, "if you survive this, you'll need a wedding present for Clara."

Jake needed to kill time at the airport with minimal risk of being seen. Bars, restaurants, and arrivals areas were out of the question. Then he spotted the Interfaith Reflection Room, the answer to his prayers.

Head bowed, hands clasped over his mobile, he purged anything tied to the missing medalists. Aside from the quiet and privacy, its comfy chairs were a welcome relief. He walked with a slight limp, like he had a stone in his left shoe.

When the video monitors showed his flight landed, he blended into the deplaning crowd. He caught the shuttle to the hotel, no one following that he could see.

Handling his luggage and garment bag was a struggle, what with his left arm in a cast and sling. That was part of Saturday's project: wrapping his arm in bandages so Erik could mold a cast from water-cured resin wrap. Once it dried, he slipped it off with difficulty and removed the bandaging underneath, leaving space between forearm and cast. They scuffed it up and added a few cheeky autographs. The damn thing itched like crazy.

Jake produced ID at the hotel check-in and asked for a room booked in his name. He requested two key cards and slipped one in an envelope preaddressed to Erik. He scrawled, "from your friend in 623," and gave it to the clerk.

"A Mr. Demidov will be checking in, please notify him there's a letter at the front desk."

"Certainly, Mr. Ockham. Enjoy your stay."

Inside 623, Jake set his suitcase by the closet, flopped his tux on the bed and checked his phone, which vibrated during check-in with an incoming email. He expected a coded message from Erik who was having his *Hero Hatr* vetting about now.

Instead, it was from Tina. Subject line: "We're through."

"What the fuck?" Jake said aloud.

He opened the message: *"Cheating was bad enough. Destroying my reputation is unforgiveable."*

Attached were two videos, a .JPG photo, and a copied email from Trent Shane dated several days back. It read: *"Your boyfriend is fucking my wife. Stop him, or I will."*

"Jesus," Jake said aloud. The photo showed Jake's car parked overnight in front of Shane's house during his ill-fated one-night dalliance with Amanda. The photo was time-stamped 2:43 a.m. It was undated.

He played the first video, probably shot from a parked car: him leading Amanda into her new apartment after meeting with the lawyer. Shortly after, it showed their embrace and brief kiss by the bedroom window, followed by Jake looking out as he closed the curtains.

"I'm so fucked."

"Yes, you are." It was a woman's voice.

He wheeled to see a young man and a woman walking from the bathroom. The woman held a pistol.

"Hello, Brad," Jake said. "My, Kristy, how you've grown."

She snatched the phone from his hand and replayed the video. "Tomcatting, were you? Well, that's the least of your problems. Let's see the other video."

It was billed as part of a "Historic Crimes" series from a Wolf News affiliate in San Francisco. It opened with reporter Travis Barnes in front of Tina Doctorow's medical office.

The ribbon at the bottom of the screen read: *"Great-great granddaughter of nation's worst serial killer returns to scene of his crimes."*

Suit bespoke, hair coiffed, Barnes had gone upmarket since his university days.

He began his stand-up: *"There's a new doctor in Washington State's gritty port city of Aberdeen, one who arrived with a deadly secret we can now reveal. Aberdeen has a long history as a logging and fishing town, but it also has an ugly past. Fans of Nirvana know this as the childhood home of frontman Kurt Cobain, who ended his life with a shotgun blast in 1994."*

The video cut to Barnes walking the banks of the Wishkah River, stopping at a sign reading "Welcome to Nirvana," in a tiny park known as Kurt Cobain Landing. Barnes heaved a theatrical sigh as he gazed over the muddy river.

"But Aberdeen was never Nirvana, not for Cobain, nor almost a century earlier when the ocean and rivers of Aberdeen bore a deadly harvest, the so-called Floater Fleet of human remains. We'll never know how many bodies were carried out to sea, murdered at the hands of William (Billy) Gohl, perhaps America's most prolific serial killer. Locals called him the Ghoul of Grays Harbor, but never to his face.

"Gohl came north from San Francisco to lawless Aberdeen, where, as the powerful official agent of the Sailors Union of the Pacific, he carried out his rampage of robbery and murder with seeming impunity. He's believed to have killed between one hundred and two hundred transient sailors and dock workers, earning Aberdeen the ugly reputation as hell hole of the Pacific."

The video cut to yellowed clippings of his trial, news pages that could only have come from the *Independent's* morgue. Barnes was the "TV guy" who'd approached Ramona. Why hadn't he asked her his name? He'd never have let that slimeball in the door.

Jake's stomach clenched, sure worse was coming.

The video cut to Barnes in front of Billy's Bar & Grill. "Modern Aberdeen perversely celebrates Gohl's sordid past, there's even a bar named in his so-called honor. Billy's ghost, and many of his victims, are said to haunt the place.

"But one woman isn't celebrating. She is Dr. Christina Doctorow, who recently moved to Aberdeen for reasons unknown, while hiding her dark secret. In turn-of-the-century San Francisco, Doctorow's great-

great grandmother gave birth to Gohl's illegitimate child."

Jake watched in horror, oblivious to the gun at his back, as Tina climbed into her car.

Barnes tapped politely on her driver's-side window. "Yes?" she said with a puzzled smile.

Barnes waved the file from the *Independent*. *"You're the closest living relative of America's worst serial killer, how long did you think you could keep your past secret? The details are in these files. How did you stop the Independent from printing the story?"*

Tina raised the window, which did nothing to hide the shock, horror and anger playing on her face, or her streaming tears. She started her car. Barnes attempted to block her departure, shouting: *"Why did you move here? Is it guilt? Is it shame? Are you trying to bury Billy's ghost?"*

She laid on the horn and revved the engine. Barnes jumped to the side as she peeled away, tires chirping on the hot asphalt.

Barnes gave the camera a shit-eating grin. *"I'll take that as a no-comment. What is known is she's romantically linked to the Independent's deposed former editor, Jake Ockham, who has his own checkered past. Did they conspire to hide the truth?*

"That's the latest in a line of unanswered questions dating back to the nameless, faceless and uncounted victims who met their sad end in Aberdeen, still haunted by its reputation as hell-hole of the Pacific...This is Travis Barnes reporting for Wolf News San Francisco."

Kristy powered down the phone, tossing it on the bed beside Jake's tux.

"You won't need either of these. Pity we didn't know about your hot doctor girlfriend, well, ex-friend. Would have invited her to the party. We'll pay her a visit later. Anyway, your old friend Lyla is ready and waiting. Surprise, ain't no wedding. Just as well, you look like shit, that crash did a number on you."

She gestured with her pistol. "We're gonna walk you out like we're old friends. Our van is in the parking garage. This will be pressed in your side so don't get any ideas."

Jake stood, knocking over his chair in rage and frustration "What about my suitcase?"

"Nope."

"I'll need clothes."

Kristy gave a derisive snort. "Not likely."

Tina dominated his thoughts as he was frog-marched to the elevator. He shouldn't have hidden from her that fling with Amanda. It was before the good doctor came into his life, but he worried it would tip the balance against him. Coward. He should have had faith in Tina's understanding.

And he should have excised references of Gohl from her file at the newspaper. True, he gave her the opportunity to do so, and she hadn't. He was editor then, she'd had faith in his discretion.

Misplaced faith. The hurt on her face and in that last email was palpable. And it would be met with his silence. Their relationship was beyond repair, even if he got out of this alive.

And that was now a big *if*.

A micro-GPS unit was hidden in his tux garment bag, and a burner cell was sewn into the lining of the suitcase—both left behind in the hotel room. He and

Erik discovered late Saturday even that small burner phone wouldn't fit between Jake's forearm and cast. Now, fifteen minutes in, the plan was unraveling. Erik, tied up with the *Hero Hatr* vetting, would be left in the dark about Jake's whereabouts.

Chapter Sixty-One

They'd led him to a van in the garage, crushing his phone under its tires. They gagged him with a rag and duct tape, and zip-tied his legs and one good arm to eye bolts in the steel floor. He'd briefly surveyed the van before Brad pulled a pillowcase over his head. Overkill. There were no windows in the cargo area, and nothing useful inside.

Kristy patted him down. She pulled his wallet out of a back pocket. and emptied the others of keys, gum and change. She yanked down his pants and boxers, looking for who knows what. Her finger flicked his limp penis.

He felt her breath on his ear. "Real men stand at attention, even before I get in their pants." She pulled up underwear and pants and gave his crotch a quick squeeze. "Sad."

He estimated they drove for an hour. Most of it on good roads, though gravel pinged off the undercarriage the last five minutes or so. The van pulled to a stop; its sliding door rasped open. His captors sliced the zip ties and hauled him out.

He deliberately stumbled on the uneven ground. Brad yanked off the pillowcase and Jake took in his surroundings. A long gravel drive bisected two fallow fields, ending at two wooden outbuildings and a sprawling white clapboard farmhouse.

The main section was three stories high. Three dormers jutted from the steep pitched roof. A fieldstone chimney climbed the outside, a covered porch wrapped two sides of the building. A stone addition was added at one end. It was built to impress, though from what Jake could tell there were no nearby neighbors. There was a weedy front lawn, and on second glance, the house looked careworn.

Jake said, "Could use a paint job."

Brad glared. "Fuck off."

Kristy gave an amused snort. "Told ya, Brad."

"Then get off your back," Brad snapped, "and paint the damn thing."

They led him to the kitchen in the stone addition. Kristy thrust a set of blue sweats at Jake. "Your room's downstairs. So is the bride."

Brad led him to the cellar at gunpoint and waved him into the dank bathroom. "You've got ten minutes to shit, shower and get into those clothes. I'll be waiting, don't get any ideas."

He piled his street clothes on his new running shoes and took an awkward shower, careful not to wet his cast. He slipped on the sweats, struggling to pull the shirt over the cast. He noticed the HH logos, wondering if Erik had been admitted to the club.

Wondered, too, if Erik knew where he was, his abduction happening a day sooner than anticipated—their plan looking shakier by the minute.

He emerged, and Brad pointed to an empty cell: bare walls, camp cot, milk crate, a bucket and roll of TP. He grabbed Jake's discarded clothes.

"At least leave my shoes."

"I guess." Brad tossed them on the floor before

bolting the door.

Jake heard footfalls on the stairs and the squeal of the cellar door hinges. He sat on the cot and pulled on his shoes. Would it have killed the son-of-a-bitch to leave his socks?

After several minutes of silence, he heard a muffled, tentative voice. "Hello, I'm Lyla Watkins. Who are you?"

"Hey, Lyla, it's Jake…Jake Ockham. So glad to hear your voice."

"Oh, Jake, I'm sorry." Her voice broke. "They made me send you that message. They were going to kill my mother if I didn't." She gave a harsh laugh. "There's no wedding. It was a trap. Why, I don't know. I'm so very sorry."

"No need to apologize. Can they hear us talking down here? Is the cellar wired, somehow?"

"Pretty sure they can't hear. Andy, you wouldn't know him but he was a prisoner like us, we talked all the time. Just don't shout."

Jake's stomach did a flip. "Andy, that's Anderson Wise, right? I know him, he was a fellow medalist, just like you."

He heard a wail, as if something had broken inside her. "They…she, that girl Kristy, she killed him. Tied us to chairs outside—and filmed us."

It was slow going, her disjointed retelling interrupted by sobs. Jake gave her what time she needed. His right hand pounded his thigh, hammering down a growing rage.

"She had a gun at my head and then she shot him instead…They'd taped a gun to my hand, too. Said they'd kill me if I didn't shoot him. Andy was all busted up from before…after he pulled me from a car just before a train hit us. These are sick people…Andy kept saying 'Shoot me, Lyla, shoot me.' I just couldn't. Maybe if I'd tried and missed somehow—I don't know. He's dead. It's my fault."

"My guess is they always intended to kill Andy," Jake said. "He'd left his fingerprints on that car. He was a liability. They wanted you alive, to get to me."

"Just great." Her words were bitter and hard. "I'll get you killed, too. How do you know about Andy's fingerprints?"

Jake lowered his voice. "I know plenty. I know they're peddling this anti-hero shit on the Dark Web for big money. I knew you weren't getting married." He forced some optimism into his voice. "I hope one day you will, though, you're one hell of a catch."

"Some catch. My hair's a rat's nest, my ribs are sticking out. I stink and I'm an emotional wreck."

"I knew what I was getting into, you left plenty of clues in that message. We'll stop this. No more dead heroes."

"There have been others?"

Shit, no point hiding it. "I fear so. But it ends here."

"How?"

Good question.

"Keep the faith, okay? I'll treat you to an amazing dinner when we're out of here. Put some meat on your bones. Or are you vegetarian?"

She laughed. "I'd kill for a steak."

His voice dropped even lower. "Could you kill for your freedom?"

There was a long pause. "After what they did to Andy? Bet your ass."

Chapter Sixty-Two

Aberdeen, Washington

Clara Nufeld marched into the editor's office and settled into a chair. "We've got trouble."

Ramona Williams looked up from her computer screen. "That damn TV guy, right? His story aired less than two days ago, and my inbox is jammed with outrage. Dozens of angry letters and emails, and you could roast marshmallows over the flaming posts on our website."

"What are they saying?"

"It's guilt by association. They blame us—me—for giving that Barnes guy the ammunition to crap all over Aberdeen and over our new doctor. I have to admit it's an interesting backstory tucked in the files, having a distant relative as a serial killer. But this jerk made it sound like she was complicit in those century-old murders. Pretty damned unfair."

"That's the reason we didn't run it," Clara said. "Jake dug up that information—he really is quite tenacious. He came to me and said 'I have this juicy information on our new doctor, but I'm not going to print it. It's irrelevant and it's unfair.' He handed me the file, and said, 'If you overrule me, I'll resign.' I wasn't about to let that happen. Besides, I agreed with him."

"Barnes said they're in a relationship, so Jake is in a conflict of interest, no?"

"They weren't in a relationship at the time." Clara laughed. "Though, frankly, if you meet her, you'd realize Jake was way too slow on the uptake. If anyone has a conflict, it's me. Tina is my doctor, and a damn good one."

Ramona buried her face in her hands. "I know, I know. The glowing testimonials on Doc Doctorow—that's what they all seem to call her—are flooding in. It's like she's a combination of saint and angel of mercy."

"I believe Jake was drawn to her more earthy attributes."

"Where is he?" Ramona asked. "I sent a *mea culpa* and got no response. He must be really angry."

"Nothing to do with you," Clara said. "Days ago, he told me he was heading out of town, chasing a piece he's working on dealing with missing Sedgewick medalists. The details were unclear to me, but I've never seen him so obsessed with a story. Said he was 'going dark,' but promised to be back for my wedding. Better be, or I'll kill him."

Relieved, Ramona blew out a breath. She tapped her computer screen to show two newspaper dummy pages, each subdivided into six standard columns and marked up with rough layouts.

Clara leaned in. "What's this for?"

"I want an ad-free two-page spread to let our readers vent. The one on the left will be their stirring defence of Aberdeen. On the right, their appreciation of Saint Doctorow."

Clara beamed approval. "I love it. I'll use my

publisher's prerogative and lead this off with a frontpage editorial defending my doctor and my hometown, while trashing that carpetbagging TV turd. I'll—"

She was interrupted by a rap on the open doorframe as Anna Mae led a weeping Amanda Shane into the room. Crumpled tissue in one hand, phone in the other. "Oh, Clara, what a mess I've made."

Clara held up her hand, stopping her as it appeared Anna Mae was in no hurry to leave. "Thank you, we'll take it from here," she said. "Please close the door on your way out."

Anna Mae harrumphed out, shutting the door with more force than necessary.

Clara patted the chair beside her. "Sit, dear. What on earth is the matter?"

"That bastard Trent," Amanda said, thrusting her phone at Clara. "He emailed this to Dr. Doctorow and copied me. And it's…it's not even true."

The email read: *"Your boyfriend is fucking my wife. Stop him, or I will."*

"Oh, shit." Clara's heart sank even before she viewed the attachments.

"I tried phoning Jake to make things right, but he won't take my call. Where is he?"

"I wish I knew, dear. Really, I do."

Chapter Sixty-Three

Clearfield County, Pennsylvania, September 1

The bolt rattled and the door opened. Kristy stood at the threshold, a paper bag in hand. Behind her and to the side, Brad stood, gun in one hand and a similar bag in the other. "Trial day," she said.

Jake pulled back the thin cover and sat up. He'd had a fitful sleep, his mind churning with doubts and fears.

He woke once during the night to Lyla's muffled sobs. He stopped himself from calling out because he couldn't think of anything that didn't sound impossibly trite. He had to get her out of here and deliver a hard stop to these assholes.

He asked himself the same question he'd posed to Lyla: could he kill? Sure. Maybe.

Who knew until the time came?

He looked up this morning at Brad, the guy he once pulled from a burning house and pounded life back into on the lawn. The same Brad who now held a gun on him. *Who knew until the time came?*

His gaze met Kristy's, searching in vain for a hint of humanity. He slipped on his shoes.

"You've got ten minutes to eat and use the bucket." With that, she turned and locked the door behind her.

The bag held a container of lukewarm coffee, a

congealed egg-and-sausage biscuit and a limp potato patty. Since last night's dinner consisted of a pepperoni stick, a bag of barbecue chips and a bottle of water, he wolfed it down.

He heard a knock on another door. "Good morning, Lyla," Brad said in a cheery voice. "I brought you breakfast." He sounded like a room-service waiter speaking to a treasured guest.

He was playing nice. Jake hoped the courteous treatment extended to microwaving her breakfast. His sat in his stomach like a partly masticated grease-ball. He could eat anything during all those years yanking oars. When six-thousand daily calories were the bare minimum, he'd appalled more than a few potential romantic interests by ordering, and inhaling, a second dinner before his date was through her main course.

He pulled the insole out of his left shoe, fiddled with what he found underneath, then tucked it for easy access between his ankle and the side of his runner.

****

He remembered to limp as they led him to a brightly lit second-floor room, zip-tying his arms to a heavy wooden chair. The restraints were unfortunate but getting out of that concrete-walled basement was a good thing. At least he hoped so.

He faced three chairs lined behind a table. Brad sat to his right, Kristy to his left.

An older man sat in the center chair. Jake put him at mid-sixties with a full head of graying hair and a neatly clipped beard. A collared white shirt and patterned tie peeked above what appeared to be an academic gown. Weird.

Two cameras on high stands stood behind the

three, the lenses focused on Jake.

"Good morning, Mr. Ockham. You may call me Dr. Dawes. You'll recall we've corresponded in the past."

Jake faked surprise, as if the realization just dawned on him. The fact that Dawes was really Stafford Crabtree was another detail to hold back.

"Before we begin, allow me to share the immutable rules of decorum for this court."

Jake snorted in disgust.

"Rule one," Dawes said, unruffled: "Any display of contempt for these hearings will be punished harshly. Rule two: you will not mention the proper names of your accusers during the televised proceedings. Three: there will be no mention of the geographic location of the tragic events of eleven years past. Nor will the name of the woman you let die pass your lips. Do you understand these rules, as described?"

Jake shrugged.

Dawes pulled off dark-rimmed glasses, revealing blue eyes blazing with electric madness. "The court interprets your silence as consent. Any breach of said rules results in the following sanctions. First violation: your fellow guest, Ms. Watkins, will be shot with a taser. Violation two: Ms. Watkins will be shot with a pistol in a non-lethal body part of our choosing. Violation three," he smiled. "Well, the rules of baseball apply to the third strike."

Jake said nothing.

"The court interprets your silence as consent," Dawes repeated. "Irregardless of the sanctions, it is futile to slip identifiers or sly messages into your testimony. These proceedings will be edited before they are released to our clients."

"Regardless," Jake said.

"Excuse me?"

"*Irregardless*, Doctor Dawes, is barely a word, and certainly not part of standard English. It is viewed with disdain by those with even a basic command of the language. Regardless is the accepted usage. I'll forgive your *faux pas*."

Dawes slammed on his glasses. "You border on contempt, Ockham. Final warning." He nodded to Kristy who activated the cameras and returned to her chair.

Dawes cleared his throat and intoned: "This court is in session. Seated before you, members of the jury, is Jake Ockham, accused of cowardice and criminal neglect causing death. That is correct, I said jury. In a departure from the past, it is you good citizens who will determine his guilt or innocence. At the end of this free and fair trial each of you will render your verdict. You vote by sending a thumbs-up emoji, or, if guilty, a thumbs-down—a modern application of an ancient Roman practice."

Jake recalled reading that in actual gladiatorial contests, thumbs-down was a signal to lower swords and cease battle. He'd save it for his appeal. *Yeah, as if.*

The judge, ridiculous in his old academic robe, read out what he called "an agreed statement of facts."

Not agreed to by him, that's for damn sure.

The statement was drawn from Kristy's rage-filled point of view. It started with the "witness" arriving on scene to find Jake "cowering" on the lawn with an unconscious young male, ignoring the frantic cries of a woman trapped in the burning house. Jake rejected pleas by the "witness" to save the woman, watching instead as she bled out, burned and died.

It made no mention of how the young male arrived on the lawn. Aware this would be broadcast to the twisted members of *Hero Hatr*, it omitted all names but Jake's, and made no reference to the kinship ties of the family or even the state where the fire occurred.

While Judge Dawes remained aloof and "impartial," Kristy peppered Jake with venomous leading questions. Jake gave nothing back but occasional eyerolls, whipping Kristy from fury to frenzy. Dawes, perhaps aware Kristy was red lining, ended the proceedings.

"Does the accused have anything to say?"

Jake, fighting to keep his anger in check, considered this for a moment. He looked to Brad, off-camera, who'd remained silent. "How are your legs? The left was the worst as I recall."

Brad, uncomfortable at the attention, looked to a Sphinx-like Dawes and then back to Jake. "Messed up."

Jake held up his hands, palms-out to the cameras. "Messed up like this? That's the thing about scars, they never let you forget. Do you wonder how messed up you'd be if not for these hands?"

Jake glared at Kristy. "Probably not, all those years she's brainwashed you."

He turned to Brad. "Do you recall how the fire started? I have a theory. A neglected pot on the stove probably held boiling oil, judging by the condition of the ceiling and the wall behind it. And the TV blaring in another room? Were you heating oil for wings or fries, busy watching the hockey pre-game show as the kitchen turned into a fireball?"

Kristy gasped.

A frantic looking Brad shook his head. "No, no, no. Not true!"

"Enough," shouted Dawes. "Enough lies. The accused will curb his tongue or face the consequences of contempt."

Jake, thinking of Lyla, tamped down his anger. Driving a wedge between brother and sister was a calculated risk. It may work to his advantage, or it could amp up the danger. He knew little about the pathology of psychopaths. He believed them predictable only to the extent they act with cunning and callous self-interest, and without remorse or control. All he could do was expect the worst and prepare.

"You must be ruthless. You must be evil if you are to survive," Erik advised on their last night together. "Bury that bleeding heart in cement, and pray your humanity survives when the time comes to chip it free."

He saw the concern in Erik's eyes. Or was it his own doubt reflected back?

Who knew until the time came?

After the kangaroo court, Dawes detoured them to his office on the same floor. With a malicious grin, he swept an arm toward five Sedgewick medals in a neat row on his desk. They were arrayed, name side up in alphabetical order: Zaki al-Jafari, Walter J Meely, Reginald R Obergon, Lyla S Watkins, Anderson K Wise.

Jake bowed his head. Any doubts about their fate were blown away. He stood rooted to the floor, paying respect.

"Can't collect the whole set, obviously," Dawes said with calculated indifference. "Just a sufficient number to cast a nice pair of candlesticks."

Jake turned, stumbling into a large vase of artificial flowers before pulling himself upright. "You're deranged, all of you."

Kristy ground the pistol into his back as he was led downstairs. He was surprised to be dumped into a shared cell, on Dawes' orders and against Kristy's wishes.

Dawes opened Lyla's cell with a flourish. "To put your mind at ease, dear, I had Brad make modifications." He gestured to two mattresses splayed on the floor. "He removed the cots, ending temptation to weaponize the frames. But," he added, with a magnanimous spread of arms, "there's the added perquisites of his-and-her buckets. We're not, after all, animals."

Dawes called the joint cell "a furtherance of the experiment that began with Lyla and Anderson." He discussed this in front of Lyla and Jake as if they were oblivious lab rats.

"The question to resolve: can we replicate the previous bonding experience of two disparate people, divided as they are by race, gender and, one senses, personality? I hypothesize that with the application of extreme pressure, it's entirely possible. I've already a working title for my monograph: *Friendship Forged By Fire: Peacetime Applications of the Foxhole Theory.*"

The show-trial left Dawes buoyant, but Kristy was in foul temper. She glared at Lyla. "In case you've forgotten, their bond got me gut-punched and tased by this bitch. Put that in your fucking paper."

"Oh, I have," he said with a smile. "It's the sort of telling example that could bring my findings into the mainstream. Under my pseudonym, of course."

Kristy glared at the prisoners. "I want them searched first."

"As you wish," Dawes said, moving toward Lyla.

"I've got her," Kristy said with an edge in her voice. "You do the gimp. He's so banged up he can't hardly walk, almost knocked over that big vase upstairs. Clumsy oaf."

She pulled Lyla's sweatshirt over her head and stripped off her bra, giving it a close examination before tossing it out the door. "It's got metal underwire propping up her tits, don't want her getting any ideas."

Jake turned his back to spare them both embarrassment as they were strip-searched. Dawes examined Jake's shoes and confiscated the cloth sling on his injured arm.

"A possible garrote," he said, in a display of vigilance meant for Kristy's benefit.

Satisfied, their captors left them alone. Jake said: "You *weaponized* a cot?"

"Andy smuggled in nail clippers from the shower, I don't ever want to know where he hid them. We used them to unscrew a support strut, which we jammed into Kristy's gut."

"And you tased her? Impressive."

"Enjoyed that, for all the good it did. Now we have nothing, no sling, and no bra, though I doubt anyone could weaponize those."

Jake considered the risk-reward of sharing plans with Lyla. Unravelling as they were, they would hardly send her spirits soaring. Still, she deserved a sliver of hope. As for what he'd planted in the vase upstairs, he'd keep that to himself for now. Instead, he'd give her something tangible.

He pulled the cast part way off his arm, reached in with the fingers of his right hand and extracted a thin, gauze-wrapped item about four inches long. He slipped the cast back on.

"A phone wouldn't fit, not that it would pick up a signal in this crypt anyway." He unwrapped the gauze. "So, we go low-tech with a skinny folding knife."

He flipped it open revealing a nasty little blade. He handed it to Lyla, who looked stunned. She slashed it from side to side. "So, your arm isn't broken?"

"Shush," he said, putting a finger to his lips. "Nine out of ten knife scientists consider pocketknives more lethal than a brassiere, and much easier to unclasp."

She folded the blade into the handle and gave it back. "What do we do with it?"

"I wish I knew."

Chapter Sixty-Four

Pittsburgh and Clearfield, Pennsylvania

Having passed his *Hero Hatr's* vetting, a truly creepy experience, Erik made three futile calls to Jake's room phone. Anxious, he used the key card and entered Jake's room, even if that risked blowing his cover.

No one was inside. A tipped over desk chair was the only sign of trouble. Three ways of tracking Jake's whereabouts—a GPS unit hidden in his tux and a burner phone sewn in the suitcase lining—sat on the bed. And his regular cell phone, wherever it was, gave off no signal. They had had other tenuous backups, but they weren't operational either. There could be several ulcer-inducing reasons for this.

Maybe the devices were discovered and destroyed. Maybe Jake was dead and buried. Maybe Jake was grabbed before he could activate them. They were to be turned on at the last moment due to their limited battery life. He'd go with the third scenario, it offered hope.

Relief of a sort came late the next day when he received an encrypted *Hero Hatrs* announcement of a forthcoming "interactive experience, the must-see trial of a fallen hero. You, the jury, will determine his guilt or innocence."

Jake was alive. Somewhere. There was a one-time charge for this "unique" offering: five thousand dollars in crypto currency. Erik paid…and waited, the forced inaction driving him mad.

****

It was mid-morning two days later when a GPS unit went live. *Finally*. It recorded a location in a rural area of Clearfield County. Erik checked out and booted it northeast, aiming for the borough of Clearfield, the county seat. He made the trip in under two hours, thanks to a recently purchased radar detector.

The signal he tracked on his phone's GPS app remained stationary. He drove through Clearfield, bore left on Route 322 and followed the signal down a series of increasingly sketchy country roads. He cruised past a gravel drive that may lead to Jake's location, or at least that of his GPS. No buildings were visible from the road.

He drove a mile farther on the potholed two-lane and saw a possible forest access to the property. Tipping his hand at this stage would be disastrous. Reluctantly, he retraced his route to Clearfield, looking for a quiet place to think.

The town was pretty enough, if not terribly prosperous. There were rows of modest homes on tiny lots, and some grand, old-money brick houses. Erik saw himself settling into a calm, quiet, service-club life here—until he'd jump screaming off the Market Street Bridge. He found a coffee shop beside a river that cut a winding path through downtown.

A waitress, early thirties but with the resigned look of a lifer, delivered his coffee and a surprisingly fine *pain au chocolat*.

"It's a lovely river," he said, thinking of the Market Street Bridge. "Is it deep?"

She looked him over, making no secret she enjoyed the view. "Not terribly deep, it tends to flood. It's the Susquehanna." Without being asked she added, "that's S-u-s-q-u-e-h-a-n-n-a, it's an Indian name. Not from these parts, huh?"

"Passing through. Know any places to stay, maybe a good B and B? I'm sick of hotels."

She brightened, swiped back an errant lock of blonde hair and looked across the room. "Got just the spot. Let me take that table's order, then I'll get you the details."

She returned with a slip of paper listing an address and two phone numbers. "It's my great aunt's house, just up the road near the Historical Society," she explained. "It's a big old pile. When my great uncle died, she turned it into a bed-and-breakfast to pay the bills. She's got two rooms upstairs, and a suite with a separate entrance. Makes a fine breakfast."

"Super. She have Wi-Fi?"

"All the mod-cons." She leaned close. "Confidentially, take the suite if it's available. I love her to bits, but aunty will talk your ears off. She volunteers at the Historical Society and knows this county—in excruciating detail. Honestly, we aren't that interesting."

"Oh, I don't know, the people seem nice. Well, based so far on a sample of one."

She blushed. "I'm Greer. Auntie is Mabel." She tapped the paper. "Her number's on top. The second is mine. Just, you know, if you have any questions."

Erik dialed his smile to a solid eight. "Greer, you're a gift from the gods. It sounds perfect."

And it was. Worth every cent of the extravagant tip

he'd tucked under his cup.

He'd wanted a B and B because the operators were invariably outgoing and proud to share a wealth of local knowledge. Mabel took this to another level.

She lived in a red-brick monster complete with a widow's walk jutting above the second floor. The house looked like it was built by a landlocked old salt pining for the sea.

As advertised, Mabel could yak. By the time they'd polished off the wine, a wholly unnecessary bottle of lubricant he'd brought along, Erik knew Clearfield's history in granular detail, the latest updates on the wayward preacher's wife and the vice principal, and finally…dear lord, finally…the saga of Fairview Farm.

Fairview was the home of Norm Morrison, a prosperous implement salesman and part-time farmer, and his wife, Beatrice Crabtree Morrison. "Both have gone to their reward." She said Fairview is now occupied by Beatrice's son, Stafford, and two adopted adult offspring.

"The less said about Stafford the better," said Mabel. Meaning it took a mere fifteen minutes to work root-and-branch through decades of rumor, innuendo and "monkey business."

He bade Mabel goodnight and walked to a nearby pizza joint. He ordered a wild mushroom and truffle oil pizza and contemplated how simple life would have been had they known Morrison was the surname of Beatrice's second husband. Much preferable to blundering around forty-six thousand square miles of Pennsylvania looking for a widow named Beatrice.

Stafford kept his name off the property and tax rolls, most likely by leaving the farm in his mother's name or by transferring ownership to a numbered company.

His phone vibrated with a WhatsApp message as his pizza arrived. The pizza was delicious, the message, cryptic: "The trial you requested airs at 9 p.m. EDT tomorrow and is available for replay in our archives."

He assumed Jake was the star attraction. And since the audience served as jury, he'd certainly be kept alive for the verdict—a foregone conclusion. The sentence would be carried out later in another promised episode. That gave him time, but how much?

As an inducement to sign with *Hero Hatr*, Erik was shown an edited teaser of Lyla and Anderson bound in chairs for their "final countdown."

The level of insanity he detected in the three anonymous voices—animals he now knew, who kidnapped, tortured and killed Jake's heroes—forced Erik to rethink his rescue plans. Calling in the authorities too soon to storm the location could easily end in a Waco-style siege of fire, murder, and suicide.

****

Erik shared Mabel's breakfast table the next morning with a retired couple from Philadelphia, happy to let them carry the conversational load. He excused himself and walked the streets and the river paths, worried and lost in thought. He returned to the coffee shop for a light lunch and some harmless flirtation with Greer, thanking her extravagantly for "the gift of Mabel."

She rolled her eyes. "A gift that keeps on giving, for darn sure."

The day dragged. Erik picked at an early dinner. He needed better intel before calling in the cavalry.

Were Jake and the GPS tracker in the same location? Was he with Lyla—if she's alive? *Give me a sign, Jake.*

At seven o'clock he was back in his room, grateful for the private entrance. He made a pre-arranged call to his main squeeze in Seattle whom he affectionately called "the boy genius," though he was just three days younger than Erik's thirty-three years.

"Hey, Rafael, miss me?"

They reprised their week, then Erik got to business.

He met Rafael Pérez months ago at a hacker's convention. He is a civilian employee at a U.S. Navy research lab. Few know the Dark Web is one of the Navy's creations and continues to be one of its funders. It was conceived to give the navy untraceable access to intel in foreign ports and hostile countries. And it's an invaluable free-speech forum for dissidents in oppressive regimes.

Those roles are considered so important the U.S. military helps underwrite such things as a highly encrypted gateway into the site. As Erik told Jake: "think of it as a manhole into a vast sewer. While sewers perform a vital function, one is required to hold one's nose."

Or as Rafael put it: "Yeah, we created a monster. But it's our monster."

While Erik was reasonably conversant on the Dark Web, he scribbled notes for twenty minutes as Rafael gave a master class on gaming the skeevy members of *Hero Hatr*.

"Thanks, my dear," Erik concluded. "I'll make this up to you in ways that will register on the Richter Scale."

"Happy to help. The U.S. Navy: taking out the

trash since 1775. Ciao, baby, come home safe."

****

Just before nine that night, he punched the coordinates and passwords into his laptop. A faceless voice announced the start of Jake's "trial."

He was relieved to see he looked no worse than when he'd left him. Erik admired his handiwork. The facial bruising and black eye were turning vivid blues and purples. He caught a glimpse of Jake's intact cast, that was good, too.

Five minutes in, Jake blinked twice in rapid succession.

Erik pumped his fist.

Jake repeated this twice more during the hour-long farce of a trial.

What seemed a nervous tick signalled he was with Lyla, and they were safe—for the moment. Had he hunched shoulders into his neck it would have meant "come in guns blazing and get us out asap."

"Your call, buddy," Erik muttered. "I hope you're right."

The trial ended and the disembodied voice of the judge announced the jury's verdict: Unanimous thumbs-down, guilty as charged. Erik, maintaining his cover, voted with the pack.

"Sentencing will be broadcast shortly," the judge said. "It will mark the return of Lyla, a fan favorite from two past episodes. Stay tuned, friends, it will be unforgettable."

Erik heaved a sigh. "I hope so, you crazy fuck."

Chapter Sixty-Five

The fight raged for hours after Jake's "trial."

Locked in their cell, they heard doors slam, muffled shouts from Brad, and Kristy's penetrating shrieks.

"Like a fishwife on amphetamines," Jake said. "A voice that can peel wallpaper."

Lyla looked puzzled. "She screamed something about 'Mom' and then 'fucking French fries.' I don't get it?"

"It means I may have guessed right," he said, looking upward. "I accused Brad, on shaky evidence, of starting the fire that killed their mother. The house was so gutted the cause of the blaze was never determined. I've written too many stories about unattended pots of oil starting housefires. There was a pot on what was left of the stove that day. I went with the odds."

Lyla cringed as they heard the crash of shattered glass. "Was that wise?"

"Don't know. I thought it useful to drive a wedge into this creepy family unit."

At her skeptical look, he added, "Yeah, I know. A calculated risk."

The risk backfired at three a.m. when the door's bolt rattled open. Brad, swaying and reeking of booze, loomed in the doorway. He had a cut under his right eye and a gun in hand.

He waved a fistful of plastic zip ties. "Truss up this lying fucker," he told Lyla. Glaring at Jake, he slurred, "Total bullshit. Prolly jess bad wiring in that shitty old house." He leered at Lyla. "You 'n' me takin' a road trip. Jump the gun, have some fun." He waved the pistol. "Before judge Dad passes sentence today."

Jake turned on his side away from Brad, eased down his cast and slipped her the knife. "No mercy."

She tucked it up her sleeve before binding Jake.

Brad checked the straps, hog-tied Jake's arms and legs, then stuffed a rag in Jake's mouth, securing it with duct tape. He looked to Lyla. "Take that mattress, don't want splinters on that sweet ass."

Jake heard a quiet sob as the bolt on the door slid home. He cursed his stupidity. His accusation over the cause of that long-ago house fire triggered a fight that sent Brad off the rails.

It took some minutes to struggle off the mattress and worm his way to the door. Using his bound legs, he pounded with such ferocity it crashed and rattled and the cell walls shook.

Chapter Sixty-Six

Washington County, Pennsylvania.

Brad gagged Lyla and led her from the basement. "Had enough female bitchin' for a lifetime."

He hauled her to his large sedan, a clapped-out former taxi. He popped the trunk, arranged the mattress and ordered her inside. He was pissed that she didn't bring the extra zip ties.

Not bloody likely, she thought. She'd hidden them under Jake's mattress.

"No inside trunk release," he said, "so don't get your hopes up."

The trunk was hot, dark and had a faint reek of exhaust. She felt every bump on the long drive, and every heart-stopping rumble as Brad strayed onto gravel shoulders. She prayed an alert cop would pull him over for a sobriety check, but she heard few vehicles at this ungodly hour.

She used every inch of the enormous truck for modified yoga poses, certain her very survival depended on keeping her muscles from cramping. Finally, the car slowed to a stop. Brad opened the trunk and grinned at her.

She scrambled out, refusing his help with an elbow jab. "I have to pee."

"Me, too. Like a friggin' racehorse. Squat behind

that tree, I won't peek."

She took in her surroundings in the faint light of a false dawn. Cornfields stretched dark and menacing behind her. Far to her right was a weed-covered mound of rubble. To her left was a two-level barn with a sway-backed roof and a wet spot on its wall where Brad relieved himself.

He zipped his fly and waved toward the weed pile. "Our family home. Best years of my life until fuckin' Jake let Ma burn."

"He saved your life."

"Sis says he curled up on the lawn, too scared to save her. She saw it all."

He pulled the mattress from the trunk. "Plan is, we're shooting a re-enactment for the web."

He waved toward the top of the barn. "You're up there. Jake's down here. He can try to save you if he has the balls or get hisself shot if he doesn't. Got a county burn permit so the fire department will leave us be."

He moved in close, still holding the mattress. "Figure we've got two good hours before Kristy and Dad notice we're gone. Left a note saying we'll be here, ready and waiting. Two hours to get to know each other."

She stepped toward him, arms behind her back. "Go out with a bang, huh?"

He leered. "That's the idea."

She lashed out, slamming the short-bladed knife into his side. It felt like she might have hit a rib the way the knife bounced back.

She'd inflicted a shallow wound at best, but still he howled in rage and pain.

She slashed at his arm. He screamed. She struck again, but Brad, coming to his senses, used the mattress as a shield. Blade and mattress fell to the ground.

Lyla made a feint toward the knife, then buried her right foot into his crotch. He gasped and crashed to the ground.

Brad struggled to his knees, bloodied and enraged. She looked at the brightening sky and plunged into the cornfield. Dawn was close. Brad was closer.

A pistol shot cracked the quiet. Brad was playing for keeps. Her uncle farmed, she knew the shot wouldn't draw attention in an isolated rural community where varmint control was both necessity and recreation.

They crashed through the corn in a nerve-shredding game of cat-and-mouse. He likely knew these fields from childhood and seemed to have an unerring instinct for cutting off her attempts to reach the bordering country lanes or the highway. The tall, full stalks obliterated her sense of direction, like being caught in a maze. She curled in a shallow hollow, her chest heaving, trying to get a read on Brad's location as he smashed on, trailing curses and threats.

His voice grew louder. Stay still or make a break?

She had to chance it.

She plucked a cob and hurled it as far as she could from a crouching position. She saw him give chase. She waited a moment, then stole quietly in the opposite direction, toward the faint crescendo of a motorcycle running up its gears.

She had to flag down a vehicle, but progress was slow. He'd soon realize he'd been duped.

She broke into a run, flying now as leaves and

woody stalks tore at her.

The highway hum grew louder. There was hope—until her right foot landed in a gopher hole. Her ankle twisted as she slammed to the ground, cursing herself for an involuntary cry that betrayed her location.

He was on her in an instant and delivered a vicious kick to her back before hauling her upright. He rained down curses as he dragged her to the barn, and up a set of steps to the hayloft.

Brad's shirt was bloodied, but her half-hearted attack accomplished little. She lacked the stomach for the ugly intimacy of a kill. His throat had been exposed, but her moment's hesitation in the yard spared his life. His wounds were superficial. Her kick had only stoked his rage.

He slapped and punched now, teeth bared in a rictus of a smile. She fought back but he seemed impervious to her punches. He yanked down her sweatpants and was pulling at her shirt when she heard a vehicle skid to a stop outside.

He threw her to the rough plank floor and peered down from an access hatch. "Goddamit," he muttered before switching to an ingratiating tone. "Hey, Dad. Toss me a rope. I got Lyla up here all ready for ya."

Chapter Sixty-Seven

Clearfield, Pennsylvania

The tracking app alarm roused Erik from a light sleep. It was three-thirty in the morning, and he faced a conundrum: The alarm meant the second GPS unit—the one hidden in Jake's cast—was finally online. Now there were two operational units to track, but their locations diverged.

The wafer-thin unit they'd tucked under the insole of Jake's left shoe beamed a stationary location at Fairfield farm where Crabtree and his adopted kids lived. The second showed movement heading southwest toward Clearfield. Still undecided which beacon would lead to Jake, he scrambled into his clothes and grabbed the keys to his rental. He'd made a series of calls last night. Skeptical local cops and the FBI, after much convincing, planned a mid-morning raid on Fairview Farm, the earliest they insisted they could assemble the necessary numbers and equipment in this rural part of the state.

This middle-of-the-night action changed everything. Was Jake on the move or was this a diversion? The second GPS unit was headed away from the farm into central Clearview. He raced to intercept, reaching State Route 879—the southern road out of town—as a white van flashed past. It was too dark, and he was too distant to make out who was inside.

He gambled on the van, fuming as he was caught behind a lumbering gasoline tanker as they merged onto the highway. He was falling behind the GPS, which had to be in the van, one of few vehicles on the road. Praying Jake was inside, he swept around the tanker, and soon saw the red pinpricks of the van's taillights. He eased off the gas and let them disappear, content to follow at a safe distance. He was committed now, for better or worse.

Erik's calls to the raid commanders went unanswered. He left messages warning half the team may have to deploy to a still unknown destination. He drove on.

Chapter Sixty-Eight

Chaos erupted after Jake's pounding on the cell door drew Kristy and Crabtree to the basement. Their mood improved only slightly after they discovered Brad's note and learned his destination. Wherever they were headed, it seemed Brad had accelerated, rather than sabotaged, their plans.

They bound Jake again with plastic ties and tossed him into their van. He shared the interminable ride with a single video camera, the slosh and stink of six ten-gallon red gas cans, and the sickening fear that he was too late to save Lyla.

"Gonna mess up that dumb bastard real bad," Kristy raged about Brad during the drive. She'd turned to Jake on the floor of the van and waved toward the red plastic cans. "Those are a little something I picked up on the Dark Web," she'd told Jake, as though sharing a cookie recipe. "Gasoline, diesel and glycerine. They call it 'poor man's napalm.' "

The forces Jake unleashed by blaming Brad for the fire had only amped the risk to himself and Lyla. He'd hoped to wake up to a police raid at Fairview Farm, praying they'd keep clear of any crossfire. Now, the ability to pivot to a new plan depended on a pile of assumptions out of his hands.

Had Erik cracked into the *Hero Hatr* site? Were the GPS units working?

He had some faith in the one he'd slipped in the decorative vase when he pretended to stumble after the trial. He doubted the one hidden in his cast penetrated the bunker-like cellar to signal a satellite. Now, out in the open, he hoped its battery, activated two days ago, still had juice and was operational.

A plan teetering on a foundation of too many shoulds and maybes risked collapse, with Lyla trapped in its wreckage.

The scene greeting Jake as he was pulled from the van made a twisted sort of sense. He recognized the barn and gave an involuntary shudder as he turned to the weed-covered rubble, so different than the bloodied, burning farmhouse that haunted too many of his nights over the years.

Kristy saw his look of recognition and spat at his feet. She noticed he'd used the camera's tripod during the drive to pry the ties off his legs. "I suppose it's fair you have a fighting chance to save your damsel in distress."

She reared back and bared her teeth as Brad poked his head out of the barn's upper hatch and asked for a rope. "Moron," she said in a low growl.

Her brother emerged five minutes later looking sheepish. "Got her trussed like a chicken."

Crabtree looked without sympathy at Brad's soiled, bloody shirt as they wrestled the heavy fuel containers out of the van. "To paraphrase Winston Churchill, that's some chicken."

"And my brother," Kristy said with a cold smirk, "is some fuck-up."

Brad pulled the folding knife out of a pocket of his cargo pants. "The bitch stuck me with this." He jerked his head toward Jake. "Must have got it from him. Probably hid it up his ass."

"And damned uncomfortable it was," Jake said.

Kristy gave Jake a long, hard look. "Bullshit."

She grabbed the knife from Brad, sliced the ties off Jake's arms. She worked the blade under his cast, sawing with a vengeance until it split open. A black plastic square fell to the ground. She handed it to her father and ordered Jake to sit.

Crabtree blanched. "A GPS unit, for all the good it did." He stomped it to pieces and clapped his hands. "Ten minutes to showtime."

Kristy handed the knife to her brother, trading it for his pistol. "Watch him while we get ready. Can you do that without screwing up?"

She set up the camera and tripod with practiced ease before helping Crabtree soak the hay and wooden support beams with the contents of all six cans. There was no sign of Erik, Jake had to slow things down.

With two of his captors still in the barn, Jake scooped sand and gravel in both hands and rose to his feet. Brad took the bait and charged with the knife. Jake flung the handfuls of grit in Brad's face. With him temporarily blinded, Jake eluded his first clumsy blow. He danced back, knowing he had to relax. Systema was all about fluidity, easier to accomplish in practice than reality. Jake moved into Brad's attack, grabbing the knife in both hands, using his momentum to sweep it out of danger. But he failed to kick out Brad's legs.

Emboldened, Brad attacked again. Jake saw Kristy and Crabtree running from the barn. He had no hope of overpowering all three captors, he was playing for time. *Where was Erik?*

This time Jake managed to turn the power of Brad's clumsy charge to send them crashing to the ground, his elbow slamming into Brad's throat.

Brad gasped for breath and Jake tore the knife from his hands. On his knees, he straddled Brad and raised the knife, seething with fury. He heard the pistol shot as a bullet punched his right arm.

As the knife fell, the pain came in waves. He was powerless to stop Brad's next assault. Yet, there was no movement beneath him, just the warm sensation of liquid as Brad emptied his bladder, soaking Jake's pants.

Kristy was wide-eyed, her mouth moving without forming words.

Jake rolled to his back beside Brad. Both of them still. Both of them staring at the sky. Only one alive to track the drifting clouds.

Stunned, Jake worked out the angles. The bullet had ripped through his bicep before burying itself in Brad's forehead.

"Fuck me," Kristy said in a whisper. "Brad, this is on you."

Jake panted and closed his eyes, trying to quell the pain. Crabtree rushed over and choked out a muffled "Jesus Christ." Then an anguished, "What do we do, Baby? What do we do?"

After a pause, Kristy said: "Brad was weak, maybe it's for the best. Help me drag him into the barn."

Jake heard a gasp, a strangled cry, and then Kristy's voice, hard and thick with contempt. "Hurry, Daddy. We gotta move. Brad left Lyla tied in the loft, haul the little video camera up there to stream her final moments—at least until it melts."

They dumped Brad's body inside. Jake, watching from the yard, saw a dazed Crabtree turn his back on his adopted son and head for the loft, looking like a whipped puppy.

Jake struggled upright. He retrieved the knife he'd hidden beneath his body after it dropped, then cut off his bloody sleeve to fashion a tourniquet, for all the good that would do.

Kristy waved the gun. "Drop the knife, asshole."

After he obeyed, she kicked it into the weeds.

Jake blew it. Everything had gone to hell. Lyla would pay with her life.

Kristy turned the van around, ready for a quick get-away. Brad's car stayed where it was. Jake surmised she'd pin the blame for the fire on her late brother.

"All set." A muffled voice came from the loft. "I'm going out the back, light it up."

"Took long enough," Kristy muttered. She wrapped a gas-soaked rag around a rock, sparked it with a lighter and tossed the flaming ball into the barn.

It erupted with a woof that almost knocked her off her feet. "Fuckin' amazing." She checked her watch. "Eight minutes and we're packed up and outta here."

She tucked the pistol in the waist of her jeans, picked up a hand-held camera and walked toward Jake. "Here's your chance, big boy, show us whatcha got."

Chapter Sixty-Nine

Erik cruised past the farm drive, tucked the car into a nearby tractor access, and crept back through the corn. Flat on his belly at the edge of the field, he took in the scene. He assumed Lyla was locked in the barn. A camera on a tripod was ready to record Jake's attempt to save her. Both were as good as dead, entertainment for an audience of degenerates.

Erik redialed the last number on his call list. This time the raid commander picked up. "What now?"

"I've eyes on Jake Ockham," Erik said. "He is not at Fairview Farm. Repeat, he's *not* there. They've moved him two-and-a-half hours southwest. I think Lyla Watkins is here, too. Can't confirm that." He read out the GPS coordinates.

"Chrissake, Demidov, we've just got the local cops in the fields staking out Fairview and a fuckin' SWAT army rolling north. You got us running around like headless chickens. Best case, we're an hour out from your location."

Like it was his fault these loonies had moved Jake.

"Not good enough," Erik said, keeping his voice low though he wanted to rage in frustration. "It's going down now. They're armed and they're going to torch a barn, with Jake, and probably Lyla, inside it. I'll try to slow things down but—"

"Okay. Fuck. Okay. I'll call in the locals. The cops

338

or sheriffs, whoever patrols out there. You stay clear, you're no fuckin' superhero."

"Hurry." Erik cut the connection and set his phone to silent.

He wanted to rush the three but the odds were against him, especially with at least one pistol in view. And Jake's priority was Lyla.

Staying low, Erik stole around to the back of the barn, relieved to see a secondary access. He slipped inside, using hay bales for cover as he made a quick reconnoitre. Seeing nothing, he crept up the stairs.

Lyla was tied to a support beam, wide-eyed with terror. Putting a finger to his lips, he flashed one of his thousand-watt smiles. She nodded in frantic agreement. He tore at the knots and pointed her to a hiding spot behind a wall of bales. He then crept to the front access hatch.

Shit, shit, shit. Jake was wrestling with Brad.

He held his own but his Systema form was rusty. Jake finally grabbed the knife and raised his arm to strike. Erik had time for a fleeting worry about Jake's ability to handle the trauma of a kill when Kristy raised the gun and fired.

Jake rolled on his back. Erik closed his eyes, muttering curses, vowing revenge.

After an agonizing moment, Jake struggled upright. He fashioned a crude tourniquet. Brad was deathly still, a dark pool under his head.

One down.

Kristy and a panicked Crabtree dragged Brad's body into the barn.

The air reeked of gas fumes. Erik heard Kristy order her father to take a camera to the loft, treating him like a dimwitted child. Erik grabbed a shovel and waited out of sight near the top of the stairs.

He didn't waste words on Crabtree. The blade gave a hollow *thunk* as it met skull at full velocity.

Two down.

He dragged Crabtree's inert form behind some bales. Alive or dead he didn't much care, but Lyla didn't need to see it. He'd grown to hate the man after hours on that website listening to his unctuous, condescending voice.

Erik put his gift as a mimic to good use. "All set," he called from behind the hatch. "I'm going out the back, light it up."

Lyla leaned against him as she hobbled down the stairs in obvious pain, the fuel fumes making them dizzy. They stood far behind the barn as the gas ignited with an explosive *woof.* Flames consumed the building with ferocious hunger. Erik gave it another beat then made a quick phone call.

"Locals are five minutes out," the raid commander said.

He cut the connection and ignited his smile. "I'm Erik, Jake's friend, pleased to meet you."

Lyla smiled, then put a hand to her mouth in alarm. "How is he?"

"He's upright, I'll give him that," said Erik, who'd made a covert check around the shell of the blazing barn. "Let's put his mind at ease."

They walked arm-in-arm to the front drive, well out of pistol range, unless Kristy was a crack shot. Which seemed unlikely.

Jake, swaying on his feet, saw them first. He slumped with relief and summoned a wan smile.

Kristy's hand flew to her mouth as she saw them, and the realization hit.

"He's upstairs," Erik shouted, he and Lyla keeping their distance. "Might want to do something about that." A rising chorus of distant sirens carried on the morning air.

"You bastard," she screamed, turning the gun on Erik.

He took a deep breath, signaling Lyla to stay. Feeling neither heroic nor super, he moved closer. "What are you going to do, Kristy, kill all three of us? Try explaining that."

She swore and ran toward the fire, but the intense heat drove her back. She gathered her cameras, a laptop and gun, and threw them into the barn. She sat on the ground, arms hugging her knees, and watched the flames.

Looking shaky, Jake walked to his friends. He nodded thanks to Erik and gave a weeping Lyla a cautious one-armed hug. "Sorry, I'm a bloody mess, drenched in various bodily fluids."

Erik wrinkled his nose. "Your bag is in my rental. I'll do us all a favor and get you fresh clothes."

Overlapping sirens built to a welcome cacophony.

Erik said, "So our stories are straight, here's how this played out…"

They nodded in agreement. Much of it was true and the rest was reasonably credible. There would be no mention that it was Erik, not Crabtree, who shouted "light it up."

The volume and intensity of Kristy's wails escalated as first-responders raced up the lane. She stayed seated, her head swinging back and forth as if waging an internal argument.

"Polishing her script," Jake speculated. Perhaps a fraction of her anguish was true, the rest was reasonably credible.

Two fire trucks were first on scene. With no available water-source fire fighters attached their hoses to their one, inadequate tanker truck. The intense heat from the blazing fuel-soaked hay and the dry timbers evaporated the streams of water into a foul-smelling steam.

Erik told the fire captain there were two bodies inside.

"Ah, shit," the captain shouted above the roar of the inferno. "This is totally out of control. We're low on water, and even if my guys could get near, I wouldn't risk them. This damn thing is gonna come down."

Other emergency vehicles had pulled into the yard, parking well back from the choking smoke and raining embers.

Two sheriff's deputies rushed to Kristy and led her back from the flames. She fell weeping into the arms of the younger male deputy who seemed highly motivated to offer solace. The older deputy began taking notes.

Erik and Jake watched the scene unfold. "She's playing him like a violin," Jake said.

"And road-testing her *daddy-made-me-do-it* alibi, I expect," Erik replied.

The barn had taken a precarious lean as burning ground-floor support beams, weakened and twisted by the heat, began to fail. Jake shivered despite the heat. Erik expected he was reliving an earlier fire. The three stepped farther back from the inferno. Jake swayed and eased to the ground, too weak to stand.

"Sorry," Erik said. "There was nothing I could do. I died a thousand deaths when Kristy shot you."

"I feel your pain." Jake looked to Lyla. "I take it Erik introduced himself?"

"My guardian angel," she said.

Erik grinned.

Jake said: "Half that is true."

Two paramedics divided their time between dressing Jake's bullet wound and wrapping Lyla's badly sprained ankle. They sat her in a wheelchair and tended to the many cuts and bruises Brad had inflicted during his wild assault.

Lyla borrowed a cell phone from one of the paramedics. She punched in a number, waited a beat as the person answered. "Hi, Mom," she choked out before bursting into tears. She hunched her shoulders and collected herself. "I'm fine. I just don't sound like it...No, I'm not on my honeymoon, not even close." She was laughing and crying at once. "Do you think I'd get married without you?"

There was a long pause, her mystified mother, no doubt, peppering her with questions. "Now Mom, don't cry, you'll only get me going again...Hey, you remember Jake, Jake Ockham, that nice boy from the newspaper who wrote that story about me way back when? Yeah, that big white boy..."

She rolled her eyes and turned to Jake, who smiled and waved. "He's here with me. He says hello...No, Mom, I'm not marrying him either."

She and Jake were laughing now. "We've got lots to talk about when I get home. Love you, Mom. Bye."

Erik was speaking on his phone to the raid commander. He heard sirens wailing as his team pounded hell-for-leather down rural roads toward the fire. He cut the connection. "Too late and a dollar short," he told Jake. "On the plus side, the secondary team now has a search warrant to rip apart Fairfield Farms."

He offered Jake his phone, but he waved it off. "Anything I want to say, I'll say in person."

Another ambulance skidded to a stop, cutting its siren and lights.

The two paramedics emerged, took in the scene, and strolled over to their colleagues, and to the woman seated in a wheelchair and the man now loaded on a wheeled stretcher.

A black guy. A white guy. Pepper and salt.

The larger of the two peered at the stretcher and turned to his partner. "Well, well. What are the odds?" He leaned over Jake. "Must be, what, ten, eleven years since our last encounter?" He gently inspected the scarred palm on Jake's uninjured arm, and nodded approval. "Not bad, all things considered."

Jake looked up, his pale face breaking into a grin. He turned to Erik and Lyla. "Allow me to introduce Hank and Frank, they're semi-famous in these parts."

Lyla left in the first ambulance. Hank and Frank insisted on transporting Jake to hospital. Erik stayed behind, bracing for the inevitable interrogation.

Behind him, the barn—with groans and snaps and roars of tortured timber—collapsed upon itself like a fallen diva. Smoke billowed up, and sparks cascaded down in an operatic finale.

Chapter Seventy

Aberdeen, Washington.

They touched down in Seattle, four hours before
Clara and Roger's big event. Jake called a hard stop to
further police questioning the night before. "I've given
you everything. My father and my aunt are getting
married tomorrow, I will not miss it."

"To each other?" a detective asked.

"Naturally," Jake said, offering no further
explanation.

They taxied to Erik's condo where Rafael waited.
Jake watched them embrace, his first look at the boy
genius. Erik, as always, went top shelf: Rafael was lean
and tall with dark Mediterranean good looks. Erik
reloaded his suitcase and donned a sleek grey Italian-
made suit.

Jake was unable to handle his stick shift with his
arm in a sling so Erik drove them to Aberdeen. Rafael
followed in Erik's SUV.

Jake was on the phone assuring his father he'd
make it to the church on time. Actually, to the wood-
panelled office of a justice of the peace, a family friend.
There were just two witnesses to the ceremony: Jake
and Em Watson, Clara's best friend and contract bridge
partner.

Eyebrows were raised when Jake arrived in his

rented tux, accessorized with arm sling and assorted facial bruising. "Long story," he said, waving off their concern.

Never one to waste money, he handed Clara the necklace purchased as a prop in Pennsylvania for Lyla's fake wedding. Clara slipped it on, dropping into her purse a set of pearls easily worth ten times as much.

"Sorry, Dad, didn't get a chance to shop for you."

Roger straightened Jake's tie. "Your arrival, almost in one piece, is present enough."

While the wedding was intimate, Clara's community standing dictated a reception at the Elks Lodge for a brutally culled guestlist of eighty, complete with dinner, open bar, and DJ.

"I hope you don't mind," Jake told Clara in the taxi to the hall. "I invited Erik's boyfriend, Rafael. Shouldn't change the seat count since I'm going stag."

"It's all good, dear," she said, fingering her necklace.

The hall was a rocking wall of noise when they arrived, Roger having ensured the bar opened early. It took five minutes to work through back-slaps, hugs, and handshakes. Erik caught his eye from a table across the room and gave a wolfish grin.

Clara and Roger led him to their six-top table. Ramona and Anna Mae were seated beside a woman with her back to the door. A woman in an elegant off-the-shoulder dress that revealed a familiar mole.

As he sat beside her, she turned with a tentative smile. "I hope you don't mind, Clara insisted."

He shook his head, groping for words. "God, Tina, you're beautiful."

They gazed at each other with silly smiles.

"Sorry," they said, simultaneously. Then they laughed.

And then they both said, "No, I'm sorry." And they smiled some more.

"A delegation of three women appeared at my office last week," Tina said and nodded toward Clara and Ramona at the table. "And Amanda, who's quite the dish, reminds me of someone famous but the name escapes me. They made me see the error of my ways." She looked across the hall. "And Erik just gave what I fear is a sanitized version of your adventures."

A flute of bubbly trembled in her hand. "I phoned about a thousand times, but you never answered."

"Would you believe a van ran over my phone?"

She nodded. A tear rolled down her cheek. Jake dabbed it with his napkin. "Sorry," she said. "I always cry at weddings." She took in his battered face and wounded arm as if for the first time, and lightly touched the hand poking from his sling. "You look like a med-school practice patient."

"Sorry about that."

Clara choked on her drink. "That's four 'sorries' in five minutes. You sound like a couple of Canadians."

Clara gave Roger, Ramona and Anna Mae the high sign. They rose to mingle or refill at the bar. Tina and Jake, heads together, barely noticed.

****

Dinner over, and Jake's heartfelt toast delivered, Roger and Clara started the first dance. They moved as one. It seemed to Jake so darn…right. Somewhere, his mother was smiling.

Tina pulled Jake to the dance floor. Erik and Rafael followed and soon the floor was awhirl as the DJ, reading the room well, plucked tunes from Motown to Mumford and Sons to, naturally, Nirvana.

There were fine dancers amid the plodders but none, absolutely none, came close to the animal grace of Erik and Rafael. When they finally left the floor to recharge their glasses, the crowd broke into spontaneous applause, Jake splitting the air with a two-fingered whistle.

Erik, drink in hand, chatted up the DJ. She grinned, nodded and gave a high-five.

When the time came, Erik introduced the night's last song. "Friends know I'm a huge David Bowie fan. I want to share tonight my favorite of his songs, one that reveals new depths with every listen. Bowie wrote this in Berlin, inspired by two lovers who'd meet beneath the gun turrets of that dreaded wall dividing east and west. 'Heroes' is a song of yearning, a song of love, a song of the unquenchable thirst for freedom. I dedicate it tonight to everyday heroes everywhere. You know who you are."

The dance floor filled. Tina moved in close. Jake asked: "Is this, technically, a slow dance?"

She said: "Shut up and hold me."

They swayed, Jake doing his best with a busted wing, Tina humming the melody.

His ear warmed with her whisper. "I know who you are."

Chapter Seventy-One

Aberdeen, Washington, January 2020

Christmas came and went. Clara marked the new year with an early move to Bend. "You've got this publisher thing figured, more or less," she told Jake. "And I miss Roger."

Kristy was in prison. His and Lyla's sworn depositions saw to that, together with the damning videos Erik plucked from the Dark Web.

As the sole beneficiary of Crabtree's estate, Kristy had the best legal team money could buy. They convinced her to plead guilty to a set of charges that were drastically reduced during bareknuckle backroom dealing with the prosecutor's office.

The price of expedited justice meant Jake and Lyla were denied testifying at trial.

They attended her sentencing. She sat unruffled beside her attorneys, dressed in a formfitting but conservative business suit, like a young executive on the rise.

"As monsters go," Lyla whispered, "she cleans up well."

Kristy's gaze swept the courtroom just once, locking on Lyla and Jake long enough for an enigmatic smile. She lowered her head, sorrowful and contrite, as the charges were read. Then she looked up, her demure gaze never straying from the judge. If not for the ache of Jake's healing bullet wound, it was difficult to reconcile this penitent with the sadistic jailor of a few months back.

He muttered under his breath the names of the victims, conjuring them into this courtroom: Zaki al-Jafari, murder victim, not suicide. Walter Meely and Reggie Obergon, reduced to skeletons by the time Kristy's plea bargaining revealed their watery grave. Anderson Wise, nothing but fragmentary remains on a railway mainline.

Judgment had already been served on Stafford Crabtree, the psychopathic patriarch, and Brad Nichol, the boy Jake saved all those years ago. If Kristy hadn't fired the fatal shot, would Jake have killed the man Brad became?

Who knew until the time came?

The judge was sympathetic to Kristy's chilling portrayal of a childhood ruined by tragedy, betrayal and sexual abuse. As for the twisted scenarios inflicted on their victims, she pinned those on Crabtree and Brad. In her telling, she was a victim, too. Perhaps she even believed it.

Added to that, police uncovered a monograph locked in Crabtree's desk: *"Nature and Nurture: Creating Psychopathy in Receptive Youth."*

Whatever Kristy's predisposition, she had no chance after Crabtree made her his live-in psychology experiment.

****

Jake spent much of the fall and early winter writing a devastating series on the ugly legacy of *Hero Hatr*. He couldn't have done it without Rafael's and Erik's skill in what they called 'deanonymizing' the site's subscribers.

He named and shamed its members, giving full credit to BitBust.

Lawsuits threatened by those Jake named never materialized. *Hero Hatr* subscribers were caught with their pants down, literally in some cases. Rafael, who kept his role on the down-low, had remotely activated the laptop cameras of many subscribers.

Beyond public shaming, subscribers suffered few legal sanctions. Murder is illegal, obviously. As is failing to report a murder you witnessed. It's a legal gray area, Jake learned to his disgust, to watch and possess such things as snuff videos.

Jake's Dark Web series was well-received and was reprinted in part by *The New York Times* Sunday magazine. But the worst of humanity still roams its sewers. No doubt a similar site has already sprung up. Jake hasn't looked.

Jake had taken up meditation at Tina's urging and found he was getting through most nights without waking in cold sweats.

There was a public outcry at the lenient sentence the judge handed Kristy. She'd be released in five years with good behavior. It was as noisy and short-lived as a summer thunderstorm. The outrage was offset by advocates for victims of sexual abuse who demanded Kristy's immediate release. The politically savvy district attorney saw no win in pursuing an appeal.

With Kristy's trial over, the medals seized from Crabtree's house were returned.

Jake stayed in touch with Lyla. "I'm feeling stronger," she'd said in a phone call. "Days go by now between my crying jags and wild rages."

Sedgewick was underwriting the cost of trauma counselling. She'd accepted a teaching position for next fall. In the meantime, she was taking extension courses to specialize as a guidance counselor. "Maybe I can make a difference."

"With that in mind," Jake said during the call, "can you do me a favor when the time comes?"

"Anything," she said, puzzled. "You know that."

****

Jonathan Foley traveled to Omaha to present Walter Meely's medal to his mother: "Sabina handed the medal to a man beside her—Walter's lover. She said, 'All I wanted was for Walter to find love and look at this wonderful young man.' Well, shit, Jake, I blubbered like a baby."

Anderson Wise was posthumously awarded a rare second Sacrifice Medallion for his heroics on the train tracks. Jake, back in Sedgewick's good books, delivered his medals to Spokane.

Sharon Key hosted the event at Sharkey's. She'd commissioned a robust plexiglass display case, "so no thieving slut walks them out the door." Jake was accompanied by a tall beauty, dazzling in a blue dress and just a bit nervous.

"Sharon, I'd like you to meet Lyla Watson. My friend. Andy's friend. She'd very much like to meet Toby." Sharon said, "Any friend of Andy's…" She waved her grandson over.

Toby had grown some and filled out since Jake last saw him, but he was very much a shy thirteen-year-old when he shook hands with the beautiful black woman in the blue dress.

Lyla rested a hand on Toby's shoulder. "I had to meet you. Andy talked about you all the time. Toby this, and Toby that. He called you his 'little brother from a different mother.' "

Toby beamed.

Sharon slipped away and returned with two glasses of soda. Lyla and Toby were now deep in conversation. "So," Lyla asked, "how are the Wildcats doing this season?"

"Not so hot," Toby said. "They've got a big hole at shortstop." Toby led Lyla to a distant table. They were still chatting as Jake prepared to take his leave.

Key looked to her grandson across the room, animated and mimicking catching a fly ball as Lyla laughed. Key gave Jake a hug. "Thank you, I think Toby's in love."

"I know the feeling," Jake said.

He worried Tina's publicized link to her murderous relative might drive her from Aberdeen. She snuggled close one autumn evening and answered his unasked question. "Your paper ran the most wonderful letters. Seems folks here don't give a toss I'm related to a serial killer. I felt for the first time that this is my home…

"Our home," she added with a smile. "I'm not atoning for Billy's sins, if ever I was. I'm working for my people. They need me and I need them. That make any kind of sense?"

"Trust me," Jake said. "I get it."

****

They moved in together in mid-January, renting Clara's century-old home. It sports what Tina called a "very Freudian" turret—Jake's favorite room.

Amanda and Sam took up temporary residence in

Jake's Wishkah River cottage, enjoying the privacy while Jann Maxwell busted Trent Shane's nuts in the divorce proceedings. After Jann warned him of Jake's photographic record of his abuse against Amanda going to his superiors if settlement talks derailed, Trent's belligerence lessened significantly.

If there was ever doubt, Jake now became Shane's mortal enemy. He'd have to watch his back.

Amanda dropped by the *Independent* in early January to give Jake a letter mailed to the cottage. The return address was a women's prison in Muncy, Pennsylvania. He opened it with trepidation.

"Jake, it looks like I have time to reflect on my errors in judgment. When I'm freed, I will visit you—and your lady friend—to atone for my tragic failures. I feel a burning need to put things right. Please note my release date. Until then…"

He shared the letter with Tina, who shook her head in disgust.

Next day, Jake found a leaf from a five-year calendar pinned to his home office bulletin board. Kristy's release date was circled in red.

And underneath, in Tina's handwriting: "Bring it, bitch."

A note from the author...

So many people helped and inspired me on this long meander from idea to fruition. I'll start with veteran book editor Adrienne Kerr, who saw promise in an early draft then suggested I reshuffle the chapters to speed the narrative and hike the tension. It was a revelation.

I'm grateful to many early readers who offered advice and support. Among them: Keri Sweetman, princess of punctuation, mystery mavens Sharon Muller and Wilf Muller, Jo-Ann Bayley, Scott Honeyman, Simon Bradbury (actor, playwright and author), and retired Canadian Forces Capt. Trevor Greene (rower, soldier, author and the very definition of hero.) To the murderous members of Crime Writers of Canada, a big thank you for your encouragement, your inspiration, and for some damn fine writing.

Work takes you so far, then you need a bit of luck. My thanks to the judges of the Pacific Northwest Writers' Association who named *Hero Haters* a finalist in their 2021 writing contest. This led me to the wonderful folks of Wild Rose Press, specifically senior editor Frances Sevilla, suspense division, and my extraordinary manuscript editor Kaycee John.

Speaking of luck, how else to explain Ros Guggi, my beloved wife, first-reader and the mother of our two great sons, Daniel and Cameron? She makes everything better, every day.

About the author...

Before turning to fiction, Ken MacQueen spent 15 years as Vancouver bureau chief for Maclean's, Canada's newsmagazine, winning multiple National Magazine Awards and nominations. He travelled the world writing features and breaking news for the magazine, and previously for two national news agencies. He also covered nine Olympic Games and drew Jake Ockham's athletic prowess from tracking elite rowers in training and on podiums in Athens, Beijing and London. kenmacqueen.com

Thank you for purchasing
this publication of The Wild Rose Press, Inc.

For questions or more information
contact us at
info@thewildrosepress.com.

The Wild Rose Press, Inc.
www.thewildrosepress.com